THE ADVENTURE BEGINS

DRAGONERA: THE DARK ONE CHRONICLES

CHARLIE ROSE

To: John

"Enjoy the
Series!"

— Charlie

Rose

BROKEN
TOWER
P R E S S

CHAPTER 1 - LAST BRAVE WORDS

*D*estruction laid before the young warrior as she ran, not just for her life, but for her kingdom. The faster she ran the more her legs screamed for mercy. It was a cry for mercy that she had no choice but to ignore As she sprinted she saw it all, images that would remain in her mind for the rest of her life. Wrecked buildings that were once homes to proud families, innocent civilians crowded the streets in terror, and dead warriors with broken weapons surrounding their corpses.

She muttered a curse in her own tongue under her breath as she ran. *Why hadn't they acted sooner?* She had worried that question around like a dog with an old bone ever since the attack began. She glanced behind her one last time to view the enemy, a large cloud of pure concentrated evil. The one responsible for the attack on the Kingdom.

It had no name, no true name. None that any of the races that it had attacked could call it by name. No one could really even say for sure what it was. There was only one title for this monstrosity. The Dark One. A being of pure concentrated evil born for one purpose - to eradicate every living being in the world.

And so far? It was accomplishing this goal.

The human, the harpy, the mage, and the elf kingdoms had all stood before this unstoppable force and all had failed. What survivors there were went either unnoticed or fled for their lives.

The only kingdom left standing before this atrocity? The mightiest of all the kingdoms. And it too, was beginning to fail before the Dark One's power.

The young woman had believed they were ready for something like this, how wrong she, and the King's council, had been. It appeared unexpectedly and began a path of destruction stretching for miles, a malevolent tornado. Many of her King's finest warriors fell in the battle against the unrelenting force of darkness and the horrible power contained within it. None were successful in slowing it down, let alone stopping it.

The young woman gritted her teeth as shame filled her. She was one of the greatest warriors of the Kingdom, the King's right hand. She had the honor of being the most skilled sword master in the kingdom, only being out done by her King himself. But against this evil she too was powerless. And so, she ran, like a coward.

"How could it come to this?" She asked herself. They should have taken the threat of the Dark One far more seriously than the other kingdoms. She should have convinced her King to do something sooner! Now, their home, their Kingdom was paying the price for her failure.

As she shook her head, the young woman continued to flee, her common sense returning. This wasn't the time to think about how they could have readied themselves. She had to reach the one who stood any chance against this evil: the King. He was the only hope the Kingdom, no the world, had left.

The malevolent force was catching up far too quickly. If she had any chance of making it to the King, she had to slow it down. Without a second thought she quickly turned to face her foe. She held her hands out in front of her, her eyes flashed with an inner power.

"*Flarnea!*" she shouted.

A blast of white fire flew from her palms. The flame reached the darkness and slammed into it at full force. The evil reacted to this attack in just the way she expected: annoyed, but not stopping its approach. However, the attack was successful enough to put some distance between the two of them for another moment.

She took the chance that her attack had bought. With an expenditure of her power she pulled her arms back to her sides, closed her eyes and focused.

"*Winlan.*" she whispered.

As she spoke, two great white wings emerged from her back, her feet lifted gently from the ground, and she rose above the darkness. Her heart soared. Even now, in this moment of terror, the joy of flight filled her spirit. So flew away from the enemy, her wings a brilliant white slash outlined against the eternal darkness covering her kingdom.

The chase began anew, but this time the young woman had a much better chance at getting away. She could see the outline of the castle in the distance. She knew her brothers would already be there, rallying the few troops still alive.

As she flew faster, the castle came closer. Behind her, the Dark One continued to approach, devouring all that lay before it under its dark clouds. The young warrior's heart felt like it would burst out of her chest as she finally reached the castle. When she landed in the castle courtyard, the first thing she saw were injured soldiers trying to treat their wounds as best they could. Other warriors were preparing weapons for battle, while some knelt in the corners of the courtyard, praying to the gods for redemption.

"Sister!" a young man's voice called out as he quickly approached her, accompanied by a taller man.

"Brothers," she replied, catching her breath as her wings slid back into her shoulders and disappeared beneath the skin. "Thank the gods that you are unharmed."

"Our bodies may not yet be injured, sister," the taller man spoke, "but our pride is most grievously wounded."

"Perhaps if we had listened to the earlier warnings, this would not have happened," the shorter man said, glaring to the taller one. "If someone had alerted His Royal Majesty we would not even be here now. The cost of this...It is far too high for any warrior to pay." He spread his hands outward, pointing to the wounded men and women littering the courtyard.

"Now is not the time to talk of injured pride or to argue among ourselves!" the woman interrupted. "Where is his Majesty? I must speak with him!"

"The King?" asked the taller man. "The last I saw of him, he was headed towards the top of the castle."

"Then I must make haste." She clenched her fists. "By all that I am, I refuse to let this Kingdom fall. Order your men to hold the Dark One back for as long as they can, I will make my way to the King!"

Before either of them could argue with her, she headed up the stairs to the top tower of the castle. As she ran, she could hear the echoes of her brothers' orders to their men. She knew that the soldiers could not hope to stop the Dark One; the best they might do would be to delay it, pray to the gods that was enough.

She cursed under her breath once again. If they had listened to the warnings from the other Kingdoms, their fate would not be the same as the fallen members of the races whose lands and people had already been destroyed.

As she ran up the stairs, she heard the sounds of battle. She hated to see warriors that she herself had trained falling in battle, but she could not let her grief blind her to what was most important. In war, good people die: it was a fact she had accepted long ago. The gods alone knew if this was the final battle for their race. Her mission now was the King; she must reach him, their world depended upon it. She couldn't fly inside though: the stairway was too narrow and the turns to quick.

At long last she reached the top of the castle, breathless, exhausted, and afraid, something she very rarely felt. The one person she had been looking for stood alone as the Dark One slowly boiled around the base of the castle, a fog of evil from which cries of despair wailed.

"Sire!" she shouted, her breath short.

The King stood silently, his back to the young woman, his face hidden in the shadows of smoke covering what was left of his burning Kingdom. He turned to the young woman behind him, the remnants of a failed smile flashing across his face.

"So, this is how it ends?" His voice drifted off at the end, fading away into the smoke, punctuated by the fall of a building somewhere in the darkness.

"No, Sire! This is not the end! We can still save you, if not the Kingdom!" cried the young woman. She was trying her hardest to encourage him to continue the fight. Although her face was hidden by the smoke, he could hear the tears in her voice.

The King sighed heavily as he shook his head. A small smile appeared on his face as he placed a hand on the young woman's shoulder.

"It's over. The other Kingdoms did not last long against this foe, and now my Kingdom falls to the hunger of the Dark One."

"It is never over, my lord. Not while we live, while we breathe, and while we fight!" The young woman continued, tears forming in her eyes, "You still have your soldiers, your guardians and me! We will never abandon your side!"

Once again the King shook his head, turning away from the young woman. He sighed as his eyes took in the creeping darkness coming closer to the tower.

"You are my most fierce and loyal warrior. You have led my armies to many victories, but this is a battle not even you can win." He finished, closing his eyes once more.

"Surely you don't believe this is the end?"

"All things end," the King answered, raising his hands against the darkness. "The Kingdoms of the other races only lasted a few days against the Dark One. It was my foolish pride that made me believe we could possibly avoid the choice that confronts me now…" His hands dropped limply to his side.

"Sire…" She reached out, touching his shoulder. His eyes opened at her touch, a resigned smile on his face.

"I will not allow our world to end. I will not let the light of magic die." The echoes of ancient kings could be heard in his voice. "If it is possible I will stop this beast from destroying our world."

With wide eyes she pulled away from her king, body trembling in fear as her mind began to piece together what he planned to do.

"You don't mean you're going to…"

"Yes, that is exactly what I am planning to do."

"But my liege, your death is certain if you do this!" she said, her voice cracking as she spoke.

A soft and surprising chuckle escaped the King's lips.

He spread his arms wide, pointing out the destruction everywhere. "You tell me: how could I live with what has happened around us? What is there left to live for? The Kingdoms have fallen, the world is ending, there is nothing that can completely stop the beast. How could I hide in the face of this, knowing that I might have made a difference and that I did not try?" He took a deep breath. "In the end it is not whether we fail or whether we prevail, it is how we face the darkness when it comes for us that matters."

His eyes narrowed, his hands bathed in a strange glow. The woman took a step back as he walked towards the edge of the tower.

The King's eyes focused on the dark shadow below.

"I may not be able to stop it," he said through clenched teeth, "but that does not mean I cannot delay it."

"You speak of suicide!" the woman screamed, taking a step towards him. Hot tears rolled down her cheeks as she reached out to him "To seal such a force away will drain you completely!"

"If that is the price then so be it. It is my decision, my responsibility. As my loyal knight, my friend, my," he paused, swallowed hard and went on, "as my dearest friend I demand that you step aside. It is my final order."

He stood, hands outstretched and whispered, "Remember me."

The glow around his hands took the form of twin blue orbs. He slammed the two together before holding the combined orbs above his head. The power of the combined orbs formed a bright beacon of light against the seemingly endless dark sky.

The beacon illuminated the faces of warriors running up the staircase. They both knew what those orbs signified One ran to their comrade, his voice filled with shock.

"Why are you standing there?! His Majesty will die if he does this!"

The young woman lowered her head, a single tear traveling down her cheek as she glanced away.

"I'm sorry, brother, but his mind is made up. The orbs are cast, it is already too late."

The third warrior, the tallest of them all, took a step forward, reaching out towards the King with one hand.

"Sire, please, no! You can't!" He shouted, his deep and powerful voice filling the darkness.

"Be silent!" the King ordered, his eyes shined with power as he glanced back at the three Warriors.

In an instant the three were surrounded by golden orbs. The young woman pounded on the orb around her, trying to call upon her powers to free herself, but nothing answered. She stopped, tears streaming down her face as she realized what the King had done.

"Please Sire! Let us stand by you one last time! Do not take this burden on alone!" She begged. "Please...don't leave me alone..."

The King only smiled.

"No," he said quietly, "this is not your end. I cannot defeat this evil, merely contain it. The three of you must find a way to stop it when the Dark One rises again. Accept my final command to you. Survive, watch for the signs and prepare. Remember me with fondness." He took a deep breath and bellowed. "Now, be gone!"

Before the warriors could protest, there was a blinding flash of light. When the darkness returned they were gone. As he took a deep breath, the King turned back to the shadowy force that had finally reached the tower. His orb of light grew larger and brighter.

"Though it cost me my life, you will not have your way on this day, you spawn of evil!"

The Dark One let loose a roar as it reared back. The King stood his ground and released his entire life force into the gaping maw of darkness. The shaft of light flew from his chest, piercing the darkness, consuming everything in the radius of its brilliance.

From the top of a broken tower, in a shattered Kingdom, the King's final words echoed across the now peaceful palace:

"When your power stirs again, they shall rise and stop you... in the next life."

CHAPTER 2 - THE LAST NORMAL DAY

iden Russell groaned as his alarm clock beeped loudly in his ear. He lazily reached over and grabbed a hold of it, eventually finding the off switch. He opened one eye to glance at the clock and grumbled as he shifted in the bed.

"What school has you get up at this awful time in the morning?" He thought.

Slowly he pulled off the covers and rose up from the bed, stretching his arms as he glanced over to the clock. He missed the days where he didn't have to get up until at least seven. But ever since he started middle school, he had no choice but to get up every morning at five.

"Aiden?" His mother's voice echoed down the hallway. "Aiden, are you awake?"

"Yes, Mom," He called out to her, rubbing his eyes. "I'm up."

"Good," She said. "I was worried that you were going to ignore your alarm clock again."

He sighed as he stood up and headed for a shower. His mother's voice echoed from the hallway once again.

"If you're planning to take a shower, please remember to save some hot water, all right?"

"Yes, ma'am." He called back, closing the door before she could call out again.

If a stranger were to describe Aiden Russell, he might say merely that Aiden was a thirteen-year-old boy, about five feet and eight inches tall, with dark ocean blue eyes and chocolate brown hair. And while he was not completely out of shape, his physic was not as impressive as most boys his age. His arms and legs were scrawny in comparison. Aiden believed that his skinny arms were not meant for lifting weights or doing chin-ups, and no one had been able to convince him differently. At least not yet.

After his shower, Aiden got dressed and headed to the kitchen for breakfast. His mother, who shared his dark chocolate brown hair, smiled at him as she flipped pieces of bacon in the frying pan.

"Good morning, dear," she said. "Did you sleep well?"

"I can't really complain," Aiden answered, taking a bite of bacon. "I mean, I got about as much sleep as a person can get before five in the morning."

"I know it's not easy, but remember: somewhere else in the world, someone has gotten up even earlier. You should consider yourself lucky that you don't have to get up at four instead of five."

Aiden shivered at the thought. He took another bite of his bacon and sipped the orange juice his mother gave him.

"Did Dad already leave for work?" he asked, wiping his mouth with the back of his hand.

"Yes, you know that his job has him there early in the morning," she answered. "But before he left he wanted me to tell you that he put a gift for you in your backpack."

Aiden blinked some as he turned to his backpack in the corner of the kitchen. He shrugged and turned back to his breakfast plate.

"Did he tell you what it was?"

"Now Aiden, if I told you, it would ruin the surprise, wouldn't it?" She smiled as she ruffled his hair. "But I am allowed to tell you that he said it's something that you'd be interested in."

Aiden glanced back to his backpack. Now his curiosity was piqued. *Something that he would be interested in?* He couldn't figure out what his father meant by that. While he and father weren't at opposite ends with each other, they did have very different interests.

Aiden's father was an extremely successful businessman, the right hand man of the CEO who ran the furniture company Pasquale. Aiden, however, was not interested in business. He wanted to learn the old, forgotten secrets of the world.

His father would often say that Aiden's mind was still "in a fantasy world." They never had a big argument over it, but Aiden knew his father would be hesitant to give him a gift to feed his interest in such things.

He finished the bacon on his plate and took a sip of what was left of his orange juice before standing up.

"Well...okay, Mom," He said, reaching for his backpack. "I better get going before the bus arrives too late."

"Ok, Aiden, but remember to stay close to the bus stop. I don't want you wandering off before your bus arrives."

"Don't worry, Mom," He reassured her. "I promise I won't leave the bus stop."

He kissed her on the cheek and headed towards the door, slipping the backpack on his shoulders as he left. He glanced back at the house as he walked. He lived in a cul de sac in an average neighborhood in a boring town. Exciting things really never happened in this town. He often wondered why his mother would worry about him getting lost; the bus stop wasn't that far from their home.

He shrugged it off as he walked slowly as he checked his cell phone. There was still time to get to the bus stop. He groaned a bit as he glared at the time it now read. Five thirty AM. What kind of sick person made a young teenager get up at this hour?

Before he could ponder on the question further his eye glanced up to the bus stop. A girl standing at the bus stop had caught his eye. He grinned as he put his phone away before he spoke up.

"I figured you'd be here early, Theresa."

Theresa Goldwin turned to him and smiled. For as long as he could remember, Theresa had always been his best friend. Many of the kids at their school envied their friendship - most of the boys had a crush on Theresa. She had bright emerald eyes that lit up depending on her mood. But perhaps the most unusual thing about her was her hair.

Unlike most of the girls at school, Theresa had never once colored her hair; it was long, straight and white like snow itself. It could have been close to platinum blonde hair, but he had known Theresa for too long to make that claim. Aiden had never seen anyone else with hair like Theresa's.

Needless to say, she was a very pretty girl. Which made a lot of the boys at their middle school wonder how in the world someone like Aiden Russell ended up being her best friend.

"Well now," she said, "you're here much earlier than I thought you would be, Aiden."

"Hey, cut me some slack." Aiden joked, taking his spot beside her. "I'm not that lazy."

"Oh yeah? Then I guess your mom never dragged your lazy butt out of bed on the first day of school, hmm?"

"Hey! It was cold and I wasn't ready to end my summer vacation!"

Theresa rolled her eyes, giving him her sternest look, the effect ruined by the snicker bubbling up from her throat. Aiden couldn't help but laugh. If there was one thing Theresa could not do, it was give Aiden a stern ook. He laughed louder.

"Face it, Theresa," he said after a few more chuckles, "you're never gonna be able to intimidate me."

"Hmph." she huffed before folding her arms, "Don't get an ego now." She turned to him, folding her arms.

"So, anything new?"

"Eh, not really. Besides being forced to wake up for another day at school, last night was just kind of bland." Aiden said, shrugging. "Though mom said that dad left me something in my backpack."

This caught Theresa's attention as she quirked an eyebrow at him.

"Really? What do you think it is?"

"Hell if I know." He frowned. "The only thing he told my mom was that it's something that would 'interest' me."

Theresa frowned; she was one of the few people who knew that Aiden and his father didn't share much in common. Aiden shook his head, dismissing the thoughts of the gift.

"So what was going on in school the other day?" He asked, desperate to change the topic. "Looked like they were looking through backpacks."

"You're not kidding," Theresa said. "They've been pulling kids out of my classes like they're looking for something on them."

Aiden blinked, turning to her once again.

"Wait, in the middle of class?"

"Yeah, some of them were the smart kids as well." She frowned once again. "It's like they're up to something, but I can't figure it out."

Aiden rolled his eyes as he folded his arms across his chest. He knew what she was up to. All too well did he know how his friend worked and how she planned things out.

"Theresa," he began, "don't tell me that you're-"

"And since no one is asking about it," she mused, a confident smile was growing on her lips now, "Then it's up to us to find out exactly what they're doing!" She turned to him, smiling. "And you're going to help me find out!"

Aiden groaned, smacking his forehead with his palm.

"Theresa, no," he said. "You remember the last time you dragged me along to investigate something?"

"Vaguely," she said, pursing her lips as she placed a finger to her chin. "We were going to see if they were changing the meat in the school lunches to rat meat..."

"Yeah, and because of that we got detention and extra homework for nearly a week!" Aiden reminded her. She merely scoffed at him and brushed his comment off.

"You make it sound like it was my fault we got caught."

Aiden sighed before glancing away from his friend as he watched the road for the bus.

"I wouldn't worry about it too much, Theresa," Aiden said, "Nothing really happens in Raymond Virginia. Especially at our middle school."

"But that's the thing, I know a lot of the students that they are taking out. They're smart kids and each of them are passing like us." She folded her arms, "Tell me that doesn't sound odd to you, Aiden."

He sighed in defeat. Theresa had a habit of proving herself right to him whenever she felt strongly about a subject. Regardless of how he felt, he had to admit that she was right. It was odd that the school was pulling out the smart students from their classes, but it wasn't odd enough for him to become involved.

But he still remembered the time they had gotten detention. And after those long days in detention, there would be a new lecture from his father waiting for him at home.

"Theresa, I am not gonna get into some investigation that most likely will end up with us locked up in detention again." He said firmly, tapping his foot.

Theresa was silent for a bit, a rare thing for her. Aiden turned back to his friend, thinking he had upset her somehow, but instead her emerald green eyes greeted him. A serious expression slowly replaced Theresa's smile, dimming the brightness of her face.

"There are worse things than detention." She said softly, almost as if she suddenly became wiser in just a few seconds. "Remember that, my friend."

He blinked a couple of times. She sounded spooky. At first he thought she was just being overly dramatic, but he had known Theresa for far too long for that explanation to fit. She never gave him that look unless she absolutely meant it. It made him uneasy, almost scared, to see that expression underneath her snow-white hair.

Theresa turned away from him, looking towards the street for the bus. Aiden frowned, tapping his friend lightly on the shoulder to get her attention.

"Hey," He started, "I didn't mean to upset you. I'm sorry if I ..."

Theresa turned back to him, her familiar smile reappearing.

"Don't worry about it, Aiden." She nudged him with her elbow.

He smiled in relief. Still, he couldn't get what she had said out of his mind. If this were one of the books that he loved to read it would be an omen. The beginning of a perilous adventure where the hero found himself on a journey. He almost expected lighting and thunder to accompany the moment, but all he heard was the sound of the bus backfiring as it turned the corner.

As the bus approached, he remembered a lesson his history teacher, Ms. MacDonnell, once taught. It was about omens in the medieval times, mostly based on the old Celtic religion, before the Druids, in the time of the ancient ones. Pieces of those stories could be seen in the tales of Scotland and England; the magic bones beneath many a medieval tale. He knew omens only happened in stories, but he couldn't help but feel that something dangerous was coming. Soon.

Then again, he always got that feeling whenever he got on the bus. Almost every morning he would have to avoid a spit-wad from the local bully, Eric, and it was no different this morning. Aiden ducked his head the moment he stepped onto the bus as a massive spit-wad hit the windshield. The driver glared into his rear view mirror.

"Eric Noakes, don't make me write up a referral on you again!"

Eric Noakes was about the same size as most school bullies. He was a little fat in the stomach area, with small brown beady eyes, and buzz-short black hair. His eyes found his target, Aiden. He grinned deviously as he prepared another spit-wad, but he then noticed the bus driver's glare and snorted.

"Lucky punk." He grunted under his breath.

Aiden grumbled as he took his seat on the bus, not wanting to look at Eric. He had been dealing with Eric since the fourth grade, and he was quite frankly getting tired of it.

"You think he'd back off for once and bug someone else for a change." Aiden said, looking out the window.

Theresa frowned as she sat down beside him, gently placing a hand on his shoulder.

"Don't let it get to you, Aiden." she advised. "You know getting into a fight with him will only make it worse."

"Doesn't mean that he should get away with it." He argued. Theresa sighed as she shook her head.

"Aiden, as much as I agree with that, right now there is nothing that anyone can do to get him suspended," She explained, crossing her arms over her chest. "He might be a bully, but he's not stupid."

Aiden sighed in defeat. Theresa was right. She always was right. Eric wasn't the typical bully who would gather a group of friends to pick on one kid. He was the smart, loner kind who would slowly torment his victims until they snapped, throwing a punch at him. In the end, he would claim innocence and his victim would get in trouble. It was that one aspect Aiden hated most: Eric always got away with it, and that was just not fair.

The bus ride was slow and uneventful, for the most part, occasionally stopping to pick up the next bunch of students, some of them greeted by spit-wads from Eric. Aiden just looked out the window and watched the scenery. It was still early in the morning; he was not really up for talking much, even to Theresa.

But as it roared down the streets all of a sudden the bus came to a halt at an unexpected red light, jerking the students forward. Aiden's backpack, fell out of his lap and as he bent to pick it up, he felt something odd, a shape he didn't expect. He blinked, confused at what he had just felt. Before he could investigate more though, Theresa tapped him on the shoulder.

"Uh, Aiden?" She asked, raising an eyebrow. "Unless you want a broken neck, how about you sit up before the bus goes again? You know the school loves to confiscate things."

Aiden nodded as he pulled himself back up into his seat. It would be best to wait to see what exactly his father gave him in secret. And that usually meant doing so at the lunch table they sat at every day. He just had to make certain that none of the teachers or administrators noticed when he did.

The bus ride continued on for a good ten minutes before it eventually reached their school, Saint Hope Lester Middle School. While the school had a fine reputation for good grades and students, bullies and rival students would often play a cruel joke on school. They would rearrange the sign's letters to say "Hopeless Middle School." It was an act that got really old, really quickly.

Today though, the sign was spared from the terrible nickname. When the bus came to a halt, Aiden did the next daily ritual: get off the bus quickly before Eric fired another spit-wad. Again, he had to duck to avoid it, hearing Eric's tormenting chuckles in the background.

"This is gonna be a long day," he said, glancing up at the sky above.

"Just relax." Theresa frowned. "Complaining about it won't make the day go any faster."

"I wish it did." Aiden told her in a sarcastic tone. "Today is the last day before spring break! No school for a week!"

Theresa giggled as they reached their homeroom.

"Always looking forward to getting as far away from this school as possible, aren't you?"

"And you're not?" The two shared a good laugh before taking their seats.

The day might not be so bad after all. Maybe if he got lucky the day would move at a quick pace.

CHAPTER 3 - NOTHING WILL EVER BE THE SAME AGAIN

*A*iden's hopes for a smooth moving day fell apart with just the very first class. The day felt like it had dragged on for an eternity, maybe even longer than that! He struggled through math, a class during which, at times, he truly felt like he was in an insane asylum where he was screaming for release. Ended up being perplexed by the odd world of science, where it felt like his brain was about to turn into mush, and barely managed to squeeze through English. However, the next class was history, his personal favorite. The reason he liked this class more than the others was his teacher, Ms. MacDonnell, a preppy Scottish woman with short red hair and a pair of bifocals that matched her personality. She was the coolest teacher in the world.

Aiden smiled as he walked into the classroom. What felt like a huge burden from the previous classes came off his shoulders as he found his seat. This was a class he always looked forward to, no matter how much the rest of school sucked. As he took his seat, Aiden noticed his teacher was wearing a strange mixture of garments put together in a haphazard fashion.

Ms. MacDonnell was a short stout woman, with streaks of

indigo in her auburn hair. She also wore a pair of large bifocals, that she kept attached to a necklace that she seldom took off. Sometimes Aiden wondered if she wore them because she had to, or if she only wore them for show.

Either way, it was one of her charms.

"Welcome class!" Ms. MacDonnell said in her thick Scottish accent. Aiden couldn't help but smile at the accent. It took awhile for him, and most of the student body, to understand her at first due to it. However she made up for that thick accent by being a very kind hearted teacher.

"Today we're going to continue our lesson about Celtic history and songs. Please turn to pages one hundred thirty five and one hundred thirty six!"

Aiden couldn't help but feel happy in Ms. MacDonnell's class. She was unlike the other teachers, free spirited and kind. Of course some students would try to take advantage of this, but that would usually end up with them getting a ticket straight to detention for their actions. As he pulled his book out of his backpack in order to read along, he found himself drawn to wrapped package inside. Aiden frowned as he just stared at it. He could see it laying there right beside his math book, undisturbed by the events of the day when he moved from class to class. He could have sworn though that the item had some kind of pull to it. Like it was tempting him to reach in and grab it now. He still had no idea was it was exactly though. Still, remembering what Theresa told him, Aiden did not give in to the temptation.

That didn't mean that his mind wasn't free to wonder. He had only gotten a small feel of it earlier on the bus, and even that wasn't enough for him to imagine what it was exactly. What he could tell though was that it had some sort of curve to it. That was his only clue.

"*Focus, Aiden,*" he thought. "*You're in school, not in dreamland.*"

"Hey, Aiden." A new voice whispered over to him. "Do you have a spare pencil to give?"

Aiden turned to the source of the voice. A small blush came to his cheeks. The person that asked for the pencil was one of the most popular girls in school. A girl that every guy would have wanted a shot at being with.

Her name was Liza Hollingsworth.

Liza had short blonde hair that reached to the back of her neck, and a pair of light sky blue eyes. Eyes that, at times, Aiden almost felt himself getting lost in. Several other guys in school begged for a chance to be with her, though Aiden couldn't recall her ever having a boyfriend.

She was smart, a bit preppy, but an amazing athlete. As far back as Aiden could remember she'd been a star on every soccer team she had been part of.

"Um, Aiden? You okay?" She asked. "You're a little red…"

Aiden snapped back to reality and shook his head. He immediately felt like he should have been kicked in the head for staring at her like a creep. While he and Liza did talk during class projects, they never really talked personally.

"Uh, y-yeah sure!" He hastily said, reaching for a spare pencil in his backpack. "I-I got one."

Aiden quickly grabbed the first pencil that he found in his backpack. Without wasting any more time, he handed it over to Liza. The latter took the pencil with a somewhat confused look on her face.

"You sure you're okay?" She asked.

"Of course I am!" He whispered, a little too fast. "Just willing to help out a fellow student!"

Liza raised an eyebrow as she tried to read Aiden's expression. With a tiny laugh, she flashed him a look that made his heart skip a beat.

"Okay then, fellow student. Thanks for the pencil." And with that she returned to her notes. Aiden wanted to smack himself hard in the head.

"Smooth, idiot. Smooth." He told himself.

He found himself returning his focus on his small crush to the lecture at hand in the class. Ms. MacDonnell was talking about Omens, a subject that often got under his skin. Especially with the way today was going. Earlier the very same day Theresa's normal cheerful attitude was replaced by a much more serious tone before the bus arrived. Aiden couldn't get the image of Theresa's face out of his mind as he stared at the page.

"Why in the world did she look so different?" His mind wondered. *"She normally is cheerful and happy. It's not like her to just turn into...well, whatever the hell that was."*

The class continued on about the omens widely held by the Celtic people. The more she went on about the topic, the more Aiden dreaded what else the day had planned for him. It was bad enough that Eric was trying to hit him with spit wads on the bus, and in classes that he was unfortunate enough to share with him, but now he made himself look like a fool in front of one of the most popular girls in school.

It wasn't until the bell rang that his eyes turned away from the word. Somehow, he had a very bad feeling in his gut as he tightly closed his book. It was lunchtime, and he was looking forward to eating something after the long hours of never ending class.

As he got up from his chair, he noticed Ms. MacDonnell turn to him. She smiled as the rest of the students left the classroom.

"You look like there's something troubling you, Aiden."

"Well, Ms. MacDonnell...yeah, I guess there's something I'm thinking about."

"Aye, I could tell that easily my young pupil." Ms. MacDonnell began clearing her desk for the next class. "You seemed much quieter in class than you usually are."

Aiden couldn't help but laugh.

"Nothing ever escapes you, does it Ms. MacDonnell?"

"In my classroom? Hardly so, Aiden. Now tell me, what's on your mind?"

"You know Theresa Goldwin, right?" he asked. His teacher smiled in a playful way.

"I'm hardly the person to go to for girl problems, Aiden."

"W-What? No! That's not it!" he quickly said. Ms. MacDonnell laughed.

"I'm just messing with you, laddie. Now then, what about Theresa?"

"Earlier today, she gave me this weird look and what she said almost sounded like an omen."

Ms. MacDonnell raised an eyebrow.

"An omen you say?" She mused, "What exactly was it that she said?"

Aiden stretched his mind to remember what she had said in the early hours of the morning.

"She said that 'There are some things in life are worse than detention, Aiden.'" he said, though he admitted that those probably were not the exact words. Ms. MacDonnell frowned.

"Ah, yes, the detention increase going around the school." She sighed. "I honestly cannot tell you why such a thing has become so common now, Aiden. It's been happening for a while though, and I don't think it'll stop anytime soon."

Aiden frowned.

"I'm confused; I thought you couldn't get detention if you did what you were told and stayed out of trouble. You just gotta do your classwork and you will be exempt from detention. Not even the troublemakers want to have it for weeks!"

"I cannot tell you more than I already know on this subject, I'm afraid," Ms. MacDonnell told him. "But remember this about omens, young one: they are not always as grave as they seem."

She smiled a crooked smile, and then noticed the other students in the hall heading towards the lunchroom.

"Ack! Look at what I'm doing, keeping you away from your lunch! Go! Eat! Recover your strength!"

Aiden smiled as he left the classroom. He was getting hungry, and it was time to meet up with Theresa at their table. Next to Ms. MacDonnell's class, it was his favorite time of the day.

Though as he approached the lunchroom, he noticed the hall monitor, Patrick Martin, down one of the school's halls. He was a big man, with short, dirty blonde hair and piercing green eyes. Aiden didn't like him one bit; with the exception of Eric, he was his least favorite person in the school.

He wasn't the only one who didn't like him either. Patrick was behind most of the students getting into trouble with the school administration. There were even rumors that it was because of him that detentions were starting to pile on in the school.

Patrick had only been working at the school for a few months now, but it didn't take long for him to become infamous with the students. They would often refer to him as 'Ticket Man' as whenever he caught students doing something that was either against the rules, or he didn't like, he would write them a referral to the principal's office right away.

Patrick glared at him as Aiden reached the lunchroom, his piercing green eyes following him through the double doors. Aiden shook his head as he reached the table where he and Theresa normally sat, happy that she was already there waiting for him.

"Hey there," she said. "What took you so long? Usually you're here before I am."

"Had a little talk with Ms. MacDonnell," Aiden told her. "Mostly about the detentions."

Theresa frowned.

"Let me guess: she didn't reveal to you why there have been so many?"

"Yeah," Aiden sighed. "Truth be told, I was kinda hoping that she would. After all, Ms. MacDonnell usually gives us some insight when there's something up at the school."

Theresa grinned, before shoving him in a playful way.

"I thought you told me that you didn't want to find out why there have been so many detentions?"

"I said I wasn't interested in one of your 'detective' games that could get us in trouble." He stuck his tongue out at her. "That doesn't mean that I don't want to find out."

Theresa laughed at his comment, noticing the lunch line finally shortening.

"Looks like the line is finally dying down." She turned to him. "Mind telling me what you want?"

"What?"

Aiden felt himself feeling really embarrassed by this question. He was never the best with keeping money on his person. Especially when it came for lunch time.

"I know you forgot your lunch money, like always," Theresa said. "I have more than enough money for both of our lunches."

"Theresa…" he said, trying to protest. Her finger laid right on top of his lips before he could say another word.

"No buts, Aiden." Theresa smiled. "I'm not gonna let you go hungry. I bet you want spaghetti, right?"

With that, Theresa stood and went to the lunch line. Aiden sighed as he watched her go. She was too kind for her own good; how he'd ended up with a friend like her he'd never know. Frowning, he sat there in silence as he waited for her to return.

Then his eyes glanced to his backpack. Once again his mind was focused on whatever it was that his father had placed inside. The event on the bus from earlier still was driving his curiosity up a tree. Aiden knew that he shouldn't open the bag up and begin to tear into what his father had placed for him, but the urge was too strong to fight! He had to know what it was!

Aiden looked around the lunchroom, making sure that Patrick or none of the other teachers were nearby. He also made certain that Theresa wasn't looking back at their table before he made his move. It was now or never, and never was waiting for school to finish.

He reached for his backpack, unzipping it slowly. Aiden reached into the bag, feeling around for the shape he had felt before. He took his time removing the paper that was around whatever the present was. His eyes flurried about as he looked over his shoulders to make certain unwanted eyes were not prying at him. And then, once the paper had been removed, he touched the curved shape from earlier that morning. Aiden took his chance to yank the item out of his bag and when he saw what it was he let out a gasp of shock. Nothing his mother had hinted at could have prepared him for what he held in his hand.

Aiden's eyes were wide with disbelief. The item that he had just pulled out, was what he had to guess as a rare collectable. A big grin came to his lips as his eyes shimmered with excitement at what he held in his hand.

The present was a pure shiny silver figurine of a European dragon with ruby red eyes, or at least they looked like rubies. The wings curved above the dragon's body, almost forming a hand guard. Unlike dragons that were depicted in most forms of fictional media, this dragon had four legs. A detail that Aiden greatly appreciated as he felt the 'wyvern' design in dragons had been over done to death. But there was a small, strangely vacant slot in the dragon's chest. He had no clue what was missing from it, or if a piece of its chest had broken off, but he didn't care. Aiden couldn't put his finger on it, but something about this dragon seemed familiar, it felt right in his hands. He absolutely loved it!

"Unbelievable!" he said, mesmerized by the beauty of the object. He couldn't believe this came from his father, someone who often told him that he spent too much time in a fantasy world and that he had to grow up. Words couldn't describe Aiden's excitement. It was the perfect gift.

Just when he thought that nothing could ruin the day, he felt a tap on his shoulder. Afraid to see who it was, Aiden slowly turned his head. His worst fears of who it was were confirmed by the sight of the tall person behind him.

It was Patrick.

"*Dammit! Not now!*" Aiden thought, noticing the sly grin on Patrick's face.

"Well, well, look at what we have here," Patrick said. "You're in possession of something that doesn't belong on school grounds. Aiden Russell, you just got yourself into some serious trouble."

"For what reason?!" Aiden demanded.

Patrick glanced to the dragon figurine.

"That looks mighty fancy for a middle school student to own," he said, his voice hinting a darker tone. "Did you steal it?"

Aiden glared at Patrick. He was truly insulted that he had been accused of something so low as stealing.

"It's a gift, and you're invading my personal space."

Patrick's eyes narrowed as he grabbed a hold of Aiden's shirt, pulling him up out of his chair rather roughly. The young boy almost let out a gasp for air as his shirt smacked into his neck.

"I don't give a damn if I'm in your personal space, buster. Now you're coming with me. You and that little figurine of yours."

Before Aiden could say anything, Patrick pulled him by the back of his shirt and pushed him towards the lunchroom door. Aiden grunted from the shove, forced to walk away from his backpack with the figurine in hand. He quickly glanced to see if Theresa, or any of the other administrators were watching the clear abuse of power. Lucky for Aiden, Theresa had just arrived at their table. The look on her face said it all: it was one she wore whenever anyone attempted to hurt Aiden.

Of course that didn't stop Patrick from being a royal jerk as he forced Aiden down the hallway. More than anything, Aiden wanted to punch the hall monitor in the face. Their size difference kept him from doing that, as well as the certain knowledge that his mom and dad would be mad if he did. Patrick took advantage of this, forcing Aiden to a door at the end of the hall.

"Open it," the hall monitor commanded, "or I'll pound your face into a pulp."

Aiden glared at Patrick as he reluctantly reached for the door. He was pretty sure that Patrick was also violating several rules about treating students, the look on his face practically said he did not care. Now would have been good for Theresa to show up with a teacher, but Aiden didn't have any chance to see if she was following with anyone. As he opened the door, he found that Patrick was leading him outside the school, by the baseball field.

"Get moving, punk." Patrick ordered, shoving him out the door with one push.

Aiden nearly tripped over his own feet as the hall monitor closed the door behind him. Patrick's grin disappeared as he approached Aiden in a much more threatening manner now. Aiden flinched as the big hall monitor pushed him against the chain link fence that separated the two from the baseball field.

"All right, you little runt," Patrick growled. "Where did you get that? And don't play dumb with me." the hall monitor spat. "That figurine you're holding. Where'd you get it?"

"What's it to you where I got it from, huh?!" Aiden spat back in anger. "It's none of your damn business!"

WHAM!

That one moment of defiance coast him dearly. Aiden gasped in pain when Patrick's fist slammed into his stomach. He tried to breathe as Patrick threw him to the ground.

"I'm not playing games here." Patrick growled. "You tell me where you got that dragon, or I'll break every bone in your damn body."

Aiden struggled to get up, coughing as he tried to breathe. Patrick's eyes seemed to glow now with a different color as he kicked Aiden's chest, driving what little breath he had out in harsh grunt.

"I'm giving you one last chance, punk: tell me where you got that figurine and I might let you live!"

Aiden stared up in shock, each breath making his lungs feel like they would burst. The hall monitor stood over him, cracking his fingers now.

"Time's up. The master will be very pleased with me when I take that thing from your limp hands, kid!"

Aiden almost asked what he meant when he said 'master', but his body wouldn't allow it. He was in so much pain!

Patrick drew his fist, ready to deliver another crushing blow. Aiden closed his eyes as he prepared to take the punch. Just when it felt like the punch was just to ram into him, the door swung open, slamming into the wall so hard it sounded like someone had fired a pistol. Both of them turned to look and Aiden felt relief spread across his face. It was Theresa. And based on how dark her normally bright green eyes looked, she was not happy.

"Back off," Patrick growled. "You can't protect this kid, girlie. Or do you WANT to join your little friend down on the ground?"

"I'll give you one warning," Theresa said, Aiden noticed there was a slight growl in her tone, before she took a few steps towards them. "Leave him and this place now, before I'm forced to take you out."

"T-Theresa, run," Aiden said. "G-G-Get the teachers..."

"Sorry Aiden," she said, clenching her fists. "This is something I have to do."

"Ha! Brave words from such a little girl." Patrick smiled. "Now get back inside or suffer his fate!"

Theresa's eyes flashed with anger as she stepped toward Patrick.

"I'll say it again: leave him alone and go, now."

Patrick's eyes narrowed as he charged towards her, raising his fist and throwing a punch that would knock a normal person out. However, Theresa easily dodged him, as if she had done it a thousand times. Aiden was shocked as he watched his friend grace-fully avoid another blow from Patrick.

Theresa laughed at Patrick's dumbfound look.

"What's the matter, beast? Your master didn't teach you what to do when someone moves?"

Before he could answer, Theresa astonished Aiden by deliv-ering a near-perfect roundhouse kick to Patrick's jaw, knocking him to the ground. The force of the kick caused the hall monitor to skid across the ground for a couple of inches. Before he could recover, Theresa ran to Aiden and helped him off the ground.

"Aiden, thank goodness I got here just in time!" She said, her kind tone returning when she spoke to him. "I'm so sorry I'm late!"

Aiden blinked, his mind still trying to process what was happening. How was it possible that Theresa, a person he'd known pretty much all his life, was capable of such quick combat moves? Right before he could ask her what was going on or about her combat skills, Patrick grunted and stood up slowly, however he hunched over in pain. He glared at the two friends, his eyes no longer green, but a sick pale orange as his skin began to crumble, revealing a shade of green underneath.

"You…" Patrick groaned, "You dragoness bitch! How dare you interfere?!"

"Dragoness?" Aiden said, glancing to Theresa in confusion. "What the hell is he talking about, Theresa?"

Theresa's eyes narrowed as she glared at Patrick, but she kept her grip on Aiden's shoulders.

"To hell with what the master wants!" Patrick roared out as his skin finished turning green, which resulted in his hair also disappearing. "I'm taking the two of you down, right here, right now!"

"Aiden, pay very close attention to what I am about to tell you," She instructed, glancing to the figurine in his hand, "Understand?"

"What? Theresa, what's going on?" Aiden asked, now more confused than ever.

"You have to trust me on this." She pointed to the dragon, "That figurine in your hands is no mere trinket. It's a weapon."

Aiden's eyes went to the figurine. A weapon? Was she serious?

"Theresa, what's-"

"Aiden, for all your life we've been friends," Theresa interrupted, her friendly smile returning once more. "You've always trusted me before, trust me now, and I'll explain everything."

Her smile did the trick. Aiden knew she was right: she had always been there for him and there was no one else that he trusted more. He nodded his head slowly, gripping the figurine in his hand tightly.

"Good." Theresa turned back to Patrick, the former hall monitor approaching them in anger. "There's a word that you need to speak in order to use the figurine, Aiden. Try to pronounce it correctly, ok?"

"Gotcha," Aiden said, the sweat from his palm making the figurine moist.

"Repeat after me, then stab him right in his heart," Theresa instructed. "*Ladbe.*"

Aiden glanced to the figurine before he pointed it at Patrick, who appeared to have finished transforming into whatever he really was. He could only pray that Theresa was right. As he swallowed the lump in his throat, he took a deep breath and concentrated.

"*Ladbe!*" He shouted.

As the strange world left his lips, it happened. A long, sharp blade extended out from the slot in the dragon's chest. Aiden's eyes widened in surprise at the sudden sword the figurine had just turned itself into. The blade itself was a mix of gold and silver metal, with the gold at the bottom and the silver at the top, shined like a bright star in the sunlight. Aiden couldn't believe what he was holding in his hand: the dragon figurine was an actual sword. With the added weight of the new metal that came out from the figurine, it became heavier than it looked, but he was able to hold on to it.

"Now Aiden!" Theresa shouted. "Stab him in the heart!"

Aiden snapped back to reality as he remembered her instructions. Patrick made a low growling sound before lunging at the two. With a quick thrust, Aiden plunged the new blade right into Patrick's heart. The green-skinned Patrick cried out in pain then burst into dust and vanished.

"W-What the hell just happened?!" he asked, his whole body trembling now. "I-I just killed him!"

"Aiden, Aiden!" Theresa shouted, shaking him. "Remember what I told you! Everything you want to know will be revealed but not here. We'd just draw in unwanted attention, now focus!"

Aiden stopped trembling, relaxing at Theresa's touch.

"Now, since we can't have a sword in school, repeat after me, and make it a habit of remembering it," she instructed. "*Regande.*"

Aiden stared at the sword in his hand as he spoke the strange word. "*Regande.*"

Just as instantly as the sword had appeared, it disappeared back into the dragon, almost as if it didn't exist at all. Theresa smiled and patted Aiden on his back.

"Good, this is very good," she said. "Now listen Aiden: things are about to really change. Nothing will ever be the same again."

Aiden turned the figurine in his hands, staring right into the ruby eyes of it. The feel of the sword and Patrick's green skin still fresh in his mind.

"Tell me about it."

CHAPTER 4 - REALITY IS NOT WHAT IT SEEMS

"Now listen very carefully," Theresa explained as she glanced at their surroundings. "Keep that figurine out of sight. Don't even think about pulling it out when we're back at the lunch table."

"Why? Besides of course the fact that it's a weapon." Aiden said, glancing at the figurine, or in this case, the sword.

"I told you, I'll explain everything after school." Theresa answered. This time she far more firm with her answer. "Just trust me, and please, keep it hidden for the rest of the day!"

The tone in Theresa's voice was something Aiden, admittedly, was not use to. Add that to the list of things that had been out of the ordinary this day.

Aiden sighed, deciding not to press Theresa's patience. Reluctantly he put the figurine into his pocket. The very moment he let go of the figurine though a new feeling of...emptiness filled him. He couldn't really explain it, but he hated having it out of his hand. He looked at the pile of dust that used to be Patrick, the hall monitor he had just stabbed with the blade. He swallowed a lump in his throat, common sense returning in a rush. It felt like the whole world was spinning.

"Theresa, I just killed a man, right there!" he exclaimed, pointing at what was left of Patrick. "We need to get out of here, fast!"

Her hand suddenly covered his mouth. This caught him off guard, as she had never been this fast before in her life. The grip she had around his lips felt like an iron clap.

"Would you be quiet?!" Theresa snapped, her eyes flashing daggers. "The only way they're gonna find you is if you keep shouting like a lunatic!"

Something about the tone of her voice made Aiden uneasy. Theresa had never spoken like that to him before or anyone like that before. He could not remember any time in his life when she had yelled at anyone, let alone him. But that was not the only thing different about her: her eyes had changed while she was speaking.

Theresa's eyes were always warm and welcoming. They were the kind of eyes that you would place your trust in. She had a new look in her eyes, one that was unusual of Theresa. It was like she had been given a mission and that she could not fail. She had always been a strong and determined friend, but this was new - different. Aiden sighed quietly and quickly nodded his head. He felt her hand pull away from his mouth as she turned to her right once again. Then she turned back to him, motioning with her head towards the door.

"Let's go. We gotta get back to our table and finish lunch."

"Lunch?!" Aiden gasped. "Finish lunch?! What about Patrick?!"

"Aiden now is not the time to explain, trust me. It will all become clear, but not now."

Before he could argue further, Theresa grabbed his wrist with a firm grasp. She pulled him back inside the school, moving quickly to avoid being seen by any teachers who might be looking out from their rooms. Aiden wasn't used to being dragged about like this, but after seeing Theresa take on a fully-grown man and make it look like child's play, he followed along.

"Whatever you do, keep quiet about the figurine. And keep it out of sight," She explained. "Their eyes are everywhere, watching for the signs. And don't you even think about asking me who those eyes belong to."

"Wasn't even gonna ask." Aiden thought. This whole situation was so outside of "normal" he didn't know what to do.

The two eventually reached their table at the lunchroom, their stuff untouched, and took their seats. Aiden frowned as his friend looked around them, expecting some kind of attack. Not that he blamed her; after what happened with Patrick, he was nervous too.

Ok, he was more than nervous. He was terrified. How could he not be? He had just stabbed some kind of...person in the heart!

"It looks like we're safe here," Theresa said, before she turned back to her lunch. "Let's hope it stays that way for the rest of the day."

"How come we have to wait until the end of the school day?! Why can't we just leave now, skip school?" Aiden asked in desperation, "Why all the secrets Theresa?!"

"Aiden, there's way too much to explain here at school." Theresa frowned. "If I could tell you right now, I would. But it's way too open here. I can't tell who might be listening. So for now, we have to act totally normal like nothing has happened. That means staying in school for the day, just like always. Believe me, this is a conversation you don't want anyone else to hear."

"Could you please at least tell me a little bit about what's going on?!" He was desperate for answers; not knowing anything was the worst feeling of all. "You had me kill-"

"Dammit Aiden! I am begging you to keep quiet about this until we are at your home today. So please, drop it!"

The two sat in silence as Aiden watched her eyes light up again up like they were on fire. Aiden timidly looked away, not wanting to cause her anger to rise up again in response to his questions. At that very moment his stomach growled. The whole commotion had made him forget that they were at lunch. Food would be a welcome bit of normalcy.

Theresa had bought him a plate of spaghetti with meatballs and an apple. It wasn't his ideal lunch, but he wasn't complaining. After what he had just went through, he could use some 'normal' food. He took a hold of a fork in his hand he began to play with one meatball, not meeting Theresa's eyes after her last comment. It was an uncomfortable silence. The two were always talking with one another during lunch. But now? He was afraid to even ask a question, let alone start a conversation.

He glanced up at her every now and then as he took bites from his lunch. She seemed less angry, but Aiden could tell that she wasn't going to give him any answers soon. Theresa must have known that he was watching her as he ate.

"...I'm sorry," Theresa finally said.

Aiden picked up the apple that she had gotten him and prepared to take a bite. Theresa's voice was no longer defensive or angry; it was kind and gentle as usual. Her eyes were also back to normal, warm and welcoming.

"You didn't deserve to be snapped at." Her smile returned. "I know you're confused and scared about what's happened. Believe me, I intend to explain it all to you when school is over, I promise."

A feeling of relief washed over Aiden. The Theresa he had known all his life had not vanished completely. A smile crept across his face.

"For a second there, I thought you weren't ever gonna smile again," he said, taking a bite of his apple.

"Not too much to smile about today, but I'm trying."

That smile on his lips quickly turned back into a frown. Man that rang true.

The bell rang, signaling the end of lunch period. Aiden groaned in annoyance; they'd lost half of the lunch period thanks to Patrick, but then he guessed Patrick had lost a lot more. He felt the figurine in his pocket one last time before gathering his backpack, but he couldn't stop thinking about what had just happened. It was so much to take in.

Here he thought today was going to be just like any other day. It started out as a normal day, but now Theresa was acting differently, Patrick had nearly killed him, Patrick was gone - and for what? A dragon figurine his father had given him? His fist began to get a bit sweaty with excitement as he thought about it..

"A dragon figurine like something from a fantasy novel and my dad found it? Where? How? Does he even know this thing is a sword? More importantly, how in the world did he even find this thing?!" He thought. "Must be more to dad than I thought." Now that was something tough to wrap your head around for sure.

"Aiden! Hurry up or we'll be late for class!" Theresa called out from the doorway. As he got close to her she hissed between her teeth, "Everything has to look normal, everything!"

With a sigh, he followed her to their next to last class of the day: science. As the two sat down at their table, Aiden noticed that Theresa was finally calming down. When he asked her why she leaned in an whispered.

"Their eyes cannot find us here," she said around the edges of a smile. "Just relax and we'll be fine."

Aiden had no idea what she meant by 'their eyes' but he didn't dare question her. Deciding to take her advice, he relaxed into the lesson. However, he knew he could not escape the final class of the day, no matter how much he wanted to avoid it.

P.E.

Next to math, P.E. was Aiden's least favorite class. He had never enjoyed it. All the coach did was tell them to put their backpacks away, grab a basketball, and go shoot some hoops. Once in a while the coach would have them do different activities, such as running track, dodge ball, and the obstacle course that was set up outside. But for the majority of the classes, it was nothing but basketball, a sport that filled Aiden with disdain.

"Ugh, I hate this class," Aiden grumbled as he put his backpack in the storage room, since the locker room by the gym were being renovated.

"It's only for an hour, Aiden," Theresa said, trying to keep his spirits up.

"An hour of boring basketball. Joy. It seems like a lifetime."

Theresa rolled her eyes at his displeasure as they joined their classmates. Coach Bryan, their P.E. teacher, walked out of his office. He was a big man; not muscular, just big, particularly around the belly. He was fatter than anyone Aiden had ever seen in his life. From his head to his toes, he was fat. His fat probably had fat. He sported a buzz cut matched with a small goatee. Aiden always wondered how someone so large could be a P.E, coach.

"All right, listen up!" Coach Bryan yelled out, getting everyone's the attention. "Today, basketball is off the list of activities."

Aiden must have been the only student, aside from Theresa, who wanted to shout 'Yes!' at the top of his lungs. But he kept his mouth shut, knowing that he would be the target of his classmates who adored basketball. Coach Bryan turned towards the ball room, taking his keys and opening it.

"Today, we are going to play dodge ball." Coach Bryan's words were punctuated by dodge balls bouncing across the gym floor.

Everyone groaned at his announcement. The coach turned around on a dime, squinting at the students through eyes surrounded by fat, like a giant pig. His entire face became covered in a bright pink red. There was only emotion that went with face whenever their coach made that expression. Anger.

"Quit your whining! Everyone get up and separate into two teams. The first person to complain is getting a referral to the principal's office!"

No one dared complain after that threat. Coach Bryan was known for having a terrible temper, often exploding at students who dared to argue back. For some reason, the school had never fired him. Theresa had joked about starting a campaign to have him effectively removed, but no one dared to speak out in fear of being in more trouble.

Aiden groaned into his palms in frustration. Dodgeball. The only other sport he did not lik in gym class. The harrowing memories from elementary school filled his mind at the mere thought of having to play this accursed sport. No matter what happened, Aiden would always be targeted by the other team. And to make matters even worse, Eric was usually on the other team.

That just made the sport even worse to him.

"Well, look at the bright side," Theresa said as the two of them became part of the first team. "It's not basketball."

"Not funny, Theresa."

And just like that, the class was forced to participate in dodge ball. Throughout the class Aiden found himself running back and forth between his team's side of the court. Very rarely was he able to find an opportunity to throw a counter attack back at the other side. He almost got hit a couple times in the head by the dodge balls while he dodged. If it wasn't a school class, Aiden could have sworn that the other team was trying to take his head off!

At least he was an expert in dodging incoming objects. Being Eric's top target as a bully victim, which was almost his entire life, had taught him how to become an expert at dodging attacks. A trait that he was glad to have, but he knew that in the end doing nothing but dodging would make him too tired to counter the opposing team.

"Give…me…a break." He panted as he dodged another ball. He had been on the defensive for some time now and he was getting tired of running all over the court. The toll of dodging nonstop was beginning to take an effect on his legs and breathing.

"Hold still already!" one of the students cried out from the other team, throwing another ball straight at him.

Once more, Aiden dodged the ball. A slight groan of frustration escaped his lips as he looked over to where his best friend was. Like he thought, she was on the offensive side.

He didn't complain about this of course. He knew very well that Theresa was better at throwing than he was. As they had grown up together, and through many MANY dodge ball games, the two of them had developed a tactic that worked well when they played on the same team. Aiden would catch the other team's attention so they would focus their fire on him, then Theresa would take shots at the person whose guard was down.

However, on the opposing team that faced them, was one group of students that were so good at dodge ball they could not be fooled that easily by their tactics. This group was known as "The Hornets," troubled students with a record for misbehavior that rivaled Eric's. No one was certain how they earned their nickname. The best guess anyone could make for the strange name was that it came from the stinging impact of their throws. Aiden, from past experiences, could one hundred percent vouch for that.

The leader of the Hornets, Jason Costain, had set his eyes on Aiden from the beginning of the game. Jason had always disliked Aiden, almost to the level of hatred. Why? Aiden, or anyone in general, knew the answer to that question. The leader of the gang gave a smug laugh as he tossed his ball up and down before he took his shot. Jason pulled back his arm and threw the ball straight at Aiden, bypassing all of the other students.

"Look out!" Theresa called out as he dodged another ball.

Before he could blink, the ball came flying at his face. Aiden cursed silently as it approached him, but he was too tired to dodge another ball after avoiding being hit by the previous one. Time seemed to slow down to an inch as he realized right then and there he had only one option to avoid being hit in the face.

He would have to grab it with both hands.

That alone was easier said than done; Jason threw harder than any student in the school. Even Eric did not throw as hard as the Hornets leader did. The best defense there was to avoid being hit by a ball thrown by Jason was to just dodge and pray he didn't have another one to throw. That option was no longer available to him though as the ball soared at him. It was either his hands or his face.

Aiden chose his hands.

It all played out like it was the fight shot in some big sports movie. Aiden threw his hands up to catch the ball speeding towards him. Reality suddenly came crashing back as the stinging impact from the ball met the palms of his hands. He winced from the pain upon the impact, but despite it all he somehow held onto it. If you dropped a needle in that gymnasium, it would easily be heard in the silence that followed. In Bryan's gym when someone caught the ball the person throwing it was out for the rest of the round. It made everyone in the class that could throw compete just to not be bored out of their minds.

"I don't believe it." Jason muttered as Aiden glanced at the ball he held.

"Jason, you're out!" Coach Bryan shouted from the sidelines. Jason clenched his fists in anger, glaring back at Aiden as he walked off the court..

"Nicely done, Aiden!" Theresa called out as she dodged a ball.

Aiden smiled briefly as he dodged another ball. Now all he had to do was endure the last few minutes of the class before the buses arrived.

The game continued on for what seemed like forever. More balls were thrown, even more were dodged, and few actually made impact with their targets. At long last, after what felt like an hour longer than a usual class, Coach Bryan finally blew his whistle, signaling the end of the game.

"All right, put the balls away, get your backpacks and get out of here!" he shouted. "Head to your home rooms before the buses arrive!"

Sighing with relief, Aiden leaned against the wall, breathing heavily. His legs felt like jelly; it had been a while since he ran that hard. Theresa jogged over to him, patting him on the back as the rest of their classmates grabbed their bags from the storage room.

"You're pretty good at catching you know," she said. "I think you should practice and see how good you can be."

Aiden scoffed at that suggestion.

"Please, I just got lucky" He stretched a bit as he glanced to the door. "You better get back to home room. I'll catch up with you."

Theresa shook her head, looking suddenly older.

"Luck is just where skill meets opportunity, Aiden."

And with that, she turned and left him alone in the gymnasium. Aiden walked pushed open the door to the storage room and walked inside to where his backpack lay against the wall, reaching down to pick it up.

At least he had made it through the day, one where he had to stab a hall monitor...monster thing. The security of the school bus never felt any better than it did right now. Aiden could almost smell the diesel fumes inside the bus. He was looking forward to the ride home. Maybe Theresa would share some of the story about the figurine. Maybe things were taking a turn for the better.

The thought died as he noticed the five shadows blocking the exit to the storage room. Aiden swallowed a lump in his throat when he saw the leader of the Hornets, Jason, with four lackeys by his side. All of them looking incredibly ticked off at the mere sight of him.

"Well now, look who's the last one to get his stuff together," Jason said, taking a menacing step towards Aiden.

"I don't want any trouble, Jason. Why don't you and your friends get out of my way already?"

"Afraid I can't do that, asshole," Jason snarled his lips back. "See, no one makes a fool of me or the Hornets. So the boys and I all came to an agreement: Your "catch" today requires payback."

Jason's lackeys cracked their knuckles, which gave off a sickening sound. That was a sound Aiden was all too familiar with when bullies tried to use numbers to intimidate their prey. He glanced over to the clock hanging over the gym door. The timing couldn't have been worse for him to mess with the school's local punk gang. And of course, there wasn't any sign of the coach. Typical.

"I don't have time for this," Aiden muttered, pushing past Jason. "Get out of my way and leave me alone."

"Do you have a hearing problem, loser?" Jason asked, suddenly snatching Aiden by his left arm, "I said, we require payback!"

Before he knew what was happening, Jason kneed Aiden right into his stomach. With a loud gasp of pain, Aiden fell back and tried to breathe. Jason and his lackeys approached again, their eyes so dark they almost didn't seem human.

"Maybe we should show you just why they call us the Hornets," Jason mused. "Screw what the boss ordered. This punk is dead! Boys, let's ditch these pointless disguises."

"Disguises?" Aiden thought, glancing up at the word.

He almost wished he didn't. What he saw made his face pale and his stomach tighten into a knot of fear. Jason and his gang were definitely not human. In the time that Aiden was keeled over the gang had suddenly altered their appearances, much like Patrick did earlier. Their faces had become more bug-like, closely resembling a hornet's face. Hornet wings sprouted from their backs. The normal pigmentation of their skin turned into an unusual combination of yellow and black. Antennas sprouted from their foreheads as Aiden watched in horror. Their transformations complete, the giant "hornet men" laughed.

"Well, I gotta be honest," Jason said, his voice buzzing on each word, "I was expecting you to go running away like a coward, like most humans do when they spot their betters, but it's obvious you're not completely surprised. Hmmm, I wonder what else you've seen today?"

Aiden glanced around, hopelessly searching for Coach Bryan; he'd already seen him leave the gym after dismissing class, but Aiden couldn't keep himself from hoping. Of course he knew that he probably wouldn't have been able to do much, but it was better than facing giant anthromorphic insects on his own!

A dash of hope swelled up in his chest as he remembered the figurine. Maybe...maybe that could turn the tables against his attackers. He would just have to hope no one would walk in to spot him swinging a sword around. Aiden quickly took off his backpack, fumbled around to get it open before he grabbed it and pulled it out, his hand tightly clenched around the body of the dragon. The heat from his palms relaxing when he felt the cool of its touch.

"Oh please, what's that supposed to do?" Jason smugly asked. "You gonna use a little toy to scare us?"

"Come on...remember the word..." Aiden searched his mind, trying to remember what it was Theresa told him to unleash the sword.

"Well, if you're done standing around like a fool, we'll teach you never to mess with us again. Boys, get him."

The Hornet gang approached, wings buzzing. Each step they took made their wings flutter quickly. Closing his eyes tightly, Aiden continued to search for the word. Before the gang took another step, it came rushing back to him. Quickly opening his eyes, Aiden shouted out.

"Ladbe!"

As it did before with Patrick, the golden and silver blade sprang forth. Jason's crew took a step back, shocked by the sudden appearance of the sword. One of them glanced to Jason, buzzing. Aiden knew that they were communicating, but he sure couldn't understand it. Jason turned to the hornet buzzing by him, and then smacked the hornet hard across its face.

"You idiots!" he shouted. "Why are you scared? He might have a sword, but you have wings. Use them!"

Aiden's face paled; he had forgotten about the wings. He tightened his grip. If only he hadn't told Theresa to head back to homeroom, maybe she could have done something to help.

Jason's gang buzzed, whether from joy or excitement he couldn't tell. Not that it mattered; they had the advantage and it looked like they were going to use it.

The hornet gang took flight, their wings humming loudly as they circled him. Aiden's face was covered in sweat.

"C-Come on you freaks!" he yelled. "If you're gonna fight me, fight me on the ground!"

"Ha! We are not some mindless animals in some stupid movie," Jason laughed, or at least it was the closest thing to a laugh a hornet faced being could make. "We fight to win! Boys, get him!"

On his command, the other hornets charged Aiden. Each one threw a kick at him from above. Aiden swung his sword in a circle, hoping to hit at least one of them. He must have hit something, because he heard a slicing sound as a hornet face shrieked in pain. Aiden glanced to his left: one of the hornet gang members had lost an insect like arm to his blade.

"You dumb asses!" Jason yelled, his antennae squirming like wild. "Don't attack him all at once. Use your brains! Wear him down and then we'll kill him!"

As Jason's voice rang out the hornets flew away from Aiden, each preparing their own strike against him. Aiden could feel himself panting now. Jason was right. The dodge ball game had worn him out. He was in no condition to fight a group of flying "hornet men." How could you even train for that? Besides, he didn't know anything about fighting anyway. He would not have the time to think about that now though, as the first hornet charged him!

Aiden swung his sword at the hornet hoping for another lucky hit. No such luck, as the hornet easily dodged his attack. Before he could turn around, he felt the hornet kick him in the back. Aiden didn't even get a chance to cry out in pain before another hornet came after him. This time, it was the hornet whose arm he had cut off. Aiden forced himself to stand up straight, readying his sword.

He pulled his arms back, quickly thrusting at the hornet. This time he hit his mark, stabbing him right in the stomach. Aiden smiled; it felt so good when his sword slid into the hornet. That feeling disappeared quickly, however, as something hit him hard in the back - twice. Grunting in pain, he fell, trying to hang onto his sword's hilt as best as he could. Jason hovered above him, with a smug look in his eyes.

"You're weak, Aiden. You should be thanking us for ending your miserable life right now." Jason's buzzing laugh came back once again as his gang, except for the one Aiden stabbed, floated above Aiden.

"I know the boss told us to not take your life, but you pissed me off. Big mistake on your part. It's time to finish you off once and for all!" Jason shouted. "Boys, ready your stingers!"

The hornet gang flew into the air once again, their lower abdomens positioning themselves straight towards Aiden. He forced himself up from the ground, gasping for breath. He was running out of options, and ideas. Maybe if he hadn't run so much during dodge ball he might have stood a chance. It was almost like they were wearing him out on purpose during PE.

"Theresa..." he whispered. "I need help..."

Jason's crew flew down towards him, ready to finish him. Aiden tried to stand back up, but his body betrayed him. Even with all the determination he could muster his strength had left his body. This was it. There would be no answers for him now.

Just stingers piercing his flesh. If only Theresa were here. He closed his eyes so he wouldn't have to watch them sting him. Then nothing.

Aiden thought the hornets were trying to scare him to death. Then he thought they must be waiting for something. He could still hear the buzzing wings, but he had not been stung. Curiosity overcame fear and he opened his eyes. What he saw nearly made his eyes jump out of his head.

Standing over him was Theresa, two large, white, reptilian-like wings sprouting from her back, covering both her and Aiden. Above her wings the hornet gang hovered. Relief and confusion swept through Aiden. He was glad to see Theresa, and even happier that the stingers were not piercing his flesh, but wings?

"Wait. Wings?" He barely managed to gasp out.

If Aiden had learned anything being Theresa's friend, it was that when she was angry, it was best to stay out of her way. He watched as Theresa pulled her elegant white wings back, flapping them once, making the hornet stingers fall harmlessly to the floor. She glared at the hornet gang, clenching her fist.

"You cowards," she growled, "attacking one untrained, one worn out from exercise, ganging up on him. You have no honor."

"A Dragoness?! Here?!" Jason shrieked. It was then that Aiden noticed that Jason and his crew had grown new stingers. He thought, "Why can't they just die like a bee after it stings someone?"

"Why protect this boy? You have nothing to gain from doing so, and much to lose!"

"I don't think I need to answer you, bug." Theresa's eyes narrowed. "Your kind never could keep your noses out of things that did not concern you."

Jason laughed again, the buzzing sound driving Aiden crazy.

"Typical," he mused. "You and your kind always had a superiority complex. Isn't that the same attitude that brought about the end of your species?"

Theresa's eyes flashed with an intense anger. Her mighty wings flapped once, which resulted in a gust of air rising up to blow right into the hornet men.

"Do I look extinct to you?"

She held her palms out towards them. The hornet gang flew back, but stopped when Jason punched one of them behind their neck.

"Get her you fools!" he shouted. "Sting her now!"

"Aiden, keep your head down and don't move until I tell you to." She didn't need to say it twice. He kept low to the ground. If it were possible, he would pull the earth up over him like a blanket.

With great reluctance, the hornets charged Theresa, stingers at the ready once again. Before they could reach their target however, there was a strange sound, like a snap. Aiden only had a few seconds to wonder what the snap was, before he felt something very hot above his head. Curiosity got to him as he raised his head, right in time to watch as his best friend aimed her palms at the flying gang.

"*Flarnea!*" Theresa shouted.

A stream of white fire seemed to explode from the palms of her hands. The fire flew towards the hornet gang, leaving a strong 'hissing' sound as it burned away at the air. The hornets proved to be slower than Theresa's attack and could not get out of the way in time. The white flames consumed each and every one of them, reaching Jason last. As he began to burn, he cried out in anger.

"Damn you Dragoness! The master will make you pay!"

The white fire consumed Jason. Just as quickly as it had appeared, the stream of white fire vanished. Unlike regular fire, it did not seem to leave a streak of smoke, nor did it burn away at anything in the gym. Even the ashes of the once threatening Hornet gang were gone. Theresa pulled her arms back, letting out a deep sigh as her large reptilian wings slid back into her shoulders, disappearing beneath her skin. She wasted no time as she snapped her fingers once, the part of her shirt where the wings erupted from began to reconstruct itself back to normal. She turned her attention to Aiden, who was utterly amazed by what he had seen.

"Thank goodness I got here in time," Theresa said, kneeling down to help him off the ground. "When I got to homeroom I had a feeling something was wrong. I ran back here as fast as I could."

"I'm just glad you came when you did," Aiden said, wincing from the pain radiating across his back. "If you hadn't, I would be dead from their stingers."

His eyes widened as he remembered the stingers on the ground.

"Theresa, the stingers!" he said. Theresa raised an eyebrow at him.

"What about them?"

"If they were like actual hornets, then their stingers had some kind of venom to them!" Aiden explained, "You took four of them in your…wings!"

Theresa giggled lightly and shook her head at him.

"You're worried that the venom from their stingers will affect me somehow?"

"Of course I am!" Aiden exclaimed. "Didn't you see how large they were? That's probably five times the amount of a normal hornet's venom!"

"Ten times, to be more accurate," Theresa said, smiling. "You don't have to worry, Aiden. Hornet demons might have extremely potent venom, but against my kind? Their venom can't affect us."

Aiden blinked, remembering what both Patrick and Jason had called Theresa. He had been skeptical. Perhaps Patrick was just exaggerating when he called her a 'Dragoness.' But now that Jason called her by the same thing, he knew she was not human.

"Your kind? Then...both Patrick and Jason called you 'Dragoness.'" He looked her in the eye. "Theresa...who are you? What are you?"

Theresa giggled again and smiled at him.

"Aiden, by now I think you should have figured out reality is not what it seems," she said as she picked up his sword and returned it to him.

"What Patrick and Jason called me though, was true." She closed her eyes briefly, and then opened them up once again. Aiden could sense the true power behind them. Quietly he whispered *regande* to retract the sword into the figurine.

"I am Theresa, the Dragoness of White Fire, second in command to the former Dragon King and leader of his armies."

She smiled. "But more importantly," she continued, "I am, and will always be, your friend."

Aiden promptly fainted.

CHAPTER 5 - WHEN DRAGONS RULED

"Come on Aiden," Theresa said, shaking his shoulders. "Get up!"

Aiden opened his eyes, looking up at Theresa's face, a face that looked the same as it did yesterday – even if nothing else was the same. He couldn't decide if today was the strangest day of his life or the greatest. His best friend was a dragon. A dragon? For real? For a moment, he felt like the coolest kid in the world. A dragon was his best friend? That was almost every kid's dream. Aiden, however, was not a little kid anymore and this was no dream. He placed the figurine in his backpack before turning to Theresa.

"If you're a dragon, then does…"

"Dragoness," Theresa corrected, helping him up. "Dragon is a term used for the males of my kind."

Aiden raised an eyebrow.

"How come I never heard the word before? If the word dragon is used for males, why do myths and legends never mention dragonesses?"

Theresa shrugged her shoulders as they walked out of the gym.

"I honestly can't tell you why," she said. "Humans tend to have the worst memories of the species from the pre-history Kingdoms."

"Pre-history!?" Aiden asked. "You're not telling me that dragons existed before the time of the dinosaurs, are you?"

Theresa laughed at his question.

"Goodness no," she said between her giggles. "If there's one thing your historians are correct about, it was that dinosaurs came eons before either one of our kinds existed."

"What about Jason and his hornets? Or Patrick? What were they?"

"Aiden, remember, I promised I would tell you everything when we got back to your house," Theresa said in a calm tone. "Hopefully you'll pay attention, because I don't want to explain it a second time."

Aiden nodded his head. He knew if he was going to get any more answers, he was going to have to be patient, but it just wasn't in his nature. After an eventful day, he was ready for some answers. His mind was going into overdrive about the possibilities. One question couldn't wait until they got home.

"Hey, Theresa?"

"Yeah?"

"If you're a dragoness, how is it that you look like…well, you know…" He hesitated to finish his question, not wanting to offend her. Theresa had no such concern, and finished his question for him.

"Why do I look like a human?" She smiled again. "Well, just like Patrick and the hornets, dragons have a choice of two forms. Our original form and any form that we wish to use for our disguise."

Aiden blinked. He wasn't expecting that answer at all.

"So then, if it's a disguise you're wearing, does that mean that it's not a real body?"

Theresa sighed at the question, but she didn't frown at it.

"No, Aiden," she said. "Our original forms go through a metamorphosis state, meaning that our human disguises are still our bodies, but just in a different shape and size."

"So you can transform into your original form whenever you want?"

"Yes," Theresa answered. "This is the last thing I'll explain before we get to your house." She looked around the hall before speaking up again. "There is a reason we should not be talking about this here. We can morph into our original bodies when we want to, but for the most part we tend to remain in our human form. Mostly because of the massive size difference when we do transform into our true forms."

She gave him a sly smile and a wink.

"And let me tell you, being at least fifteen feet tall isn't exactly the ideal body size to be in a building."

Aiden's eyes grew wide. Theresa's original form was over fifteen feet tall? He had never been so excited in his entire life. He wanted to ask another question, but held back when he saw her eyes giving him a defiant 'shut up' expression. After a short walk back from the gym room the two reached their homeroom door, but before they entered Theresa turned to him.

"Now listen to me, Aiden." She spoke in a more serious tone. "You can not reveal to anyone what I really am or what has happened here today. Understand?"

Aiden nodded his head.

"Good."

The two of them entered their homeroom, taking their seats in silence as the rest of the class remained caught up in the endless chatter about what they were planning to do for their spring break. Aiden himself was in the middle of picturing what Theresa's dragon form looked like. Maybe it would resemble the European Dragons he'd read about in old fables. Or she could resemble one of the Chinese Dragons, which had serpent-shaped bodies and long whiskers on their noses. He thought he could probably scratch Chinese Dragons off the list though since Theresa had wings. Chinese Dragons did not possess wings, at least not in books.

He closed his eyes as his mind began to wonder away from the reality of homeroom. He pictured himself riding on the back of a dragon, flying high above the rest of the world. Free from any cares or worries. He had always wondered what it was like to fly; maybe now he was going to get the chance.

His daydreaming was cut short by the school bell. Reality came back to him as he stood up from his desk, and he and Theresa walked to their bus. He glanced over his shoulder, noticing that Eric was not preparing a spit wad for him.

"Hey, Theresa," he whispered. "Is there any chance that Eric is a monster as well?"

"If you're thinking that Eric isn't human, I hate to tell you he's no monster."

"Dammit. The way he acts you would think that he was one of them."

Theresa smiled and patted his back.

"You want to know how I know he's not a monster? It's simple really: All mythical beings are capable of telling a human apart from a creature in human form," she explained.

"Then how come Patrick and The Hornets couldn't tell who you were?" he asked.

"Patrick and The Hornets eyes are not as good at such as my kind, harpies, griffons, the usual fantasy creatures you would find in those Dungeons and Dragons games you play."

"Hey, I don't play D&D!" Aiden proclaimed, pursing his lips. "My father and I already have enough arguments about me being into fantasy things. If I played D&D he would blow the roof off our home."

Theresa smiled as she leaned her head back on their bus seat.

"Well get this fact into your head, Aiden, fantasy creatures do exist. They always have and always will. You'll need to learn how to tell them apart from regular humans, but you'll learn that eventually."

Aiden smiled as he shook his head.

"You'll have to teach me after you tell me everything," he reminded her.

"I know, I know. Believe me, I have every intention to explain what is going on," she told him, putting a hand on his shoulder. "You just gotta remember to keep your mouth shut about all this. Not even your parents get to know."

Aiden had no problem with that. Although he loved his mother dearly, he would never tell her anything that could possibly make her scared for his life. As for his father? Well, they rarely talked as it was, so he didn't see any reason to let his father know what had happened.

"Today started out just like any other morning and now I find out that fantasy creatures are real. This is the kind of thing I could only dream about."

"Well it's no dream," Theresa said. "Now, keep quiet about it until we get to your house. We don't want anybody eavesdropping on us now, do we?"

"Good point," Aiden said, knowing that many of the students of his middle school were excellent at listening to conversations that were supposed to be private.

He glanced back at Eric, making sure that the bully was not preparing anything special for him. For once, it seemed like he was going to stay quiet. Aiden sighed in relief, then almost on instinct ducked as a spit wad flew into the windshield of the bus.

"Eric!" The bus driver shouted. "The first day you come back from spring break, I'm giving you a referral for detention!"

Aiden kept his thoughts to himself as he heard Eric's groan. If there was one thing he liked about Eric, it was the constant detentions he got for himself. The bus started up and slowly drove away from the school. Aiden's eyes grew tired as the bus moved on. He tried to keep them open, hoping to stay awake as long as possible. Theresa turned to him, a small frown appearing on her face.

"Go ahead and take your regular bus ride nap, Aiden," she said. "You summoned your sword more times than you should today. You need to recover your strength."

"But what about the bus stop?"

"I'll wake you when we get there." Theresa flicked his forehead with one finger. "Now go on and get some sleep."

Aiden wanted to say something else, but his eyelids finally gave out and his eyes closed.

As Aiden slept he saw strange images. Clear as day he saw Theresa, giving him her familiar smile. Beside her, though, were two figures completely shrouded in shadows. He tried, but he could not make out their facial features. He turned back to Theresa's image; behind her was a large creature of sorts, shrouded in shadows so thick he could not make out what it really was.

With a thunderous boom a voice in his head suddenly spoke.

"One has been found, yet two remain," it said. *"Time runs short, young one."*

Aiden looked up at the giant shadow, trying to pinpoint the location of the voice.

"Who are you?" he asked. "What do you mean by 'two remain'?"

"Who I am is of no importance for the time being," the voice said. Aiden could tell that it was not coming from the large creature he saw in his dream, but it was beginning to fade away.

"Focus on finding the remaining two..."

"Wait!" Aiden shouted, but it was too late. The voice vanished into the shadows of his dream. He turned back to Theresa and the two shadow cloaked figures. Two remain? He tried to process that. Did the voice mean that there were other dragons besides Theresa?

"Aiden?" Theresa's voice rang out in the dream. "Aiden, wake up."

"Huh?" Aiden woke with a start; they were at their bus stop. "Oh, thanks Theresa."

The two of them got off the bus just in time as far as Aiden was concerned. He wanted answers to all his questions. It was more than about the sword and Patrick now. He realized he was more involved than he thought. Theresa noticed the confused look on his face, frowning at him.

"What's wrong? I thought you'd be happy to finally be back home?" she asked.

"Sorry," he replied, "I just…it's really a lot to take in."

"I know it's a lot," Theresa said, "but you have to understand what is really going on."

Aiden smiled as they began walking towards his house.

"Do your folks know that you're coming over?" he asked.

"Don't worry about them." Theresa smiled. "I sent them a text saying that I was gonna help you with a history report and that I would be home soon."

"That's good to know," Aiden said, but then another question came to mind.

"Are your parents dragons as well?"

Theresa gave him a look, almost as if she were offended.

"If you mean my original parents, then yes, they were dragons," she answered.

"Oh, no no!" Aiden quickly said. "I meant your other parents!"

The insulted look on Theresa's face vanished as her familiar smile came back.

"My modern family is human," she said. "Just like your family."

"But…how is it that you're a Dragoness and they're human?"

"It's a long story." She glanced over her shoulder quickly. "Add it to the list of things that need to be explained."

Aiden smiled. It wasn't every day that Theresa explained

herself. It was like a rare historical event, like Haley's Comet passing over the Earth. He shook his head: no, that wasn't right; the comet came around way more often than that.

At long last the two arrived at his house. They entered to the sound of a teapot screeching on the stove. Theresa wrinkled her nose as the smell of herbal tea floated in the room. Aiden's mother was known for making really good and fancy teas, though the smell of some of them was often so strong they made one's eyes water.

"Mom, I'm home!" Aiden called out.

"I'm in the kitchen honey making dinner."

"I see your mother still has a taste for fancy tears, I mean teas," Theresa said, her nose still wrinkling.

"Oh come on, Theresa," Aiden joked. "Mom's teas don't smell that bad."

Theresa pursed her lips at him.

"You try having a sense of smell that's stronger than a wolf's and tell me that," she grumbled as she folded her arms across her chest.

"Is that Theresa with you, Aiden?" his mother asked from the kitchen.

"Yes, Mom," he called back. "She and I are gonna work on a history report for a while, OK?"

"Would she like to stay for dinner? I'm making roast, potatoes, and carrots tonight."

Both Aiden and Theresa's faces went pale at the mere mention of that meal. Theresa shook her head quickly. Aiden's mother was a very fine cook, there was no denying that. But one meal neither of them could stomach: roast, potatoes, and carrots.

There was a little history to this. When Aiden's mother had learned how to cook the meal, it was a brand new dinner to try out and it wasn't bad. But then came a very long and cold December. While Theresa's parents were out of town, she stayed with them for the month. The snow had hit the roads really hard and no one could drive anywhere. Aiden's mother though had prepared a big dinner that night of roast, potatoes and carrots. It was so large that they could not finish it in one serving, or even one week of servings. For the rest of the month, they had leftovers from the meal.

And it got really old, really quickly.

"Not tonight, Mrs. Russell," Theresa said finally. "I promised my dad that I'd be home as soon as I was done studying with Aiden."

Aiden shot her a nasty glare. She knew how much he disliked the meal, especially if he had to eat it alone.

"All right, if you're sure!" Aiden's mother called back, "You two have fun studying now, OK?"

"OK, Mom!" Aiden said as they went to his room. As soon as he closed the door, making certain that his mother could not hear a word they were going to say, he turned his focus to Theresa. A less than pleased expression graced his lips.

"You're evil, you know that?"

"Hey, I already went through one month of eating that meal day after day. I am never eating it again."

"Oh, so I should have to suffer alone?"

"When it comes to roast, potatoes, and carrots? Yes."

Aiden rolled his eyes as he closed the door to his room. He sighed and sat down in his comfy chair. Theresa sat on the foot of his bed. It had been a very long day, but at last he was finally going to get some answers.

"Are you ready?" Theresa asked.

Aiden nodded his head, trying to keep his excitement to a minimum as Theresa began.

"Long ago, before the time of recorded ancient human civilizations, there existed an era that has all but vanished from the world. It was known as the Era of Paradise." Theresa explained, closing her eyes. Aiden couldn't help but wonder what memories she was reliving in her head.

"It was a peaceful era. Our kind were strong, proud beings that lived in peace among each other. We were proud blacksmiths, builders, and craftsmen. Our hard work created the jewels of the ancient world." She smiled sadly.

"Were the dragons the only ones around back then?" Aiden asked.

Theresa shook her head.

"We were not the only ones, but we were one of the oldest." She sighed. "In those ancient times, in that era of great works and deeds, there were four Kingdoms of great power and beauty. The first was that of the Elves, fairest and wisest of all the Elder races. Next came the Harpies, vicious backstabbers, faithless and evil, shunning males. The third Kingdom was not a race, but a group: the mages. These were members of the Elven and Human race that were especially tuned the ways of nature. They could literally feel the movement of the natural world and were connected to animals and plants in way that has now been forever lost. Ancient legends of Druids, shape-shifters and witches are based on a broken understanding of that ancient Kingdom."

She closed her eyes before continuing.

"Last was the youngest of the great Kingdoms, the Kingdom of Man. It was the first truly civilized realm that your kind ever knew. Unlike the other Kingdoms though, who were united under one ruler, the Kingdom of Man had several different kings. Four of them for each different region. One in the north, one in the south, one in the west, and finally the youngest in the east. Back then, mankind was in its infancy. Far more accepting of things around them, not judging or hating the other races." She sighed as she folded her arms. "Still, it was a Kingdom of man, and eventually the inner darkness of your hearts would rise up from within. And it all started from a murder of one wife of the youngest human King."

"H-Hey wait a second." Aiden interrupted for a second. "Elves, mages, dragons, and humans...but there's no dwarfs?"

Theresa blinked in bewilderment at the question. Aiden felt awkward for a moment as she quirked an eyebrow at his question.

"Of course there were dwarfs." She said blandly. "They mostly kept to themselves back then. They were so reclusive and secretive that most of the time we forgot they existed. They always hid in their mountains, building, tinkering, and such. As such we never really saw their civilization as a kingdom because of how they just did not interact with the rest of the world that often."

"O-Oh." Aiden blushed in embarrassment. "S-Sorry, it's just-"
"It's okay, Aiden." Theresa said with a short laugh. "You got curious, and I guess I did forget to mention them. That's how forgettable the dwarfs were for most of us."

Aiden frowned as he leaned back in his chair. The tone of the room taking a more serious tone now as he asked his next question.

"Peace couldn't have lasted forever, though, right?"

"Yes, peace did not last forever. Humanity had the best intentions when they become one of the Great Kingdoms, they truly did. For over a hundred years the peace we had was upheld...until one day." She frowned. "The first incident was between them and the Kingdom of the Harpies. It was not pretty and unfortunately the humans paid for it."

"What do you mean, 'paid for it'?" Aiden's curiosity peaked again. Theresa sighed as she opened her eyes.

"Harpies were never the strongest of the ancient Kingdoms, but they were known for being tricky, particularly when it came to their prey, and the humans became their prey quite easily." Her face turned grim. "Remember what I said before? About humanity having an innocence back then? Well that ended on a grim fateful day when...when one of the queens of humanity was killed by a harpy. The...reaction from the humans was not a pleasant one, as the human they killed was the youngest king's wife."

Aiden shivered at the thought. He had read about how vicious harpies could be in the ancient Greek stories. But those were just stories. The reality would have to be even worse. There was no need to explain to him what they would do when they captured their prey.

"When word got wind of what happened to said Queen, the humans became enraged. And they demanded justice for what had been done. And so..." Her face soured. "War broke out between the humans and harpies. Once it began chaos soon consumed the land. At first, the other Kingdoms were not involved, but slowly that changed. First the Kingdom of Mages allied themselves with the Human Kingdom. Soon, the elves joined the conflict, taking the side of the more brutal harpies due to their connection to nature. But then came the time for our Kingdom, the oldest of them all, to choose which side to take."

She paused for a moment, hesitating before continuing her story.

"It was at that time, when the war reached us, that our leader, the Great Dragon King, decided that if there was to be proper order among the Kingdoms, we could choose no side." She sighed. "We stood alone, neutral during the war. No one was happy about it, for we were the most feared among the Kingdoms. Our power was unmatched. After nearly a hundred years of war, it all came to an end suddenly. A summit was ordered by the Great Dragon King. He demanded that the leaders of each Kingdom to meet for peace, form a truce, one that each race swore never to break. Tensions died down, but never really died off." She smiled slightly. "Peace had returned."

Aiden smiled as well, but remembered something Jason had said when Theresa revealed her wings.

"But Jason said something happened to the dragons. That you were supposed to be..."

"Extinct?" Theresa finished for him, she sighed heavily. "Yes. My kind was driven to the edge of extinction, as were the rest of the Kingdoms." Sadness filled her eyes. "We didn't expect it, but the magic and hatred unleashed during the war created a pure force of evil that took the form of something that I...I can't even mention it. It is too terrible. Sometimes when you speak a word aloud, even after all this time, it has power to bring things back into the world that are better left hidden."

"Theresa," Aiden said, frowning as concern for his friend rose. She put her hand up to stop him.

"The first Kingdom to fall was that of the mages. They were followed by the elves, barely any of them are alive today. Then the harpies, who had gone into hiding ever since the Great Evil arose. The human Kingdom got the worst of it, I'm afraid. All their lore and ancient ways were lost; the humans today barely resemble the potential of their great ancestors. As for...as for the dragon Kingdom..."

She stopped herself, biting down hard on her lip as she clenched her fists.

"We allowed our pride to blind us, to believe that we could stand alone against the Great Evil when it came for our Kingdom. But we were wrong, and we paid for it dearly. It cost everything."

She turned to Aiden, her eyes filled with an emotion. Such sadness. Such loss. It should not be born, let alone seen by others.

"Our kind was wiped out. But our king sacrificed himself to seal the evil away, and only three of us remain."

Aiden had never seen pain like he saw now in Theresa's eyes. He was used to seeing her smiling and joyful. Not like this, so filled with tragic sadness.

"And that is the story I promised you. At least, part of what I can tell you at this point and time." Theresa placed a hand on his shoulder. "I hope you understand why I've never told anyone about it before today. As far as I know, there are only three of my kind, when I include myself, that remain in the modern world. If I know them, they will keep their true identify hidden so not to cause a worldwide panic. No offense, but humanity always goes overboard when they make a new discovery of life on this planet. There is more that I could share, but please believe me that what you don't know could hurt you even more if you knew it right now."

He nodded.

"I do. Theresa, to keep this locked up within you for years and still smile everyday..." He couldn't help but feel some bit of her sadness. Theresa, however, gave him her familiar smile.

"That was my life before. The Dragon King sealed me and two others away. We are to wait and return when we once again sense the Dragon King's power reborn into the world, when his power is felt again." She glanced at the dragon figurine Aiden had on his desk. "That sword there, it was his sword. But now, Aiden, it responds only to you."

Aiden turned his attention to the figurine. The king's sword was now his own.

"His sword?" Aiden took the figurine, cool to the touch. "Are you certain? I don't even know how to use one."

Theresa giggled and shook her head.

"Believe me, Aiden, the sword chooses its master. No one else can wield that blade.

"When your spirit came into this world, I sensed it from my seal. Knowing I had to make haste, I found a family to be my human parents, merging my essence with the essence of their unborn child."

"So they really are your parents," Aiden mused.

"In a way, yes." She glanced away. "I felt bad, taking the body of a child who had not been born, but I've come to accept my human parents, all the while watching out for you."

Aiden began to piece it together slowly. He could understand Theresa's story of her past and how she had human parents, despite being a dragoness. But he still didn't understand why the sword would respond only to him. Why wouldn't it respond to

Theresa? She was the better fighter, there was no doubt about that.

"Theresa, what if it made a mistake?" He began to feel nervous. "I'm not exactly the best fighter."

"No one is the best when they first begin, Aiden," she said. "As for the sword, for some reason your hidden power is similar to the Dragon King's. The sword does not make a mistake."

Aiden took a good look at the figurine in his hand. The sword had picked him, out of all the people in the world, to be its master. He couldn't describe what he was feeling. Was it fear or excitement? His grip on the sword's hilt tightened.

"What's it called?" he asked.

"Warfang," Theresa said. "It served the King faithfully for many years, and now, it belongs to you."

"What were those two words you taught me?"

"Beginner spells," Theresa explained. "*Ladbe* is Dragonic for sword summon, *regande* is for dismissal."

Aiden raised an eyebrow.

"Beginner spells? I felt drained when I summoned it the second time."

"Yes, you'll feel like that for a while when you begin to learn spells." Theresa smiled. "But the more you practice it, the less fatigued you'll become."

He sighed, but smiled as he turned his attention back to the dragon figure. Theresa chuckled lightly as he took and held the handle of the sword.

"Tomorrow, your training begins. You cannot have this magic inside you and not learn to use it. If you don't master it, it might master you. Not to say how it makes you a target...."

Aiden turned to her wide shocked eyes. Did she say 'training?' or was his mind playing tricks on him? As if she was reading his mind, Theresa once again cut him off. "If you're wondering what you're training for, it's to protect yourself. Like you saw with Patrick and Jason there are creatures out there that hide all too well in human society and they will attack you if they have a reason to."

"But what about Warfang?" He asked. "Why would my dad give me a sword?"

"That, I am not certain of." She answered, "He *probably* doesn't even know it's a sacred blade. Now meet me where we used to camp out. We've got a lot to cover tomorrow…"

CHAPTER 6 - SWORDS AND MAGIC

*T*hat evening Aiden sat in his room alone, working on some math homework. Theresa had long since left, which meant he would have to face his mother's roast, potatoes, and carrots by himself. She might be a Dragoness, but it looked like even she could be defeated by that meal. He grumbled in annoyance as he tried to focus on one problem that was giving him trouble.

"Whoever first thought of fractions must have been a demon with a sick sense of humor," he muttered, "because no one can solve this problem!"

After what seemed like hours of struggling with this one problem, Aiden tossed his pencil in frustration. He couldn't concentrate. How could he? The day he had just had was like something from a dream. His best friend was a mystical creature and there was a history the world had forgotten about! As far as he cared, math homework could wait until later.

He kept thinking about his dragon figurine, eventually giving up on anything else, putting his homework away to finish it later. Aiden couldn't stand it any longer and picked up the figurine, holding it, admiring the fancy details. He turned his attention to the slit in the dragon's chest. At first glance, no one would imagine a sword coming out of such a tiny space. He had to admit, it was really cool to own.

"Warfang," he mused as he flicked it gently. "If you only respond to someone whose power is so similar to this Great King's, then why did you chose me?"

The figurine's eyes flashed at this question. Aiden nearly jumped out of his chair. Just like everything else that had happened today, he did not expect the figurine's eyes to flash. Gently placing the figurine on his desk again, he thought about what Theresa had told him and the strange dream he had on the bus.

A part of him wondered if he should have told Theresa about his dream. There couldn't be any harm in telling her. After all, she knew a lot of things about the ancient past. Perhaps she could help him figure it out tomorrow.

"Aiden!" his mother called out from the kitchen. "Are you done with your homework yet?"

"Almost, Mom!" Aiden called back. "I'll try to get it done soon!"

"Well don't take too long. You've got to eat sometime!"

That was almost a good enough reason for him to take as much time as possible to avoid dinner.

"Curse you, Theresa Goldwin, for making me face this dinner alone," he muttered.

He turned back to his computer to search the Net to keep his mind off of the impending meal when he heard a car door slam. Aiden didn't need to look out his window to know his father had returned from work. He had trained his hearing to listen for when his parents were back when they were out. It was a very useful skill he happily worked to his advantage whenever he wanted to be a sneak.

Aiden glanced back at Warfang once again. As cool as it was to own such a sword, he still was plagued by why his father had given him it. Maybe Theresa was right? Maybe he had no idea that it was a weapon and found it somewhere in a local pawn shop or store that sold fantasy items?

"So, Dad," he mused as he took Warfang into his hand. "Let's see what story you have for this gift of yours."

As if on cue, he caught the sound of the front door opening. Tightening his grip around Warfang, Aiden stood and walked out of his room.

Aiden's father, Connor Russell, considered himself a very stylish man. He stood tall with slicked black hair and the same ocean blue eyes as Aiden. Connor wore a tailored business suit and carried a large briefcase, bringing work home with him every day.

Connor's eyes glanced to Aiden as he walked down the hall-way. He smiled at his son before placing a hand on his shoulder.

"Evening, son," he said. "I hope you've had a good day today."

"Can't really complain," Aiden said, holding Warfang to show his father. "Thanks for the gift by the way."

"Ah, your gift." Connor gently took the figurine from Aiden's hand. "I'm glad you like it. I found it in an old antique shop. I thought you would enjoy it."

"I was right," Aiden thought. "He doesn't have a clue what it really is."

"So, tell me about your day, Son," Connor said, returning Warfang as he walked towards the kitchen. Aiden sighed. It was going to be a long dinner.

"And so the negotiations went through as planned," Connor said, smiling as he took a bite of the roast. "It was quite an accomplishment for the company, Helena."

"That's wonderful, dear." Helena smiled. "I'm happy for you."

Aiden poked his roast with his fork as he listened to his parents. Not only did he not have anything to say about his father's company, he had to listen to it. That was two things

Theresa left him to face alone. He slowly took a bite of the roast, wishing that he could make the meal disappear.

"So, Aiden," Helena said, "what did you think of your father's gift?"

Aiden smiled as he took Warfang from his pocket.

"I think it's amazing," he said. "Though I have to admit, Dad, I wasn't expecting it from you."

Connor smiled as he took a sip of his coffee.

"Well, Aiden, I'm glad you like it," he said. "I thought you would, even though it isn't what I would choose for myself of course."

Aiden rolled his eyes. He wasn't going to get into an argument about his interests, not tonight at least. If his father wanted to berate fantasy, he would have to do it when Aiden wasn't around. Especially since what happened to him today proved that the 'day-dream creatures' did exist. Aiden took one last bite of his roast, doing the best he could not to cringe. Finally, he swallowed it before standing.

"Thanks for dinner, Mom." he said politely. "I gotta get back to work though."

"All right, hun." Helena frowned. "And don't stay up too late. You might be on spring break, but I will not have you ruining your sleeping habits."

"Your mother is right, Aiden," Connor added. "The last thing we want is for you to oversleep because you stayed up too late reading one of your fantasy stories."

Aiden wanted to snap at his father. But he kept his cool, nodding his head at his mother.

"I understand, Mom," he told her. "I won't stay up too late, I promise."

And with that, Aiden was off to his room. The last thing he needed was to engage in an argument. He already had far too much on his mind.

Just as he reached his room, his cell phone buzzed with a text message from Theresa. Aiden smiled as he picked it up to read it.

"Bring a towel, workout clothes, and Warfang tomorrow. Training begins."

He sighed as he put his cell phone away. He still wondered why Theresa felt she had to train him. Did she expect him to not be near her every day? The more he thought about it, the more he realized that he looked like a fool with how he was handling Warfang in combat. Still, he couldn't deny that today had been somewhat of a joyride. Aside from being attacked by a giant hall monitor and some hornets, it had been a really good day.

"Training tomorrow, huh Theresa?" he asked quietly, placing Warfang on his table. "Let's see what you have to teach."

"Theresa, just why are we here at the forest where we used to camp?" Aiden asked, holding Warfang.

Taking her advice from the night before, Aiden dressed in his best workout outfit, a blue exercise shirt and black shorts. Theresa wore a pink exercise shirt with light blue shorts. She tied her long white hair in a ponytail and turned to him.

"Quite simple," Theresa said. "A forest has many obstacles: holes, branches, and cliffs."

"And the towels?" he pointed to the four towels they had brought.

"One of them for sweat, the others for when we begin your magic training," she explained, turning her back on hi.

"Magic training?"

"Mhm," Theresa smiled over her shoulder. "Now summon your blade and attack me."

"But you've got your back to me," Aiden protested.

"I know, but remember who's training you," she said. "Now do as I say."

Aiden blinked as he glanced to Warfang, then to Theresa. He was hesitant to strike her, but if she told him to attack, then it was probably best that he didn't make her upset.

71

"*Ladbe*," he said. Instantly the sword appeared from the slit once again.

Gripping the hilt of Warfang tightly, Aiden pulled his sword up and swung it down towards Theresa, praying that she would do something. Then he heard Theresa whisper.

"*Ladbes...*"

Before he knew what was happening, Aiden's sword was blocked by something he couldn't see. Suddenly he found himself pushed back by Theresa. Surprised by her strength, he tried to regain his footing, but instead found himself flat on his back. Before he could get up, Aiden felt a cold touch across his neck, and he realized it was the kiss of steel as it lay across his throat.

Theresa stood over him, a short sword in her right hand. Aiden stared up the blade, noticing that the sword's hilt looked like a Dragon's head, the blade coming out of the mouth. It was like staring down a very long tooth into a very grim mouth. He glanced down to see another sword in her left hand, shaped just like the one Theresa held in her right. Both of them shared the same color of gold for their design. Twin blades. Aiden swallowed as she pulled her sword away from his neck; luckily he had not been cut.

"Crude and slow, Aiden. That's something we're going to have to work on," Theresa said, extending her hand to him.

"That was incredible," he marveled, taking her hand as he stood up. "I couldn't even see that happen!"

Theresa smiled as she walked away from him, spinning her swords around in her hands. "Speed and sword play are my specialty," she said. "These two blades have been my faithful companions for as long as I can remember."

She held her two short swords to show him. Aiden blinked, noticing that one of the blades had red eyes in the eye sockets of one dragon head, and the other had blue.

"They were gifts from the Dragon King himself. The one with

blue eyes is Snow; the one with the red eyes is Fire." She smiled. "Together they make…"

Theresa slammed the pommels of the swords together. At first Aiden thought she was breaking the two swords, but then he noticed that their pommels merged into one. Theresa spun the joined blades behind her back, slicing thick tree branches down with them.

"Snowfyre."

"Whoa." Aiden was mesmerized by Theresa's swords. He had never seen a weapon like Snowfyre before.

"Now, first things first: we need to develop your speed," Theresa instructed, her weapon splitting into two short swords. "To do that, your posture needs to be correct."

"My posture?"

"Yep. You're too stiff and still," Theresa explained, stabbing her swords into the ground as she moved over to him. "Now, bend your knees."

Aiden did as he was told, bending his knees slightly. Theresa frowned.

"Lower," she said.

He bent his knees more as Theresa studied his posture. She placed a hand on his shoulder gently.

"Not too much, you'll lose your balance if you bend your knees too much," she smiled. "Ease up some."

"I feel silly."

"Silly or not, you won't complain when you survive attacks from your enemies. Now ease up a little more…good."

Theresa went back to her twin blades, pulling them from the ground. Quickly turning to Aiden again, she went into her stance.

"Now, hold your sword in your right hand. Only use both of your hands when you're planning a power strike."

"Got it," Aiden said, holding Warfang tightly in his right hand.

Theresa nodded as she placed Snow against the metal of his blade.

"First thing you're going to learn is proper sword play. Try to parry my next blade. Ready?"

He nodded as Theresa pulled Snow back, quickly bringing Fire at him. Aiden barely had time to react as he took a step back, quickly bringing Warfang to block Theresa's sword. The two swords clashed, the sound of ringing metal bounced through the forest. Aiden smiled at his accomplishment, a smile that disappeared as Theresa's second sword followed its twin.

"Don't get cocky and let your guard down!" Theresa shouted.

"Oh crap!" Aiden wanted to shout, but he didn't have time as he brought Warfang to block Snow. He took another step back as Theresa continued her assault against him, he was able to block each sword strike, but he couldn't get himself set to attack. While he was busy trying to set his feet, Theresa swung both of her swords. The impact forced Aiden back completely and he fell to the ground again. He groaned.

"Dammit." He quickly stood up. "That's the second time today."

"Better get used to it, Aiden," Theresa said as she spun her swords idly. "Before this day ends you'll fall more than twice."

Aiden sighed as he looked down at Warfang. If what she said was true, Aiden knew he was going to look like a fool all day.

"Hey," Theresa said in a much kinder tone, "don't worry, you're doing well for your first time."

Aiden smiled a little before resuming the stance Theresa had shown him.

"Ease up a little," she instructed, taking her own position. "Now, on guard!"

The rest of combat training went like Aiden thought it would: Theresa always had the upper hand. Each round Aiden's blocking got quicker, however he couldn't go on the offensive successfully. Each time ended in disaster. Two hours passed and the combat training seemed to drone on. Aiden was gasping from the heat and exhaustion. Theresa barely seemed to break a sweat.

"All right, it's time for a breather," Theresa said, stabbing her swords into the ground. "You worked hard, Aiden. You deserve the rest."

"If by 'worked hard,' you mean at falling down, I have to agree. I've gotten very good at that," he said, leaning against the nearest tree. Theresa pulled two water bottles from her backpack, tossing one to him.

"Have some water," Theresa opened up her own bottle as Aiden caught his. "You beat yourself up way too much. You're not doing nearly as bad as you think you are."

"Thanks, Theresa," Aiden said drinking almost half of the bottle. "All I can say is that my butt feels like it's on fire."

Theresa laughed as she sipped her water.

"So, what's next?" Aiden asked.

"We've done enough combat training for today." Theresa held up her palm; a small, white fireball appeared in her hand. "The next lesson is about magic. Every living creature is connected to magic; it is quite literally the force binding us all together. The supernatural surrounds us."

"I thought only mages could use magic."

"That is only half true." Theresa closed her hand, extinguishing the fireball. "Mages were the first humanoid beings to discover magic, but dragons have always had access to it. We just decide not to use it as often as they do."

Theresa picked up her two swords and whispered *regande* to dismiss them. She picked up her backpack and turned to Aiden.

"Follow me. This part of the forest isn't ideal for learning magic," she said, walking off before he could ask why.

Aiden shrugged as he picked up his own backpack and followed her. Whatever she had planned, he was certain that it couldn't be as hard as the combat training. He was curious to learn magic, although he didn't see how he would be able.

Theresa was a few feet ahead of him as they hiked what seemed like seven hills, each step exhausting his legs that much more.

Aiden heard a rushing sound as they got closer to their destination, and he wondered what it could be. It didn't sound anything like cars in traffic, so he scratched that off the list. Aiden gave it some more thought, and before they arrived, he finally figured it out.

A river.

"This right here, Aiden, is a secret part of the local river that literally no human knows about. It's the perfect place for you to train your magic skills." Theresa explained.

The rushing water splashed against the rocks along the shore. Theresa smiled and set down her backpack.

"This is why I told you to bring extra clothes and a towel," she said. "The river is a perfect place to learn about magic."

"Uh...how?" Aiden asked, raising an eyebrow. "What's so magical about a river?"

Theresa sighed and shook her head.

"Water is a source of life, Aiden. All living things need water to survive; even the dragons could not survive without it," she explained, taking off her shoes and socks. "But water also is one of the main elemental forces of magic. Hence, a river is perfect for learning how to use it."

"So what are the other forces?"

"I'll explain that the next time." Theresa took a step into the river and walked out to the middle of it. "For now, take off your shoes and stand here with me."

Aiden didn't hesitate long. He took off his shoes and did as she told him. The two stood in the middle of the river as the water rushed past them, nearly knocking Aiden over.

"Ok, I'll bite," Aiden finally said. "Why are we standing in the middle of the river?"

"For you to feel magic," Theresa answered, closing her eyes.

"Close your eyes, shut out all your surroundings, and focus only on the water."

Aiden closed his eyes and took a deep breath, forgetting everything that had happened the day before, and the rough and long combat training from earlier. Strangely enough, he actually felt at peace as the cool water flowed against his legs. Then, just around the edges of his senses he felt a new sensation.

He couldn't describe it accurately, but the water was more than cool now. It soothed his aching muscles as it flowed around him. Aiden had never felt more rejuvenated as he opened his eyes.

"That was incredible," he said, smiling. "My arms and legs aren't tired anymore."

"Good," Theresa said. "Water is one of the elements that can heal the body and the soul. It gives new energy to those who use its soothing touch. However, water can do more than heal."

She flicked her wrist at the river. Almost instantly a big wave exploded at Aiden catching him off guard. Before he could find his balance, Aiden fell into the water as the wave splashed over him. Scrambling to stand, Aiden pushed wet hair out of his eyes.

"What was that for?!" he asked.

"It was an example," Theresa said. "Water can also be used as an offensive force. Never underestimate its power."

"I'm resisting the urge to splash you back," Aiden said, "because you realize that was an act of war."

Theresa laughed as she flicked her wrist again. Another wave splashed into Aiden, knocking him off his feet.

"Dammit, Thes!"

"Focus on the water, Aiden," Theresa instructed. "Find that feeling you had before, when your body was rejuvenated, and use that same force to push the water away."

If he thought the combat training was hard, Aiden had no idea how trying it would be to learn magic. He would have to endure being splashed by wave after wave for nearly an hour. Each time he thought he had the feeling he had before, another wave splashed into him. He was getting annoyed with being drenched over and over, especially when he had the sensation, but immediately lost it when the water hit him.

He was about to give up and leave the river to dry off, but then he felt the sensation once again. This time he was determined. Theresa flicked her wrist one last time, sending another wave at him. Aiden stayed put for the briefest moment. Then he felt the sensation turn from soothing to what he could best describe as heat. He swung his hands into the air; his own wave of water came up and splashed into Theresa's, preventing her wave from crashing into him. Theresa smiled.

"Very nicely done," she said. "You've discovered the feel of water's offensive power."

"I...I don't even know how I did that," Aiden admitted. "All I did was move my hands..."

"What you felt was a force of motion," Theresa explained. "Once you felt the water's soothing touch turn to heat, you had control over a small force of magic. Thus, when it was ready to be released, your instinct took over and forced your own wave up against mine."

"Wow," Aiden marveled. "What kind of spell was that?"

Theresa giggled. "That was no spell, Aiden. That was just a force that you used."

"Wait, then when do I start learning spells?"

"When you're ready," Theresa explained. "For now, we'll use the river and the elemental magic flowing through it to hone your magical skills. Now, let's get back to shore and dry off. We're going back to combat training."

CHAPTER 7 - THE LADIES' MAN

"One, two, three…one, two, three," Theresa chanted as her blades clashed with Aiden's sword. "Keep that posture balanced, keep up with the rhythm."

"Easy for you to say," Aiden groaned as his sword blocked each of Theresa's attacks.

Each time their swords met, the clash rang through the forest. Theresa swung Fire from above before it was blocked by Warfang. Aiden took a step back, but held his ground as Theresa's second sword, Snow, thrust towards him.

Aiden had to admit, Theresa's training had its benefits. He was out of the house, free from doing any chores his parents had planned to ruin his spring break. His parents weren't too worried about where he was, but would worry when he showed up later than he promised. Not that Aiden could blame them worrying; they were just doing their jobs.

He wasn't good enough to disarm Theresa yet, but he was developing his speed; each day he grew faster and faster. One thing was for sure, he did end up exhausted every day after his combat training.

Aiden found magic somewhat harder to wield than a sword. It

seemed random whenever he was able to make his own wave of water splash up from the river. When he felt the magical energy from the river, he knew, but it seemed to have a mind of its own. Aiden swore that he had never gotten as wet as in this one week of magic training.

This was the fourth day of their spring break that they were out in the forest training. Theresa had not taken it easy on him, despite their friendship, but she wasn't going for any cuts or killing blows. Aiden knew that she was stronger than she let on.

"Watch your feet," Theresa instructed. "Keep your balance and continue with the rhythm."

After the first day of training he started to fall less and got better at standing his ground. His swordplay also improved as well. The more he improved the more confident he grew in his abilities. While Theresa still had the edge in their training, as expected of her, he was getting better at knowing when to parry and attack.

However for all his training with her, Aiden could tel that she was holding back. That was obvious though. She was an ancient Dragoness, he was just a regular boy with a King's sword. But at the same time, he felt more empowered by his growing skill. Each day he felt himself getting better and holding the sword, remembering postures, stances, and keeping a good balance. He could feel something else over his shoulder, watching and guiding him. He'd only had the sword for a few days, but it was already such a part of him that he could not imagine life without it.

Adjusting to this posture and staying in it for combat was the most uncomfortable part. His body wasn't used to holding a combat stance at all, so he often made mistakes when his body gave out. Aiden could feel his muscles ache as he continued to block Theresa's blows.

He took a glance behind him to see that Theresa had pushed him to the edge of a small hill. If he was going to avoid rolling down, he had to hold his ground and fight back. Aiden planted his feet on the top of the hill, determined to not lose his balance. Theresa's eyes narrowed; she brought her blades up simultaneously and swung both at him.

Aiden quickly brought up Warfang up to block her blades. As the sound of metal rang through the forest, the impact forced Theresa back. Taking his chance to finally get on the offensive, Aiden swung his sword. Theresa blocked his blade, but he didn't stop, attacking again and again.

Aiden knew Theresa must be tiring from his assault, but she showed no signs of fatigue; her swordsmanship continued to surprise him. Aiden decided to try something different. As she swung her swords towards him once again, Aiden waited for the right moment.

Gripping the hilt of his sword tightly, he pushed back both of Theresa's blades. He smiled as he swung his sword at Theresa from below, an uprising slash.

"Not bad," Theresa said as Aiden swung his sword, "but not good enough."

Aiden blinked just once before Theresa blocked his slash with Snow. He tried to bring Warfang back to counterattack, but Theresa's second blade immediately followed. The twin blades locked around Warfang, preventing any escape by Aiden.

"What the?!" Aiden gaped, trying to pull Warfang out of the lock.

"Rule number one on rising slashes," Theresa said calmly, twisting her blades quickly to disarm Aiden "never let your guard down!"

Warfang flew from his hand as Theresa's swords forced it from his grip. Aiden watched as his blade plunged into the ground; he swallowed a lump in his throat before turning back to Theresa. Fire's point was inches away from his forehead.

"If this was for real, you'd be dead already." She pulled her sword away, allowing Aiden to pick up his weapon.

"I'm beginning to think that no one could ever best you, Theresa."

"Why's that?"

"Well for one thing, you have a plan for everything you come up against. You know everything about sword play, and all the swords masters I've read about online don't even hold a candle to you and your skill. "

Theresa smiled as she spun her blades, stabbing them into a tree easily before sitting down.

"You think so? I personally think I've lost a bit of my skill over the years."

"A BIT of your skills? You mean you were better before?"

"Best sword fighter in the ancient Kingdoms," she said. "I could cut the heads off of a multi-headed beast in seconds flat. Being in that seal and growing in a human body without any partner to help train with seems to have dampened my skills."

Aiden shivered at the thought of Theresa being far better than he had assumed. But just how good was she with a blade? He sighed and stabbed Warfang into the ground before sitting by her.

"Everyone must have feared you then," he said. "If you were that good with a blade, then you wouldn't have any equal."

"Well while I can say that I am the best sword fighter in the old Kingdom, I'd be lying if I said there weren't other skilled warriors." Theresa corrected him, frowning. "I wasn't the only great warrior in our Kingdom, Aiden. There were others."

She glanced away. Aiden could tell she was remembering days that she obviously missed. "Two of them to be exact. They were my closest friends, my brothers. We were the Dragon King's fiercest and most loyal warriors."

"Two?" Aiden blinked, recalling his dream before, "Theresa, what was your band called?" He was relieved to see her smile at his question.

"Our band had a simple title: we were *Aba Itoa Eltragas*. The Three Warriors."

"*Aba itoa eltragas?*" Aiden repeated very poorly. Theresa laughed at his very poor pronunciation.

"That was a good first try, but let's save learning the Dragonic language for another time." She smiled. "But yes, *Aba Itoa Eltragas* literally means 'The Three Warriors.' We were a very powerful team...and we were close."

Theresa sighed before she stood back up.

"I'm sorry, Aiden. It's just sometimes memories can be painful."

"Don't be sorry." Aiden stood up after her. "I wasn't trying to dig up old wounds. I hope you understand that I didn't mean it like that... It is just so incredible to have you here and for you to have been a part of that."

Theresa nodded as she stood up. There was a moment of silence before she turned back to the tree.

"I don't doubt that they're alive, Aiden." She pulled her swords from the tree. "When the king cast his spell, he put all three of us away to wait for the return of either his power or someone bearing a power very similar to his, like you."

"But if that's the case, wouldn't they have been drawn to me as well?"

Theresa sighed, shaking her head.

"Aiden, my fellow warriors don't have the patience I possess. For a thousand years they've waited alongside me in slumber, but in that time they grew impatient." She put a finger to her chin, thinking hard. "If my memory serves, it was around the time when Rome fell that they gave up waiting and returned to the world."

"Wait, wait, wait." Aiden put his hand up. "Are you telling me that they're the dragons that spawned all the old tales from the dark ages?"

Theresa blinked at this statement and then broke out laughing.

"Aiden, you really need to stop going back to those silly old stories about how my kind acted. We didn't fly around kidnapping young maidens or hoarding treasure. How do you like stereotypes when they are applied to you?"

"Hey, couldn't hurt to ask. But I have a reason for why I'm asking these questions."

Aiden then went into detail about the dream he had on the bus: the two shadowy beings beside her, the great shadow behind them, and the voice that had told him only 'two remain.' Theresa listened intently, nodding her head as he spoke.

"I see," she said finally. "This voice, when it said 'two remain' it must have been referring to my brothers. Though this great shadow you speak of is unfamiliar to me."

"Can you take a guess at who it was?"

"Afraid not. My kind's abilities go only so far, you know. Identifying a voice from a dream is not our territory."

"Damn. It was worth a shot." Aiden sighed before whispering *regande* to retract Warfang. "I don't know about you, but I am bushed."

"Yeah, we have been training much harder today than before." Theresa dismissed her blades as well. "Since you've been working so much, how about we get cleaned up and head to the mall's food court? My treat."

"Sounds like a plan to me." Aiden smiled. It had been a while since they went to the mall. He was looking forward to stopping by his favorite store, The Griffon. "I'll meet up with you at the bus stop."

"See you in a half an hour!" Theresa said as they emerged from the woods at their cul de sac, and headed to her house.

"Finally, something that actually resembles spring break." Aiden said as he reached his home. He was looking forward to it.

The bus ride to the mall was long and tiring but it was worth the trip. "The Sunshine Mall," was the local hangout for every middle school and high school student. It had everything that could interest a teenager. Multiple game stores, plentiful cloth stores, an arcade that still somehow was kept up, a movie theater, and hobby shops. Aiden and Theresa always came to the mall whenever they had free time. It was full of happy memories of days that had gone by.

Aiden chuckled as the bus drew closer to the mall. He had just recalled one event with Eric when he was nearly embarrassed in front of everyone in the food court. The bully was about to push Aiden into the fountain from behind, but Theresa had managed to stop him before it happened by tripping Eric into the fountain instead. Everyone, save for Eric, got a big laugh at that day.

As the two arrived at the food court, they noticed the mall was a lot less crowded than during their last visit. Depending on whom you asked, that was either good or a bad. For Aiden and Theresa, it was a good thing. Less was more in their opinion. It gave them more space to talk and more of a chance to avoid trouble.

"So, Aiden," Theresa said as they entered the food court. "Where are you going to go first?"

"I figured I'd stop by The Griffon and see if there's anything new."

"Don't tell me that you think their fantasy books and games might have something in them connected to what I've been teaching you."

"Course not!" He laughed. "I mean, there's no way that stuff could be connected to your past."

Theresa laughed as she gave him a slight nod.

"All right, I'm going to see if there's something we can use for your magic training. I'll meet you at The Griffon when I've found what I'm looking for."

Aiden nodded as the two went their separate ways. He didn't know what she could find in a mall for magic training, but he knew that he shouldn't question his mentor and best friend at this point. He couldn't help but feel excited and gleeful at the thought of being trained by a dragon. Then he remembered the ache in his muscles.

"Ow..." He gently rubbed his arms. "That's the only bad thing about this training."

The training had been long and hard, but he couldn't argue with the results, even after just a few days. He had been fooled by the fantasy stories he'd read and movies with sword fights. He would never be fooled by swordplay in movies ever again. And besides, Theresa was better than any swordsman he had seen. No movie star could touch her.

His eyes soon spotted his favorite store in the mall and he grinned: The Griffon. It was a haven for fantasy lovers. Not only did it have fantasy books, but also everything a lover of the fantasy genre would want to own: classic movies, table-top games, collectible figurines, models, decorative weapons, and custom costumes for the Renaissance Fair. As far as Aiden was concerned, it was the perfect store.

"Ah, look who's here!" said the owner of the store as Aiden walked in. "One of my best customers!"

"Hey, Mr. Rutherfurd. It's been a while since I came by."

"It has been, hasn't it?" Mr. Rutherfurd said, smiling as he leaned on the counter. "I hope your school work hasn't kept your love for fantasy down now."

"Not at all." Aiden grinned. "They'd have to beat it out of me."

Mr. Rutherfurd laughed.

"In any case, take a good look around. We've gotten some new stuff while you've been gone, my boy."

"I bet." Aiden smiled. "Looks like you've been collecting some more decorative weapons as well."

"Ah, yes we have." Mr. Rutherfurd grinned. "Now don't go thinking that I'm gonna sell you one of those. You're way too young."

"Oh, if you only knew what I had now," Aiden thought, wanting to show him Warfang. But he kept his restraint. He thought of Mr. Rutherfurd as an uncle, mostly because he encouraged Aiden to read fantasy and admire it, unlike his father.

Aiden made his way to the figurine section of the shop. There was a large collection, often used for the table-top games Mr. Rutherfurd carried. They were nicely detailed and some were incredibly rare, valuable collectables.

Aiden looked for certain sets of figurines: the dragons. Ever since Theresa revealed herself to him, Aiden couldn't help his curiosity. If he could find a figurine with Theresa's wings, he might have a more accurate image of her dragoness form.

Sadly, he had no luck. He hadn't expected to find an exact match, but he had hoped to find one that at least had her wings. Aiden sighed as he went to the front of the shop, looking at some of the books. Just as he was about to open one, he heard something in the mall.

"Let go of me, jerk!"

Aiden looked up from his book to identify the source of the voice. A girl in her late teens was pushing a big, husky guy away. The guy had a sly grin on his face and kept his grip easily on the girl's arm.

"Hey don't be like that, baby," he said. "I promise we'll have a good time if you just come with me."

"I said back off!" the girl snapped, pulling her arm as best as she could.

Aiden's eyes narrowed. He hated these types of guys. They were cowards as far he was concerned. It took all that he had to not storm out there to tell the jerk to leave her alone. But after what happened with Patrick, Aiden was more intimidated by big guys than ever before. He reached into his pocket, clenching Warfang tightly as the husky guy continued to hold the girl back.

"Give me a good reason you ass." he thought bitterly.

"Let me go!" the girl shouted, slapping her attacker with full force. This made his eyes flash.

"Oh, big mistake sweetie." He smiled with dark intentions. "I'll enjoy breaking you."

"Ey there, laddie," said a new voice from behind the husky man. "The lady asked ye to let her go. I suggest ye move yer fat arse away from her now."

Aiden turned to the source of the voice: a young man who looked to be about sixteen. He had light red hair that was a mess, almost shaggy, and light brown, sandy eyes. He was of average size, not too scrawny, not too muscular. What stood out the most about him was his jacket, a red hooded jacket. While that may not have been impressive on its own, it was the lining inside that really caught Aiden's attention. Even from a distance he could see the dark blue lining, glittered with stars that seemed to twinkle on their own. It was almost like its own personal galaxy. Complimenting those were a pair of star medallions, with matching glimmer, that dangled from his pocket.

Aiden couldn't quite place the thick accent. The husky man turned towards the newcomer, his eyes flashing dangerously.

"And just who the hell do you think you are?"

"The name's Seamus O'Grady, and I believe the lass told ye to leave her alone." Seamus folded his arms. "I suggest ye take her advice 'fore this turns ugly."

"Well, Seamus, ever heard of a private conversation?"

"Depends on what ye mean by private," Seamus gave a cocky grin, "Don't reckon it applies here since the fine lassie was screamin' her lungs out to get away from yer ugly mug."

What happened next occurred almost too fast for Aiden to see. The big man took a step towards Seamus to throw a punch. Seamus, however, dodged the punch with little to no effort. Then it happened, as if Aiden could spot every single movement like it was a frame by frame shot from a movie. Before Seamus' attacker could turn again, Aiden noticed a short, stick-like object appear from his sleeve, which seemed to "grow" into a staff.

Seamus whacked the large guy hard across his back with this stick. Taken by surprise, the larger attacker fell to the ground. Filled with a victorious vigor, Seamus simply laughed before he rolled his defeated foe over with a foot.

"Now laddie, are ye gonna leave this fine lassie alone now? Or do I have to kick yer sorry arse again?"

Standing up with a grunt, the defeated offender slouched off. Seamus grinned as he turned to the young woman, bowing slightly.

"All in a day's work," he said. "I apologize that you had to see such a poor example of what a man this low life be."

"Thanks," the young woman said as a grateful smile grew on her lips. "It feels like security here is always asleep."

The young woman walked off, leaving Seamus to himself in the middle of the mall. While an ordinary human would have never noticed that Seamus used a weapon on the rude attacker, Aiden's training with Theresa had taught him to watch everything carefully. Aiden watched in silence as Seamus walked away. His curiosity getting the better of him, Aiden followed, trying to remain as quiet as possible, so he could to see what he could learn about this new person.

As he followed, Aiden noticed that every time Seamus walked by a pretty young woman he would bow politely and exchange a few words. While it was interesting to watch the first few times, it began to get annoying. Every time Seamus stopped to make idle chats with any woman he saw, Aiden was forced to find a hiding spot. If he ever had a chance to get this guy away from every girl, Aiden could approach him directly.

Easier said than done. Despite becoming annoyed at his target's antics, Aiden had a gut feeling that he must meet Seamus. At the same time his mind doubted that he was ready to meet someone that could easily knock him out. After seeing him deal with the husky man, he wouldn't want to get on this guy's bad side.

A part of him wondered then why he was following this Seamus. What would he gain if he managed to talk to this guy? How do you approach someone hiding a weapon in his sleeve?

Aiden noticed Seamus heading towards the exit of the mall. It was the perfect chance for Aiden to corner him. He knew he would have to be careful though; he had seen Seamus take out a very big man with what looked like a staff.

Once Seamus left the mall, Aiden finally got his chance and moved quickly. Pushing his way through the mall crowd, he reached the exit. As he pushed the door open he saw Seamus leaning against one of the building columns, with a small frown on his lips. And he was looking directly at Aiden, who nearly jumped back in surprise as he faced Seamus.

"And what do we have here?" Seamus said in a calm tone. "Did ye think that I did not know that ye were following me?"

"How did…there's no way that you could have noticed me following you!" Aiden managed to say.

"Let's just say that I've got some skills." Seamus pulled away from the column. "Name's Seamus O'Grady. Who might I be speaking too?"

"Aiden Russell," Aiden answered. "And I know who you are."

"Oh ye do?"

"Yeah, I saw what you did back there."

"Ah, ye saw that lil scuffle, did ye?" He grinned. "That bastard got what he deserved. No one treats a fine young lassie like that."

"Yeah…and no one carries around a staff in his sleeve," Aiden said, folding his arms. Seamus' small smile had long disappeared.

"Ye got some good eyes there, laddie," he said. "Not many know that I got a staff with me."

"It was fast, but let's just say that I've been improving my eyesight."

"Oh, is that so?" Seamus cracked his fingers. "And what would ye like to know about me weapon now?"

"H-Hey I didn't say that you had a weapon on you." Aiden

pointed out, trying to figure out how to question him, maybe he should put a brave face on it. "I know about items that can become weapons. There's no way you could carry a staff in your sleeve otherwise."

Seamus frowned as he opened his palm. An orb of white light appeared and stretched out about seven feet. Once it stretched completely, the light faded, revealing a metal bow staff with strange wing markings, with a European styled dragon at the top, its legs wrapped around the tip of the weapon. The bow staff itself was a mixture of silver and bronze, opposite coloring to Warfang's gold and silver. Aiden glanced around him, making certain that there weren't any people that were close to the two of them. When he noticed that there weren't any around, he turned his attention back too Seamus.

"So you got some good eyes on you," Seamus said, his thick accent disappearing. "Not bad for a mere human."

"I had help." Aiden admitted. His palms began to sweat as he kept his directly on the staff. He wondered if he should have reached for Warfang just in case he had to. But before he could pull the figurine out of his pocket, Seamus' staff was already pointed at his throat.

"Helpful little tip for you, laddie." He smiled. "When someone's getting their weapon out, you better have yours ready."

Seamus pulled his staff away from Aiden's throat, twirling it before it disappeared.

"Now if it's a fight you're looking for, my advice to you is this: Don't bother. I'm out of your league, kiddo."

Aiden's eyes narrowed as he pulled Warfang out of his pocket.

"You're confident, aren't you?" Seamus laughed. "Kiddo, when you get older you'll learn the difference between confidence and skill."

"You sure you're not just chicken?" Aiden asked.

Seamus glared at Aiden. He looked around before motioning his head to the right.

"Follow me."

Aiden nodded as Seamus turned away. He had no idea what kind of creature Seamus was, but he wasn't going to ask now. All he knew was that Seamus was no mere human.

He soon found himself in an alley beside the mall. Aiden raised an eyebrow as Seamus turned to face him.

"What's with the alley?"

"Tell me kiddo," Seamus said, summoning his staff, "how would it look if two teenage boys were reported to mall security fighting with weapons?"

Aiden groaned. As much as he disliked it, Seamus had a point. He readied Warfang, quickly whispering *ladbe* to summon his sword. Seamus spun his staff around quickly before slamming it on the ground.

"Interesting sword you have there...you'll have to tell me how you got it after I beat you into the ground. But for now, let's see what you've got, kiddo."

Seamus charged towards Aiden with his staff above his head. Remembering his training with Theresa, Aiden placed himself in a good battle stance. Seamus swung his bow staff at full speed. Aiden quickly countered, blocking the swing with Warfang. Taking the advantage to counter, Aiden pushed Seamus away. Now on the offensive, Aiden ran at his opponent, ready to swing his sword.

Seamus countered, though, and swung his bow staff, smacking Aiden in his side. Caught off guard, Aiden fell to the ground with a thud. He groaned in pain when his eye caught sight of Seamus pulling his staff up to strike him. Just as the staff came flying down, Aiden blocked the staff with the sharp end of his blade. Both of them grunted as they pushed their weapons against one another.

"I gotta admit kiddo," Seamus said through gritted teeth, "you're not too bad, for a human."

"Guess you let your ego get in the way, huh?" Aiden laughed.

The two continued their contest for what seemed like hours to Aiden. Despite his training with Theresa, Seamus had the advantage. His staff was a much longer weapon than Aiden's sword. If there was a chance for Aiden to win this little skirmish, it was vanishing quickly. Putting all his remaining strength into his arms, Aiden pushed his sword against Seamus' staff.

"A fighter, eh?" Seamus grunted, his arms trembling slightly, "but don't expect this to end well for you!"

"*NOMARAN*!" A familiar voice echoed in the alley.

Both of them froze. Theresa stood at the end of the alley, arms crossed across her chest. Seamus blinked as he pulled his staff away from Aiden, allowing him to roll away and stand up. Before he could attack again, Theresa put a hand on his shoulder.

"Stop, Aiden," she said. "There's no reason for you two to fight."

"And why is that?"

Theresa turned to Seamus. For a few seconds no one said a word. Then she smiled at him.

"I see you haven't changed a bit, Seamus."

There was a moment of stunned silence from him, but then Seamus grinned at her.

"Did you expect me to?"

"Wait, time out," Aiden said. "You two know each other?"

"Of course we do," Theresa said, shaking her head. "If there's one thing about Seamus I will always remember, it is the fact that he thinks he's a ladies man."

"Wait...how do you know him?"

Theresa and Seamus looked at each other. Seamus hesitated, but Theresa spoke.

"Aiden Russell, Seamus is no mere human, as you expected. But he is not your enemy."

"Then what is he really?"

Theresa smiled as she patted his back.

"He is one of my kind. A member of the *Aba Itoa Eltragas*."

CHAPTER 8 - TWO AGAINST ONE

"*He*'s WHAT?!" Aiden asked.

Seamus gave Theresa a puzzled frown.

"Theresa, that's really not information that a human should know."

Theresa turned to him, arms folded across her chest.

"Aiden is no mere human, Seamus," she retorted, "I'm sure you've already seen it in your little scuffle."

Seamus scoffed, folding his arms as he gave Aiden a wary side-eye, still unsure about his capabilities.

"And what's so special about this human, hm? More importantly, how did he get that weapon? It seems so familiar..."

Theresa narrowed her eyes and turned to Aiden. She held her hand out, gesturing for him to hand over his sword. Aiden hesitated, but eventually relented and passed Warfang over to her. Seamus raised an eyebrow as she turned back to him.

"C'mon think, brother," Theresa began, "You've seen this blade before."

Seamus was quite for a moment. His eyes widened in shock as he ran his index finger over the blade.

"Drakon Tenara..." He said in the Draconic tongue, promptly leaving Aiden lost in translation.

"Seah." Theresa nodded. "Brother, I promise you that Aiden is not like most humans. He is capable of wielding our King's weapon."

Seamus glanced to Aiden, raising an eyebrow at him.

"You certain? He's a little scrawny to be wielding a sword like Warfang. This not just any weapon, after all."

Aiden pursed his lips and furrowed his brow, glaring with frustration. Just what was Seamus implying?

"Yeah? Well, this scrawny human did pretty damn well against your staff 'buddy!'"

"Ha!" Seamus scoffed. "Kiddo, if I was really trying, you'd still be on your ass, if you weren't dead, of course."

"Seamus." Theresa said, her tone now far more mature and commanding than it usually was. "Don't you remember our code? It is not for us to judge the power that reside within others. Our calmness is our strength. Our humility the sharpest sword of all."

"Oh come on, Theresa," He attempted to argue back. "He's just a mere human boy! I've watched his kind rise to power throughout the ages. The Roman Empire, The Middle Ages, and even their so called "World Wars One and Two". I bore witness to their best warriors! They weren't impressive then, and they're not that impressive now."

"You were there for every single one of those ages?" Aiden asked, "You were around for that long and you still look like a teenager? Theresa hasn't been here that long, I've known her my whole life! So why do you look so young? You don't look like you've been around that long!"

Seamus blinked at his question. Then gave him a dark look like he had just been insulted.

"What are you saying huh? That you think I should look older?"

"I didn't mean to-"

"Enough, you two!" Theresa interrupted. "This is no time to argue with one another."

She turned pointed the tip of Warfang's blade at Seamus face. He staggered back as he stared directly into her emerald green eyes.

"Put away your staff before you bring unwanted attention to yourself, 'ladies man.' Now." Theresa tossed the sword back to Aiden. "And you, put away your sword. We're going to have a talk when we get back to our training camp."

Aiden didn't say anything as he clumsily caught Warfang. He couldn't tell if Theresa was upset with him or Seamus, or both. Behind Theresa, Seamus dismissed his staff silently.

"I certainly hope you know what you're doing, my sister. I've seen the horrors humanity has done to those they suspect of being unnatural."

Theresa gave him a look. "And your point is?"

"They are not the humans you remember," Seamus argued. "The terrors they committed upon innocent men, women, and children wrongfully accused of magic are inexcusable!"

"Brother," Theresa said, "I may have not have awakened when you two did, but I heard the stories from my human mother when I was little. I have learned of their accomplishments and failures during our absence. So believe me when I tell you this. I am fully aware of what humanity has done."

She gently placed a hand on his shoulder.

"But those dark times are in the past. If we continue to judge them by their past actions, then we are no better than the worst of their kind. Do you understand now, brother?"

Seamus said nothing as he glanced to Aiden. They nodded at each other. Although it was clear to Aiden that the two would not be friends any time soon, they wouldn't kill each other. Neither one of them wanted to see Theresa angry, particularly at them.

"All right, sister," Seamus sighed. "You've made your point."

"Good." She smiled. "Come, let's get out of this alley before somebody notices."

Aiden dismissed his sword and put the dragon figurine in his pocket. He still couldn't believe Seamus was one of Theresa's oldest friends! A so called "lady's man" that happened to give him an attitude. This guy? HE was a dragon from the lost past of civilization? He glared at Seamus as he and Theresa talked with one another. For some reason, he couldn't stand the idea of him talking to her instead of him. Jealousy?

"So, how are we going to get back to this training ground?" Seamus asked.

"That's a simple answer," Theresa said. "We take the bus."

"Oh, come on!" Seamus complained, "Theresa, we're not humans limited to ground travel! We're dragons! We can easily fly there!"

Theresa gave him a dark look for complaints. Like he had dared to disobey a direct order.

"And how do you suggest we fly there, when we surely will draw attention? In a small place such as this?" she asked.

Seamus gave her a condescending grin.

"Simple: we take off into the air behind a building and let the kid ride the bus back."

"I'm standing right here you know!" Aiden retorted.

"I know~." Seamus sang in a smug voice.

Aiden was about to say something, but Theresa's hand covered his mouth. Her brow was furrowed in annoyance at their petty little squabbling.

"Enough you two," she said as she turned to Seamus. "We're taking the bus and that's final. I do not want to cause mass panic among humans who see two flying creatures that they can't explain."

Seamus frowned, but gently lowered his head.

"As you say, *Rexkin*."

Aiden frowned. If Seamus was going to speak this language he did not know, the least Seamus could do was translate. Theresa seemed to notice Aiden's frustration.

"Do not worry, Aiden," she said. "During our training courses, Seamus will teach you how to speak our language."

"Excuse me?" Seamus asked, and yelped in pain as Theresa stomped on his foot.

"That's not a problem, right, Seamus?" she asked through clenched teeth. Aiden swore he saw all of her teeth suddenly turn into sharp canines.

"None...at...all..." Seamus answered, eyes watering at the pain coursing through his foot.

Aiden grinned with glee at the pained tears coming from Seamus' eyes. It was nice to see Theresa scold someone else for a change. His grin faded when she turned back to him. He knew he was going to be chewed out when they were out of hearing range of normal people. It was almost more embarrassing to be scolded by Theresa than by his mother.

Maybe it was the fact that Theresa was actually much older than she looked. Even Seamus seemed intimidated by her hidden temper. As Theresa made her way onto the bus Aiden glared at the newcomer, who gave him the same glare in return.

"I'm watching you, Seamus." he whispered.

"Same to you, human."

The bus ride back to their neighborhood was a very awkward one. Aiden was forced to sit by Seamus and the two engaged in an elbow butting competition the entire way home.

After what seemed like ages on the bus, the trio finally arrived at the cul-de-sac. Theresa led them to the training part of the forest quickly, not giving them a second glance. When they reached their spot, Theresa motioned them to sit down.

"I see that your taste for training grounds hasn't changed, Theresa," Seamus said, sitting on a log.

"Why choose a different training ground?" She smiled. "It was where we were trained, dear Seamus."

Seamus grinned at Aiden.

"You've got some luck, kiddo," he said. "Human training could never match up to a dragon's training."

"What's that supposed to mean?" Aiden asked.

"See, kiddo, back in the Medieval times your kind would train out in open fields. Hell, they still train out in the open fields. They drill things into their soldiers' heads, how certain things are done, how to use the battlefield to their advantage. They think every battle is the same every time."

Seamus gazed off into the distance, eyes fixed in a stare that did not invite comment.

Aiden waited with patience, not wanting to say something possibly enrage the dragon before him. Eventually Seamus took a deep a breath and shook himself, like a cold man coming back to the fire. He caught Aiden with a hundred yard stare and continued.

"Back in the day, we didn't train in the field. We lived in the field. Combat was not a game; it was our life. You fought every moment you were awake, and sometimes fought again in your sleep. You learned or died. Each battle is the same. War is always the same, but each battle is different."

Seamus slowly stopped talking, his eyes again drifting away into the darkness, his smile sliding off his face. Aiden could tell that Seamus was remembering battles that had gone the wrong way.

"What you can't learn until you have been through it is that no matter how hard you prepare, the best battle plan in the world never survives contact with the enemy. Young soldiers hope that everything will go according to plan; old soldiers know that it never does. The only thing for sure is that all hell will break loose. The tide of battle turns, plans fail, and the naive die."

Aiden could almost see Seamus' arrogant attitude fading away. He leaned in to listen as Seamus continued.

"I am certain that Theresa doesn't want you to be one of those young ones. The only chance you have for survival is to train until your eyes won't stay open. And then do it some more."

Theresa frowned, placing a hand on his shoulder.

"*Avena*, brother," she said. "Those battles are behind you now. Do not dwell on the past."

Seamus sighed as he nodded slowly.

"Perhaps." He stood up slowly. "So, what do you want me to teach this kid?"

Aiden turned to Theresa, raising an eyebrow.

"Wait, he's gonna be training with us?"

"Correct," Theresa answered. "Sometimes in combat you are attacked by more than one foe."

She summoned her twin swords. Nodding her head to both Aiden and Seamus slowly.

"But sometimes, you'll be fighting together against one strong foe. So, let's make it even; you two against me."

Seamus held out his hand, wind spinning around in one spot.

"You won't admit it, but you think highly of yourself, sister."

Theresa gave him a slight smile.

"Come now, brother. Would it be fair if the two of us went up against him?"

Aiden growled at Theresa's slight joke. With the skill he was growing he didn't like being the butt of their jokes. After all the sword came to him, a gift from his dad that fit him perfectly. He might be new but he knew he was powerful.

"Hey, I'm not that new!" Aiden snapped, summoning Warfang.

"Kiddo, until you've proven yourself, don't get your head in the clouds," Seamus said.

Aiden wanted to shout an insult back at Seamus, but kept his mouth shut. Seamus' staff materialized from the wind. The two of them faced Theresa, who was spinning her twin swords in her hands. Seamus was the first to make a move. With his staff in hand, he swung hard at Theresa. She blocked his staff with both swords and pushed back against them. Seamus continued to press his attack, swinging from left to right each time he stepped forward.

Theresa skillfully blocked each of his swings; Fire blocked attacks from the right, while Snow blocked from the left. Seamus narrowed his eyes and thrust the tip of the staff at her. What Theresa did then made Aiden's eyes widen; she gracefully jumped over the staff and landed on top of it.

"Show off," Seamus scoffed.

Theresa just smiled as she balanced atop the staff and charged toward him, both of her swords ready to strike. As she swung them down, her blades were blocked by a new weapon: Warfang. Aiden managed to push her swords away from Seamus, and then swung his sword at her. Theresa blocked his attack with one sword, and then followed up with the second; all the while maintain her balance on Seamus' staff. Aiden ducked his head quickly to avoid her attack. Pulling his blade back he slashed downward, but Theresa jumped off the staff. Aiden's sword clashed against the metal of Seamus' weapon, sending a strong vibration through both of their arms.

"Hey!" Seamus shouted. His staff shook violently. "Watch where you're swinging, kid!"

Aiden glared at Seamus.

"You could have moved your staff out of the way, you know!"

"Focus, you two." Theresa said as they gave each other dark glares.

She combined her two blades into Snowfyre and charged toward Aiden, spinning the combined blades behind her back before slashing at him. Aiden managed to block the first blade, but he felt himself pushed back. Theresa's attacks were still quick and often heavy hitting, especially when her blades were combined into Snowfyre. When Theresa delivered a quick horizontal slash that he barely blocked, Aiden felt his footing slip.

"Dammit!" He knew what was coming now: she would deliver a slash that would knock him over from the sheer force.

Theresa drew back her weapon and prepared to attack once again. She swung at him and Aiden readied his weapon to block again. Just as her blade was about to clash with his, Seamus' staff blocked her. Aiden glanced at him before muttering under his breath, cursing in annoyance.

"Watch and learn, kiddo, there's a pattern to Theresa's attacks."

He pushed his staff against Theresa's blade. Aiden watched carefully as Seamus spun his staff, creating a gusty wind to push against Theresa. Seamus stared as the wind grew stronger and stronger. Aiden watched in amazement; Theresa was forced to stab her double-bladed weapon into the ground to keep from being blown away.

"Ha!" Seamus laughed. "Where's your skill, sister? Did you lose it from all your years in slumber?"

Theresa smiled gently as she whispered; Aiden's well trained hearing caught the word.

"*Tineat.*"

Snowfyre separated into the twin swords again. Seamus blinked in surprise at Theresa's choice as she let the wind push against her freely now. Aiden watched carefully as Theresa's smile grew into a confident grin. Then it came to him: she was going to use the wind to her advantage.

"Seamus, wait!" Aiden shouted. "The wind! She's going to use it! You have to stop before she turns it against you!"

"Hush up, kiddo!" Seamus snapped. "I know what I'm doing!"

Aiden clenched his hands tightly at Seamus' response. How could this arrogant guy be one of the three warriors that were the best fighters in the dragon Kingdom? All Aiden could see was someone who was not only a lecher, but also an egotistical jerk.

Just as Aiden predicted, Theresa's wings opened up as she let the wind push against her. Then, with a mighty flap of her wings, she sent the wind right back at Seamus. Aiden expected the wind to knock him over, embarrassed by his own attack.

But Seamus just smiled and his back began to morph. Aiden's pupils shrunk in shock and awe as he saw two wings sprout from Seamus' back. The wings were exactly like Theresa's, except the color was not white; they were a dark, forest green. Seamus flapped his wings once to send him flying into the air above. Aiden and Theresa glanced up as he spun his staff behind his back.

"Did you forget that the power of flight is not only yours, Theresa?" he asked.

"Of course not, Seamus." Theresa narrowed her eyes. "But this is not aerial combat. Come back down!"

Seamus grinned as he swung his staff hard in the air. A strong wind blew over the trees. Aiden stabbed his sword into the ground to avoid being blown away. He glared up at Seamus before the wind finally died down. Theresa folded her arms in annoyance.

"Seamus..." she said.

"Oh, all right, all right," he relented, landing on the ground in front of Aiden. His wings folded back in and became part of his human form.

"She'll do whatever she can to ruin any fun. She's such a spoilsport."

"On that, we can agree," Aiden said.

Seamus gave him a small smile. The two readied their weapons again as Theresa ran towards them, swinging her weapons. Aiden blocked Fire while Seamus parried Snow. The two gave each other a small nod before they began pushing back against Theresa's attack, this time going on the offensive. Seamus kept one of Theresa's blades from making any quick movements, while Aiden dueled with her second sword.

This was the first time that Aiden had kept Theresa on the defensive since their training began, though he knew it was because of Seamus' help. Even so, Theresa still wasn't breaking a sweat.

The sound of clashing metal continued to ring through the forest. Aiden and Seamus were slowly tiring from the battle, Aiden more so than Seamus. It seemed almost futile to continue. No matter what he tried, she always had some kind of defense against his attack. Seamus thrust powerfully at Theresa, hoping to disarm one of her swords.

Theresa managed to evade the attempt and then kneed Seamus hard in the stomach. Aiden lunged at her, swinging Warfang with all his strength. Time seemed to slow down as both of Theresa's swords blocked Aiden's weapon with ease. Then Theresa surprised Aiden, throwing him over her head into the ground behind her. Pain surged through his body as he coughed hard. He struggled to get up and continue fighting, but Theresa held Fire to his throat.

"Stand down, Aiden," Theresa told him. "You fought well today, but don't push your limits."

"I can still fight," he lied, but he didn't want to give up. Theresa shook her head.

"Your body is tired, you're sweating buckets, and I just threw you to the ground. One of the things you must learn Aiden is when you have reached your limit."

Aiden groaned, still on the ground. Seamus pushed himself up with his staff, coughing a bit as he glanced to Theresa.

"Was there really a reason you had to knee me so hard?" he asked.

"Yes." Theresa smiled. "That was for underestimating me."

"How did I underestimate you?" Seamus asked, dumbfounded.

"Simple," Theresa answered. "You assumed that because I have human parents and prefer to be in my new body that my skills would not be as good as they once were."

She offered one hand to help Aiden up. He took it without complaining. Theresa smiled and spun her swords.

"But the truth is, dear brother, I am and always will be the best swords master."

She turned and grabbed a water bottle from their backpacks. Seamus nudged Aiden in the shoulder with his elbow.

"Modesty is probably the only weakness that she has." He said with a tiny smile, "She acts like she's the best, but there was one being that she could never beat." Aiden was hesitant to ask, but his curiosity got the better of him. "And that being was?"

Seamus gave him a sly little smile. "Why, it was the previous owner of the sword you wield, of course. The King of Dragons."

CHAPTER 9 - TASTE OF REAL COMBAT

A few days passed as the training continued. To Aiden's dismay, Seamus did not leave during those days. During combat training Theresa would switch out with him in the middle of a fight. When Aiden asked why, Seamus gave him a smug answer.

"Simple, if you're outnumbered you're going to be tag-teamed by opponents. Now shut up and focus!"

It was almost unbearable to have to listen to Seamus' taunts. Every time Aiden messed up, he would hear Seamus' mocking laugh. Aiden told himself not to let it get to him but that proved difficult. He already had to endure taunts from Eric at school; having a dragon mock him was almost as embarrassing.

Despite Seamus' heckling, Aiden began to improve against both him and Theresa. While he couldn't take them both at the same time, and often lost during each round against one of them, he would employ a new tactic each time they faced off with him. The more he improved, the more he began to feel stronger due to being Warfang's chosen one.

His magic training, though, was not going over so well. While he had gotten used to creating a wave to block Theresa's, which she had him do just to simply get an understanding of magical flow, Seamus made things more difficult than they should have been.

Aiden could see the differences between the two of them easily. Theresa was an expert at combat and seemed good with magic. Seamus was an expert at magic and was all right with combat, though he preferred to use magic to his advantage.

Because of his magic skills, Theresa ordered Seamus to help in Aiden's training. Seamus initially refused to help him learn magic. That is until Theresa "convinced" him by setting his hair on fire.

On Saturday, the three of them stood together in the forest once more. Sunday would be the last training day before school. A part of Aiden was glad spring break was almost over, but another part of him wished it could go on.

"All right, kiddo," Seamus said as he spun his staff, "today you'll learn your first spell at last. Think you can handle it?"

Aiden glared at him.

"If I can handle your smart ass retorts, I can handle a spell."

Theresa frowned as she watched the exchange.

"Focus, Aiden," she told him. "Casting a spell requires full concentration. It's not like pushing up a wave of water."

"She's telling the truth," Seamus said, stabbing his staff into the ground. "Spells can be very useful if they're done right and you pronounce them correctly, but if you lose your focus, they can bite you back."

Aiden gave a slight nod. In truth he was actually nervous to begin really learning about magic. Making waves rise up from water was hard enough, now he had to do actual spells? For Theresa's sake, he wasn't going to argue with Seamus. The second of the Dragon Warriors pointed to a pile of tree branches he had gathered.

"See those dead branches over there?" He asked. Aiden gave another nod. "What about them?"

"While you and Theresa went back to your parents, I spent the entire night looking for branches that would be suitable for your first spell." Seamus gave a yawn. "Let me tell you, having to fly in my dragon form at night isn't exactly easy. While I love it and all, you humans and your electric lights at night make it hard to find a good landing spot without being noticed."

Aiden's imagined Seamus' dragon form. He tried to picture it like Theresa's form, but all he could see was a very ugly dragon. Theresa shot Seamus an angry look.

"Seamus, you know fully well that being in dragon form in this age is idiotic. What if somebody saw you?"

"Oh relax, sis." He teased. "No one could have seen me. I stayed close to the forest. Besides, being at a higher altitude requires much stronger wing strength, and you know it."

"Don't lecture me about wing strength, Seamus." She folded her arms across her chest. "I'll let it slide this once, but no changing into our dragon forms unless it's absolutely necessary. Understand?"

Seamus gave her a small nod.

"Now then, back to our lesson." He swatted Aiden hard on his back, nearly knocking him over. "You ready, kiddo? Good. Now, hold your right hand out and point your palm at the branches."

Aiden felt reluctant to do what Seamus was telling him, but he held his arm out and aimed at the branches. Seamus observed his position and stance, scratching his chin slightly.

"Good stance, though you want to shift your weight onto your legs in case the spell nearly knocks you over," he said, pushing down on Aiden's shoulders.

Aiden felt his legs become heavier as he was forced to hold the position. He turned to Theresa for some help, but she just gave him a slight nod.

"Seamus knows what he's doing, Aiden. Just listen to him like you listened to me."

Aiden wanted to protest, but decided against it. His trust in

Theresa outweighed his dislike for Seamus, though his legs might kill him later.

"Now that you've gotten your position, let's talk about the main element that dragons use when we're in our true forms." He grinned. "Fire."

"If this is a lesson about fire, why am I in this ridiculous stance?" Aiden asked, earning a whack to the back of his head from Seamus.

"Don't question the teacher!" Seamus paced back and forth behind Aiden. "Sometimes in a fight you can't always jump into physical combat if the enemy possesses ranged weapons or if they have some spells of their own. Us dragons now, we have the ability to breathe fire. So we got that covered."

Seamus grinned as he cracked his fingers.

"Now, since you're no dragon and you don't possess the ability to breathe fire, this spell will be one of your main offensive magic spells. Since your training with Theresa has already taught you to feel magic flowing through your body, the next step is to use that flow to your advantage."

"How so?" Aiden asked. This time he was actually interested in what Seamus had to say.

"See, everyone's got their own elemental magic that matches their spirit. While it's common knowledge that almost every dragon can breathe fire, our main elements are different in our human forms. For example, Theresa has white fire as her element and I have wind as my own. Until we know what your main element is, we'll practice with different spells each time we get the chance."

Seamus picked up his staff and pointed it at the branches.

"Now, focus your thoughts on the one element that can make those branches into ash. If you hadn't guessed, it's fire."

Aiden glared at Seamus for the insult to his intelligence. But he turned back to the pile of branches, trying to feel the same energy he felt when he was in the river. His forehead began to sweat as he focused all his thought onto the one element.

At first he felt nothing. Seamus frowned as he watched.

"Picture the fire in your hand; focus on getting it ready before firing the spell," he instructed.

Aiden wanted to ask how he could picture his hand surrounded by flames, but he kept that question to himself. Slowly he thought of the simplest fire: some logs burning in a fireplace. As that picture began to form in his mind, Aiden felt a new sensation flow through his body. Unlike the soothing feeling he got from the cool touch of water, this sensation was bubbling with hot energy that felt like it was burning his arms.

Aiden's forehead began to sweat more as he felt his palm heat up. He wanted to stop the spell, but his will refused to let go as the bubbling feeling took form in his hand. With a grunt escaping his lips, a small orange flame formed around his hand. He nearly shouted in surprise when he saw his hand was on fire.

"Excellent, Aiden!" Theresa said, smiling widely.

Aiden watched the fire dance around his hand, mesmerized by its glow and warm touch. He glanced to Seamus, wondering if he was holding onto the flame for too long.

"Relax, kiddo," Seamus said, "you're not gonna burn from a tiny spark like that. Now, point at the branches and say slowly, '*Flarnea.*'"

"Flare what?" Aiden asked, and Theresa sighed at Seamus' quick pronunciation of the word.

"Seamus…"

"What? I pronounced it correctly."

"You said it too fast for him." Theresa placed a hand on Aiden's shoulder. "The word is pronounced 'flare-nea.' Just remember to say it slowly and don't rush the word."

Aiden smiled at Theresa's help. He was glad that she was still on his side. She pulled her hand away as he aimed at the branches again. The flames dancing around his hand began to merge into a small fireball in his palm. He could only pray that he didn't mess up.

"*Flarnea!*"

When he said the spell's name, he heard a small pop from the fireball. It flew from Aiden's hand towards the pile of branches. Pride surged through him as he watched the fireball fly closer to his target. But as it grew closer to the branches, Aiden noticed that it was beginning to die down. The fireball grew even smaller until eventually it was a small ember, dying out.

Seamus erupted with laugher.

"Oh man! So close, kiddo!" he said between laughs.

"Seamus!" Theresa snapped, glaring at her brother.

"What? Oh, come on, Thes. You didn't really expect him to get it on the first shot, did you?"

"I never said that he would," she pointed out, "but laughing at someone lowers their morale, and we don't want that."

"Oh, a little rough mentoring can't hurt too much!" Seamus responded with a know it all grin.

Aiden glared at him. "I'm so happy you think this is funny."

"Aw, suck it up, kiddo!" Seamus said, whacking Aiden's back rather hard. "You know what they say: If at first you don't succeed, try again until you can't stand!"

"That's not how the saying goes," Theresa began to say, but Seamus interrupted her by helping Aiden's arm back into position.

"Anyway, the point is that you just need to try again. Casting magic doesn't come naturally to anyone the first time. Even for experts like those bookworm mages. Now try it again."

Aiden groaned as he turned back to the branches. Once again, his hand was engulfed in flames. He aimed carefully, determined to hit his target as the flames merged into a small fireball.

"*Flarnea!*"

The fireball flew from his hand, but just like the first, it eventually died out. He clenched his fist before firing another fireball, which again died out before it could reach his target. Aiden conjured more failed fireballs, panting heavily each time.

"Come…on…" he said in between breaths. "What am I doing wrong?"

"Don't blame yourself, kiddo." Seamus said as he took a kinder tone. "Magic isn't exactly something you're not used to yet. You also just started to learn how to use it."

"But why do I feel so tired?" Aiden asked. "It's like I'm trying to move something twice my size every time to make it erupt from my hands."

"Simple. Magic is the strength of mind and patience. Unlike your biceps or your triceps, your ability to use magic is all mental. Those without a strong mental force tend to become exhausted." Seamus explained, Aiden gave him a perplexed look. "Think of it like this. When you're a novice in the arts, Magic makes you tired, so keep in mind that as you use magic, it will physically and mentally exhaust you."

"All right, all right," Theresa said, interrupting the lecture before Aiden could ask another question. "Let's get back to focusing on your…training…"

Theresa's words trailed off as she looked around. Aiden noticed that Seamus was alert as well. Something had caught their attention, but he couldn't tell what. Theresa's eyes widened as she turned to Aiden.

"Get down!"

Theresa tackled him to the ground just in time. Aiden saw an arrow sticking into the tree where he had been standing. Seamus pulled it out, examining the arrowhead carefully before snarling.

"Goblin arrows," he said. "I knew their kind was still around!"

Aiden looked at Theresa, confusion all over his face as she stood.

"You never told me there were goblins," he said.

"There were many kinds of lower monsters during the days of

the old Kingdoms," she explained, summoning her twin blades quickly. "Goblins are the lowest of the low."

"They're more like rats than anything else," Seamus growled, holding out his hand as wind began to spin in place. "Come forth, Hurricane!"

Seamus' silver and bronze staff materialized in his hand. Aiden stumbled to get up as Theresa readied herself for battle. He reached for Warfang in his pocket, quickly summoning the blade. Aiden turned to Theresa, nervous now as the forest began rustle.

"Back to back!" she shouted to them.

They stood together, their backs touching. Aiden swallowed a lump in his throat, his arm shaking from fear. Theresa noticed his shaking and frowned.

"Hey," she said softly, "I was scared before my first battle as well."

"Scared? I'm not scared," Aiden lied.

"Listen, goblins are unorganized in their combat. They're small, weak, and can easily be beaten," she said in a reassuring tone. "Even with the little experience you have, you'll be able to beat them. I promise."

She gave him her signature smile and Aiden's arm slowly stopped shaking. His confidence began to grow and the trio readied themselves as the rustling in the forest became louder.

"All right kiddo, listen good," Seamus said, spinning his staff in front of him. "Goblins do nothing but swing their weapons wildly around. It makes it easier for you to hit them hard and fast."

"Just remember your training," Theresa finished, looking to the forest. "Here they come!"

As if on cue, goblins swarmed at the trio. Aiden couldn't tell how many there were exactly; he managed to count at least ten, but he knew there were more as the group approached, and the rustling grew louder.

They were nothing like Aiden had pictured or anything like

the stories described them to be. They certainly were short crea-tures, about three feet tall at most. Their skin was not green, however. It was more of a pale yellow that didn't even seem to shine. Their eyes were a dark orange color that could pierce the soul. Their noses were huge, with two small nostrils underneath. Other than being very short, the only thing that they had in common with fairy tale goblins was that they had really bad teeth. The armor they were wearing was pieced together leather, covering their upper body and legs.

All of them carried very crude, make-shift swords that looked dull. They had almost no organization. Aiden gripped the hilt of his sword tightly as the goblins came closer. This would be his first time in actual combat when he knew how to swing a sword.

"Steady," Theresa advised, bringing up her twin swords. "On my signal."

As the goblins neared, they yelled something in strange gibberish. Aiden swallowed a lump in his throat and took the battle stance that Theresa had taught him. Seamus grinned as he swung his staff down hard on the ground, sending a powerful wave of wind at the goblins. The force of it slammed into the ugly creatures, knocking them down. Theresa shouted.

"Now!"

The three of them charged at the goblins, weapons held high as she led them into the group. Metal once again rang through the forest as their weapons clashed with the goblins'.

While Theresa and Seamus were busy slashing goblins down the chest or whacking their skulls, Aiden was facing off with one nasty goblin. The ugly creature snarled, swinging its sword at him. Remembering his training, Aiden quickly blocked the attack. The two swords clashed against each other, Aiden grunting as he pushed against the goblin's blade.

Aiden pulled Warfang back and threw a horizontal slash at his opponent. The goblin yelped when Aiden's sword cut into its skin. Green blood flowed from the wound. Aiden knew he couldn't let the goblin make a counter attack and gave a powerful thrust to the goblin's chest.

The goblin made a gurgling sound as Aiden drew his blade away. As soon as his sword was out of the goblin's chest, the ugly creature fell over. A wave of confidence and pride washed over Aiden: he had just defeated his first opponent in combat. The feeling was almost intoxicating, like he could do anything in the world and not fail.

That feeling didn't last long. Aiden saw a second goblin coming at him, swinging its sword wildly. Aiden quickly blocked the weapon, going on the defensive as it swung repeatedly. His training came back to him as he parried the goblin's sword into the air. With a quick yell, he slashed the goblin's chest, neck to belly.

Once again the blow he delivered was fatal. The goblin fell, gurgling on its own blood. Aiden glanced to see how Theresa and Seamus were doing, and smiled in relief when he saw that they had the upper hand.

Theresa was easily blocking goblin attacks, as well as slashing into them with her twin blades. One goblin tried to sneak up on her, but Theresa was prepared. She held her blades back-handed and stabbed the goblin through its stomach. Theresa pulled her blades away, then she slammed the pommels together, forming Snowfyre. She spun the double-bladed sword in a circle, hacking into goblins with ease.

Seamus had an altogether different style. Based on all their training Aiden wondered if Seamus could even land a fatal blow with such a blunt weapon. Seamus proved him wrong, taking the lower end of his staff with both hands and swinging the weapon into the heads of five goblins at once. There was a sickening crunch as each goblin head hit his staff.

"Come on you ugly little bastards!" Seamus taunted, spinning his staff behind his back. "I can do this all day!"

Aiden's sight-seeing came to an end as two goblins came at

him at once. He managed to cut into one, but the second tackled him to the ground. Aiden swung his fist at the goblin's face, punching it hard in the cheek. The goblin's skin was rough and leathery, but the punch seemed to catch it off guard for a moment. The goblin hissed at Aiden, baring its jagged teeth. Before it could strike at him, however, a sword slashed through its neck. The goblin's head rolled off its back before its body fell away.

Aiden glanced up to see who had saved him. Theresa once again was wielding her swords. She nodded once as he quickly stood up.

"Thanks," he said in a quick breath.

"We're not done yet," she said. "Keep your balance and don't fall down!"

Theresa stabbed an incoming goblin before kicking another away. Aiden knew that now was not the time to talk. He steadied his weapon again, parried an attacking goblin's sword and stabbed it in the chest.

As the fight went on, Aiden noticed that the goblins were slowly backing off. Their large numbers seemed intimidating at first, but they clearly lacked any true combat skill. The three of them continued to press back against the goblin force, each goblin that fell scared another away from the battle. Aiden knew that their retreating numbers meant only one thing:

Victory was near.

In a final attempt to mortally wound one of them, the biggest goblin of the group, carrying a make-shift staff with several skulls on it, ran at Aiden. It growled and shouted something in gibberish. Aiden raised his arms up, ready to strike the goblin, but before he could attack, a blast of lighting surged from the goblin's staff.

Aiden's eyes widened as the lighting flew at him. Although it wasn't the same as the magic Theresa and Seamus knew, it was definitely magic. It all happened in a second as a giant white wing quickly shielded him from the spell. Theresa's dragon wing had once again saved his life.

"Seamus!" she shouted. "Counter attack now!"

Seamus nodded as he slammed his staff on the ground. A powerful gust flew from the staff and slammed the goblin mage hard into a tree. At the sight of their mage dead, the rest of the goblins retreated, shouting fearful gibberish.

"Yeah, stay away you little punks!" Seamus taunted. "Remember your place on the food chain!"

Both Aiden and Theresa groaned at Seamus' lame allegory. Theresa's wing pulled back, unscathed. Aiden was flabbergasted that her wing was still in perfect shape after taking a magic attack. Theresa smiled at him.

"Goblin magic is very weak to dragons," she explained, "but to someone who's just understanding magic, like yourself, it can be deadly."

"I owe you again," Aiden said. "Someday I want to pay you back for all you've done, including saving my life."

Theresa sighed. She gently flicked his nose.

"Aiden, you're my friend. You don't need to repay me in any way, shape or form. Understand?"

Theresa's wing folded back into her back. Aiden sighed, but gave her a nod.

"Theresa?"

"Yeah?"

"Would it be all right if I fell down now?"

She laughed lightly at his question. "Go ahead. First taste of real combat rattles the nerves."

Aiden plopped down on the ground, covered in sweat and breathing hard. Every muscle in his body felt like it was on fire, far more than when they were training. Seamus smiled as he stabbed his staff into the ground, dusting his hands off easily.

"Not bad for your first fight, kiddo. I was expecting you to get squeamish with all that goblin blood."

Aiden rolled his eyes. He would be lying if he said that the sight of blood made him comfortable. However, something in him had told him to ignore the blood and focus on the task at hand: winning. Though Theresa and Seamus had done most of the work, he felt proud that he was able to take out a couple of goblins on his own. Theresa sat down beside him.

"Excellent job, Aiden," Theresa said as she put a hand on his shoulder. "Excellent job."

The pride they had in that moment came to an end though as Theresa frowned. Aiden and Seamus looked at her in confusion as she glared to the seemingly endless forest before them.

"Something's wrong though. Goblins don't attack unless they have a master. And this place is pretty secluded." "Rexkin?" Seamus asked in confusion as the white haired girl's brow furrowed.

"Someone knows that we are here."

CHAPTER 10 - RAVEN

*A*fter a spring break of nothing but constant training with Theresa and Seamus, the time came to return to school. Aiden looked forward to it like a cat looked forward to a bath. He had probably just had one of the best weeks of his life, despite the hard training, and now he was going to have to endure school until the summer.

"Why can't school just go away?" Aiden asked Theresa as they waited for the bus to arrive.

"For once, I might agree with you," Theresa said, her arms folded across her chest. "After yesterday's goblin attack, who knows what will come our way. You've just barely begun your training and we're forced to push them back to the weekend."

"I still can't believe those things even exist," Aiden said. "Tell me, do they always try attacks like that?"

"Goblins are simple-minded foes, Aiden," she explained. "They'll try anything they think will work, believing nothing will go wrong."

"So, yes?"

"Yes and no." Theresa smiled.

Aiden just chuckled and shook his head at her answer. He had to admit, she was good at cryptic answers. He glanced around the bus stop, trying to find Seamus.

"So, where's the so-called, 'Ladies Man'?'"

"He should be here already." Theresa frowned. "He better not be delaying his arrival on purpose…"

Aiden noticed the slight change in her tone. When Theresa was annoyed, she could easily show it. He remembered once when she set Seamus' hair on fire when he was refusing to train Aiden.

"What do you think he's doing anyway?"

"If I know Seamus, he's either doing morning exercises or readjusting his appearance to fit in middle school." Theresa answered.

Aiden raised an eyebrow.

"Readjusting?"

"Remember what I told you before? That Seamus thinks of himself as a ladies man? He'll change his appearance so that he'll look attractive to any female that catches his attention."

"Does that mean that you could do the same thing?" Aiden asked.

"Normally, I could. But since I was born in a human body, I have my limits," she told him.

Aiden tried to imagine Theresa changing her form in different ways. The different outfits she could choose, the different appearances one could take with that kind of power. It was both awesome to think about, but at the same time he couldn't help but have a sleezy grin on his lips, something he unintentionally learned from Seamus. Theresa noticed his expression and smacked him in the back of his head, eyes closed in annoyance.

"Ow!" He rubbed the spot that she smacked. "What was that for?"

"You know damn well what it was for." she grumbled.

"All right, all right, I'm sorry," Aiden admitted. "I wasn't trying to offend you."

Theresa sighed and her left hand glowed white. She gently rubbed the spot she smacked. The pain Aiden had felt slowly went away.

"Apology accepted." she said.

The flapping of heavy wings sounded from above. Aiden reached for Warfang in his pocket, but Theresa grabbed his arm. She shook her head as he gave her a questioning look. As the heavy flapping got closer, Aiden's grip around the figurine weakened. They looked up and Aiden's mouth dropped when he saw what was flying towards them.

A dragon.

Just like the goblins, the dragon looked completely different from what he had imagined. The head of the dragon had no horns at all. In fact, it was clean and smooth, with eyes the same color as Seamus', shining brightly in the early morning. The dragon's skin was a dark emerald green, while its under belly was a light green. The colors were so vibrant that even in the very early light, they gleamed brightly. Its wings were incredibly long, easily longer than a limousine.

"Is that really...?" he began to ask, but stopped when he saw Theresa's smile.

"Yes, Aiden, that's Seamus' dragon form."

Seamus' large dragon form landed on the open grass field behind the bus stop. The ground shook briefly, around the area where he landed. To Aiden's surprise, Seamus stood on his hind legs, his front legs more like arms for the most part. Seamus let out a slight roar, and his body prickled with a strange white light that forced Aiden to shield his eyes..

"Oi, kiddo," Seamus called out, "you can uncover your eyes now."

Aiden squinted as the light died down. Seamus was once

again in human form, looking exactly as he had before. Theresa shook her head at his dramatic entrance.

"Was there any real reason why you flew here in your dragon form?" she asked. Seamus gave a toothy grin as he scratched the back of his head.

"Well, let's just say that after the two of you went home, I went out on the town to have some 'fun.'"

Theresa sighed in annoyance.

"Seamus, please tell me that you didn't transform in front of anybody."

"Oh, no worries, sis." Seamus grinned. "The kind lady I met last night was cute and all, but she couldn't hold her alcohol."

"Seamus!" Theresa gasped, putting her hands around Aiden's ears.

"Hey! I'm not a kid!" Aiden protested.

Seamus gave him a smug look. He lightly punched him in the shoulder as he joined up with the two of them.

"Kiddo, compared to us, you're still just a tiny cell that hasn't even developed."

"What was that?!" Aiden glared.

"Let it be, Aiden," Theresa sighed, gently pulling her hands away from his ears. She turned back to Seamus with a frown.

"Next time, Seamus, when you're out trying to court women, please keep in mind that you have a duty to do."

"Of course, *Rexkin.*" Seamus sighed. "I'm sorry for being late."

Aiden couldn't take it anymore. For the past three days, Seamus would deliberately use words from their language just to annoy him. If he was going to have to listen to them speak in Dragon, or whatever it was they called it, they could at least have the decency to translate for him.

"What does *rexkin* mean anyway?" he asked, pronouncing the last part of the word differently. Theresa turned to him, her familiar smile reappearing.

"*Rexkin* is the Dragonic word for leader, Aiden," she explained. "Though you nearly pronounced it right there."

Seamus nodded his head with a slight smile.

"It's 'rex-*kin*.' Not *keen*," he explained. "Think of it as combining two words from your human language. Rex and kin. Thus, you get *Rexkin*."

"So, wait," Aiden followed, "one of your words from your language is actually just two words put together from the human language?"

Seamus glared at him. No matter what he did, Aiden always seemed to annoy Seamus.

"Do you keep forgetting that our kind existed way before yours? Maybe humans stole the word and separated it for their own uses," Seamus argued.

"Enough, you two," Theresa said. "We can't exactly be talking about the history of dragons when we're at school."

"Remind me why I'm coming along anyway?" Seamus asked, and for once Aiden had to agree with his question.

"Well, Seamus, the last time we were at that school, Aiden was attacked not once, but twice," Theresa answered.

"And that concerns me why?"

"Because one of his attackers was an ogre and the others were members of the hornet clan."

Seamus fell silent at her answer. For once he didn't have a smart comeback. Aiden couldn't help but be glad. That came to an end as Seamus smiled.

"Well, looks like the kiddo's got some bad luck if that's the case," he said smugly.

"I think it's more than that, Seamus." Theresa's eyes flashed with the same wisdom that Aiden saw before. "Someone's after Aiden for some reason. The ogre wanted the King's sword and the hornet men wanted to kill him."

Seamus shrugged. Aiden was almost stunned how laid back he was about the problem. Despite his status as a 'great' warrior,

Seamus didn't seem to take his job seriously at all. Theresa's eyes narrowed.

"Seamus...," she said in a dangerously low tone.

"Oh relax, sister," he said, leaning against the bus stop sign. "I know that we have a duty to do, but don't think I'll be playing babysitter all day."

Aiden could only pray that he wouldn't have to be watched by Seamus for the rest of the school year. He was having enough trouble standing next him. The familiar sounds of the bus came from the lower part of the street.

"Sounds like your ride is here," Seamus said, his wings spreading out once again. " Don't worry, Thes, I'm not transforming into a full blow dragon again. I'll use some magic to keep me invisible to most eyes while I fly above you guys."

"You're not riding with us?" Aiden asked.

"Why should I?" Seamus said. "I have the advantage of changing my body. That means I don't have to go to school. You two, however, got the short end of the stick."

"*Lo hitokan*, Seamus," Theresa said, nodding her head at him. Seamus nodded back.

"*Spaveteran ka, Rexkin*." With that, he flew back into the sky above them, still in his human form. Aiden looked helplessly at what they said.

"I told him to be careful," she explained. "He told me that he always is."

Aiden would have continued the conversation, but the bus arrival cut him off. He sighed as they began to climb the bus' steps. But before they climbed up, Theresa handed him a small book and winked.

"Let's see you put your training to good use against Eric's spit wads, shall we?"

Aiden's smile grew into a devilish grin. He was going to enjoy smacking Eric's spit wads back at him.

"Ugh, what I wouldn't give to get this day over with," Aiden groaned at their lunch table, spinning his fork in his hand.

"Oh, it hasn't been that bad," Theresa said, trying to keep an optimistic tone. "At least it's going faster than we thought it would."

"Easy for you to say," Aiden grumbled. "Math class dragged on for what seemed like an eternity. That teacher has it out for me, I swear…."

Theresa laughed as she shook her head.

"Aiden, you fought goblins yesterday that wanted to kill you," she pointed out. "I think a math teacher is a piece of cake."

He sighed before taking a bite of his lunch. She had a point. Goblins were much more intimidating than the math problems his teacher would set up for the class.

As lunch slowly progressed, the two of them took notice of a new hall monitor. Since Patrick's disappearance, though only Aiden and Theresa knew the real truth about what happened, four new hall monitors were patrolling the halls. Aiden couldn't help but wonder what the Principal thought about Patrick suddenly vanishing.

"Why do you think they're not asking questions about Patrick?" Aiden asked. "I mean, the guy isn't sick. He's dead."

"Who knows why?" Theresa answered, taking a bite of her apple. "Though I have a feeling that he would have attacked this school sooner or later before you gained Warfang."

"What do you mean?"

"Ogres aren't known for their patience." She opened a milk carton. "If they stay in one place they've been ordered to watch for too long, they could go crazy with impatience."

"And if he did do that?"

"I would have stopped him." Theresa took a quick sip of her milk. Aiden looked back at her.

"Don't you think that people would find it odd that a thirteen-year-old girl fought a hall monitor twice her size?"

"Are you forgetting that I'm no mere girl?"

Both had a good chuckle as they continued their lunch. So far, things had just been normal. It had only been a weak since Theresa revealed to him what she was, and he still felt like he was dreaming.

His mind wandered back to what her dragon form looked like. After seeing Seamus' form, his curiosity grew again. The thought of Seamus began to sour his mood, however. If there was one thing he hated, it was an arrogant and egotistical personality. Theresa noticed his smile turn into a small frown.

"What's wrong, Aiden?" she asked.

"It's nothing, really," he said. "I'm just still having a hard time imagining Seamus as one of your order."

"Let me guess: it's because of his personality," Theresa predicted. Aiden just stared at her.

"Are you certain dragons can't read minds?" Aiden asked jokingly, both chuckling a little.

"I know what you're feeling," Theresa said as their laughter died down. "When the Dragon King first told me that Seamus would become one of our greatest warriors, I doubted more than you."

"You questioned your King's word?" Aiden asked.

"I was more loyal to him than any others, Aiden, but that doesn't mean I didn't have my...disagreements with him." She sighed. "But yes, I was concerned that the Dragon King was wrong about Seamus. His arrogant attitude was certainly worse back then, and he never stopped flirting with any of the dragonesses."

Aiden tried to imagine Seamus with an even worse attitude. It was something that he couldn't even picture without shaking his head in disbelief.

"I take it that none of the other dragonesses were happy with his attempts?"

"Not one bit." Theresa tried not to laugh. "One time he almost lost his wings because he told one of them that she had a large tail. To a dragoness, that's like saying we're fat."

"Sounds like the dragonesses had bad tempers." Aiden smiled, taking a bite of his apple.

"Only when we're angered enough, or haven't you noticed how angry I was when the hornet men tried to kill you?"

"Point taken," Aiden said after swallowing the piece of apple. "But if he tried flirting, has he ever tried that with...you know, you?"

Theresa folded her arms across her chest.

"Aiden, I was his trainer and leader. What do you think I did when he tried to flirt with me?"

"Kicked his sorry little ass?"

Theresa laughed. He couldn't help but make that retort, especially since it was talking about Seamus when he wasn't around. Before either of them could continue, however, Aiden heard a familiar voice behind him.

"Hey loser! You're dead in gym class today!" Eric taunted.

Aiden groaned. He had almost forgotten that Eric was now taking a gym class with him and Theresa. As if he wasn't enduring enough taunts from his old bully on the bus, now he had to put up with him in gym class.

"You think he would shut up for once..." Aiden mumbled.

"Don't let him get to you, Aiden," Theresa advised. "Your skills have grown since your training began."

"I don't think combat training or swords will be allowed in class, Theresa." Aiden frowned. She gave him a smile before finishing off her milk.

"Whoever said anything about physically fighting him?" she asked.

"What are you talking about...."

He cut himself off as he noticed her tooth filled grin. Then a sly smile grew on his face as well. Aiden knew what she was talking about now. There was another way to put their training to good use.

While swords were not allowed in school and fighting would get you suspended, no one ever said that he couldn't use a brush of small magic to knock Eric down in sports like flag football or dodge ball.

"You're not worried that it'll cause some people to wonder?"

"Just as long as you don't hurt him." Theresa smiled. "Besides, I think he has a little payback coming to him." Aiden chuckled as he finished off his lunch.

"Hey, move it newbie!" Eric's voice rang out from behind him. "I'm walking here!"

Aiden couldn't help but turn to see to whom he was talking. It wasn't anybody that he or Theresa knew. No doubt it was a new student and, unfortunately for him, he was a new target for Eric.

The new kid had messy dark black hair, which covered one side of his face, and hazel eyes. He wore a black shirt and jean shorts, complete with black boots. As Eric walked away, the new kid gave him a dark glare. Obviously he didn't take kindly to being pushed around.

Aiden watched the new kid carefully. Something about him was off, and not in a good way. He could feel it in his gut that this new student wasn't just an ordinary person.

Suddenly the new kid turned towards him. Aiden's entire body felt frozen on the spot. The new kid stared at him for only a few seconds, then he left the lunch room. Aiden let out a sigh of relief; his entire body was shaking.

"Phew...," he said. "Something about that new kid just really felt wrong."

"Agreed," Theresa said. She was growing concerned as well. "I sensed it the moment I saw him."

Aiden turned back to her. "What do you think it means?"

"I honestly don't know," she mused, "but he's no normal human being. That's for damn sure."

"You think he's a monster in disguise?"

She shook her head. "No. If he were a monster, I would be able to sense it. He's human. But he's got a feeling to him that I don't like."

Aiden didn't like what he was hearing. It wasn't like Theresa to be unsure. It made him very unsettled.

"You think he could be trouble?" Aiden asked.

"If he is, we'll have to be careful." Theresa frowned. "If he turns out to be a dangerous threat, Aiden, I don't want you fighting him without any help."

"I hear you, I'll try not to jump the gun!" he said right as the bell rang.

One more class to go and they were done with the first day. He couldn't wait for it to end. The new kid was still on his mind as they headed towards the gym. Aiden didn't consider himself skeptical about new kids. Usually he would just notice them and get use to them being around.

The new kid, though, was different. The way that he stared at Aiden made him uneasy. It made him even more uneasy that Theresa was feeling unsettled as well. And she was a dragoness. What would unsettle a dragoness?

He sighed as they reached the gymnasium. Maybe some dodge ball, or whatever Coach Bryan had planned, could clear his mind.

Then he felt like punching himself. He was actually looking forward to whatever the coach had planned? Aiden was more uneasy with that thought than the new kid's strange glare.

"So, what do you think the coach has planned for us today?" he finally asked as the two of them placed their backpacks in the storage room.

"Who knows?" Theresa replied, sighing. "I'm not really focused on whatever he has in mind."

Both of them went to their assigned spots in the gymnasium and waited for the coach to come out from his office. Aiden was still bothered by the black-haired boy, even if the two of them were separated from him.

"I said move it, punk!" Eric's voice shouted from the storage room.

Aiden groaned at his old bully's voice. His curiosity forced him to glance back to the storage room again, and he almost wished he didn't.

Eric shoved the black-haired boy into the wall. Aiden's spine got chills as he watched the scene. On one hand, he wasn't happy that Eric was bothering the new kid. On the other, the black-haired boy was clearly not his friend.

He turned to Theresa, who watched the scene as well. Her eyes told him not to get involved. Aiden gave a slight nod, like he could read what Theresa was thinking. Eric's laugh echoed through the gym as he walked away from the new kid.

"Man, what a wimp!" he proudly said. "That just proves that I'm the toughest kid at this school!"

At first the rest of the class was silent as he approached them. Then they broke out laughing, except for Aiden and Theresa. Eric's eyes narrowed in anger at their laughter. His fists clenched tightly.

"What's so funny?!" he snapped.

"Oh nothing, bunny boy!" one of the classmates said through his laughter.

Eric blinked. Then he glanced down at his pants. They had fallen to the ground, revealing him in his black boxers with pink rabbits. His cheeks flushed as he struggled to pull his pants back up.

"S-Shut up!" he stuttered through clenched teeth. "I'll beat every one of you up if you don't stop your laughing!"

As the rest of the class continued to laugh, Aiden turned back to Theresa. The two of them knew that Eric's pants didn't fall without a reason. It would take either a skillful and silent hand to undo the belt that held his pants, or something more. They both glanced back to the black-haired boy.

There was a sudden change in the new kid's eye color. It was brief, but both of them could see it as his eyes went back to their hazel color. Aiden scratched his head in confusion before shrugging at Theresa. She gave him a slight nod, a sure sign that she knew what had happened.

"All right, listen up!" Coach Bryan called out then noticed Eric struggling to get his pants back on. "Eric, put your pants on right now or I'll have you in detention for the rest of the year!"

The bully grumbled in anger, his cheeks still covered in red. The new kid walked over to the rest of the class, taking his spot two students away from Aiden. Coach Bryan nodded his head as he began writing on his clipboard.

"Since it's your first day back from spring break, it's a free day. Tomorrow though, we are doing laps. I want no complaints from any of you. Understand?"

"Yes, Coach Bryan," the entire class, minus the new boy, said together.

"Good, now get going. I got paperwork to do."

Everyone went his or her separate way in the gym, most taking a basketball while others walked around the gymnasium. While the rest of the class seemed content with what they were doing, the new kid walked alone, paying attention to no one. Theresa looked around her before turning to Aiden, not wanting anyone else to hear what she had to say.

"You saw it too, didn't you?" she asked. Aiden nodded his head.

"Yeah, he used some kind of magic to make Eric's pants fall." He frowned. "Think he's a mage?"

"It's possible," Theresa mused, "but mages aren't really the kind to use their spells or talents out in the open. Even back in the days of my kind, they barely used spells in the open unless they had to."

Aiden raised an eyebrow. It didn't make sense. He couldn't imagine why a mage would not use spells out in the open.

"Is there something wrong?" Theresa asked.

"I'm just trying to figure something out," Aiden said. "It makes no sense to why mages wouldn't use their powers out in the open."

"In today's society, they'd be considered freaks. But there's another reason," Theresa explained.

"What's that?"

Theresa looked a bit hesitant to answer. But eventually she swallowed hard.

"Demons."

Aiden felt his spine freeze at that word. He always knew that demons were something mankind feared. All the time he spent training with her, he never thought to ask Theresa if they existed as well.

Then again, after battling a bunch of goblins, hornet men, and an ogre, he shouldn't have been surprised.

"Demons are some of the most dangerous enemies of all living things, Aiden," Theresa said. "They're immensely powerful beings, even dragons do not take them lightly."

"What do they have to do with mages though?" Aiden asked.

"Mages are more vulnerable to demons' influences than anyone else. Their powers are great, and demons are attracted to immense magical powers. Dragons are not so easily persuaded by their words, but mages can fall victim to them."

"Do they possess the mage?"

"No, but the way that they influence a mage is almost like they are controlling their minds" Theresa sighed. "Only the weak-willed mages allow themselves to be controlled by a demon."

Aiden glanced to the new kid again. He was still ignoring everyone that he passed.

"I wonder if he's already got some kind of demon watching him," Aiden mused.

"If he has, then I would have sensed it."

Aiden continued to watch the new kid carefully. He couldn't help but wonder about his story. Theresa noticed the new kid getting closer to them. Her body seemed to tense as he got closer; Aiden could feel the tension coming from her.

Finally the new kid walked between them. As he did, Aiden could see a slight smile on his face as he whispered.

"I thought this is where you two went to school at. Nice to know I was right." He said, his voice calm, like he had gained sudden control. "Can't do anything here, don't wanna upset the master and cause a scene. Anyway, the name's Raven. I'll see you two very soon."

With that, he was off and away from them again. Aiden's stomach tied into a knot at the name. Theresa's eyes narrowed dangerously as she stood closer to him.

"We best keep our eyes on that one," she advised. "Something tells me he's going to be trouble."

It was the weekend, and Aiden's training resumed. After a long school week, he was glad to be away, especially math class. Still, there was one thing that concerned both him and Theresa: the new kid.

"So what do you think this new guy is?" Seamus asked as the three of them headed to the forest.

"I honestly don't know." Theresa frowned. "He had a familiar feeling around him...but I can't place my finger on it."

"Well, look at it this way," Seamus said, "if you keep away from him, you'll never find out."

"That's not what I do and you know it," Theresa said in annoyance.

"Let's not make it our main focus," Aiden suggested. "We came out here to train today, didn't we?"

Theresa smiled at his question. Seamus just rolled his eyes as he walked ahead of them.

"Yeah, well let's just get started, shall we?"

Aiden was more than ready to have some training. He felt like he had lost a lot of time being in school. If he had gotten rusty after only a little while, that spelled trouble.

As the three of them arrived at their training spot, they were greeted by someone that they didn't expect.

It was Raven.

CHAPTER 11 - NEW ENEMY

*S*eamus stood dumbfounded at the appearance of Raven. Aiden's gut felt tied into a knot again. Theresa was instantly defensive the moment Raven came into view.

"Well, now, look at what we have here," he said. "I told you that we'd be meeting up soon."

"How did you find this place?" Theresa asked. Aiden noticed a low growling sound from her throat.

"Let's just say that I get around," Raven answered her, "mighty dragoness."

Aiden quickly grabbed a hold of Warfang in his pocket. Theresa's body tightened. Seamus already had his staff ready for combat before they arrived at their spot. Raven just stood there, hands in his pockets as he watched them carefully.

"You're not human, are you?" Seamus asked. Raven gave a slight laugh at that question.

"Oh, I'm human all right, but I'm not dumb like most people. I could tell you apart from everyone else the moment I saw you two in school," Raven said.

Theresa summoned her two blades. Her grip around them tightened. Aiden's blade came from the figurine. The trio watched Raven carefully to see what he would do. The intruder, however, made no move.

"I had to see for myself if there were still any other dragons left out there, especially since they've been considered extinct for years." He said a hint of danger in his voice.

Seamus' eyes narrowed in anger at that comment. He stabbed the end of his staff into the ground hard.

"Buddy, does it look like we're extinct?" he asked. "We're not dinosaurs or anything else you humans find deep in the earth."

"You assume that I'm being rude," Raven mused. "I apologize for that. But a powerful race like yours doesn't just reappear for no reason."

"Choose your words carefully, Raven," Theresa warned him. "If you know as much as you think you do, you know of our fearsome strength."

"Do you take me for a fool, dragoness?" Raven asked. "I am well aware of the powers of your race. It's a shame that there're only a few of your kind left."

Aiden liked Raven less and less as he continued to talk. Theresa was his best friend, and listening to this possibly new foe speak ill about her kind was beginning to make him mad. His sword hand clenched tighter around the hilt of Warfang. If he had to, he would charge at Raven.

"Pardon my interruption," Seamus intervened, "but would you mind telling me how the hell that you know all of this in the first place?"

Raven laughed at Seamus' question.

"I suppose I could tell you how I know," Raven mused, "but what good would it be just to reveal everything I know without you having to earn it?"

Theresa's nostrils seemed to flare at Raven's sarcastic question.

"Would you rather I beat it out of you?" she asked, and Aiden could have sworn he saw her breathing fire. Raven's smug smile stayed on his face.

"I've heard good things about the fighting skills of the dragon race. Let's see how well they've hold up to legend. Come, Zeratar, Zantul!"

He snapped his fingers once. Two dark lighting bolts slammed into the ground beside him. At first glance it looked like nothing had happened, but then the two bolts of lighting began to form into shapes. Aiden, Theresa, and Seamus tensed their bodies tightly as they watched.

On Raven's left, the first form completed transforming from the lighting it was once was. The creature was monstrous. Its skin seemed to lack any color at all, more dark gray more than anything. Its eyes were pure red, no pupils or irises. There was no hair on the monster, but smoke danced around its skull. The creature was clad in dark armor with gold outlining, a serpent head on the chest piece.

The second creature on Raven's right was just as monstrous. Though instead of dark gray skin, it was an icy blue color. Its eyes were pure green, as a cool mist rose from its skull, and it wore the same dark armor with gold outlining and a serpent's head.

Both creatures had long tails, sharp teeth, non-existent noses, and flat ears. They were nothing like Aiden had seen before. None of the monsters or the demons that he had read in his stories could match up to these.

"Zeratar," Raven said, a dark smile on his face, "the demon of gray fire."

The demon on his left, Zeratar, clapped its hands together, forming a gray fireball between its palms. Raven turned to the demon on his right.

"And Zantul, the demon of the frozen mist."

Zantul cracked its neck at the mention of its name. Each

crack sounded like ice shattering. Frozen claws extended from Zantul's hands, sharp and extremely cold.

"Demons," Seamus growled as he lifted his staff. "Their kind still stains the planet, does it?"

"Is that jealousy I hear in your voice?" Raven asked. "It's a shame that your mighty race isn't as expansive as it once was."

"So you are a mage then," Theresa concluded before Seamus could counter Raven's comment. "Did you fall for their lies?"

"Fall? Ha!" Raven scoffed. "I don't do their work. They do *mine*."

At that moment, Zeratar and Zantul charged the trio. Theresa quickly brought up her two blades to block Zantul's razor sharp claws. Seamus swung his staff at Zeratar, who caught it in its fiery hands.

Aiden quickly moved into action. He swung Warfang at the back of Zantul, hoping to draw its attention away from Theresa. The metal of his sword seeming, at first, to bounce off the demon's armor, but the trick worked: Zantul glared at Aiden with annoyance. Now, Aiden was its target.

Cursing under his breath, Aiden dodged one of Zantul's claws and parried the second one that came after him. The demon didn't relent on its assault as it continued to slash at Aiden, who was able to block each swing. If he was going to survive this fight, he had to get on the offensive. Positioning himself, Aiden held his sword with both hands, waiting for the right moment to turn the tide in his favor.

Zantul made a frozen-sounding roar as it raised its claws above its head. Aiden immediately knew what it was going to do and swung Warfang to block Zantul's downward slash. The sword's metal clanged against the icy claws. The demon was forced to step backward, its ice claws pushed back into the direction from which they came.

Aiden saw his chance. Raising his sword above his head he put all his strength into a vertical slash at Zantul's right arm. The attack hit its mark, cutting deep into the demon's skin, severing the arm. Zantul hissed as it pulled away from Aiden.

"Not so tough now, are you?" Aiden in a voice filled with bravado.

"Don't be so quick to judge, little swordsman," Raven said from his spot, a smile on his face.

Aiden looked at Raven quickly before turning his attention back to Zantul. What he saw made his heart nearly stop. Zantul was smiling.

From the spot where its arm used to be, a kind of icicle now formed. At first it was small and stubby, but it grew larger as only a few short seconds passed. Zantul roared as the icicle shattered, revealing a new arm.

"What the hell?!" Aiden said, flabbergasted.

"Didn't expect that, did you?" Raven asked smugly. "These two demons are no ordinary demons."

"Kiddo!" Seamus called out, smacking Zeratar across the face with his staff. "Don't bother de-limbing these guys! They're like lizards! Cut off a limb and it grows right back!"

"Now you tell me…"

Aiden ducked to avoid a slash from Zantul's newly grown claw, forced back to the defensive. He was able to block two slashes from the demon, but couldn't stop it from kneeing him hard in the stomach. This made Aiden stop for only a brief second, which was more than enough time for Raven's demon.

Zantul clawed across his right arm, cutting deep into his skin. The pain nearly made Aiden drop his weapon; this type of pain was new to Aiden. He had taken a few beatings from Eric when he was younger, but that was nothing compared to the open wounds on his sword arm. His vision blurred. Zantul made some sort of laughing sound as it raised its claw up once more, ready to strike at him again.

"*Flarnea!*"

A white flame slammed into Zantul's side at full force,

pushing the demon away from Aiden. It howled in shock and pain from the sudden attack. Eventually, the powerful flame slammed the demon into a tree. Aiden squinted through his blurry vision. Theresa had both of her wings out as she ran to him.

"Don't move," Theresa told him as she checked his wound. "You got lucky there; it could have cut your arm off with that attack."

"I got...careless..." Aiden said through clenched teeth.

"No," Theresa said calmly as she took a cloth from her pocket. "You didn't expect Zantul to grow its arm back. It was my fault that I didn't warn you before."

Aiden remained silent as she wrapped the cloth around his arm. Theresa put her hand on the cloth-covered wound and closed her eyes.

"*Emalla*."

A pale, peach-colored light engulfed her hand as she pushed onto the cloth. At first, Aiden flinched at the pressure, but the pain surging through his arm died down as the light from Theresa's hand soon covered the cloth around his arm. He blinked in amazement as his arm began to feel better again.

"A small healing spell," Theresa explained. "It'll take care of your wound as you fight, but don't tax your body more than it can handle or the pain will return."

"Right."

On cue, Zantul, pulled itself free from the tree. The demon snarled at Theresa. Claws raised high, it charged at the two with bloodlust in its eyes. Theresa was ready for the attack, quickly clashing her blades against the demon's claws. Aiden raised his sword arm again, but stopped when he felt the pain threatening.

"Dammit," he cursed under his breath.

"Theresa! Kiddo! Duck!" Seamus said from behind them.

The two gave each other a quick look of annoyance before ducking as Zeratar was thrown over them. The demon of gray fire quickly stood up, smoke flared from its flat ears. Seamus quickly joined Theresa, staff at the ready.

"Sorry for the wait," he said hastily. "I was busy dealing with ugly here."

"That's no excuse," Aiden said through gritted teeth, clenching the spot where his sword arm was slashed. Seamus turned to him, noticing the cloth around his arm.

"So you got your first battle wound, did ya? Good for you kiddo!"

"Seamus, focus!" Theresa ordered, spinning her blades in both hands.

Despite the slight pain in his arm, Aiden stood at Theresa's right side. His hand still had a good grip on his weapon; he wasn't out of this fight just yet. All the while the two demons conversed with one another on their next move.

"I don't get it," Aiden said. "You told me that demons used mages for their own good. How come these two are taking orders from him?"

"That was only half true," Theresa admitted, carefully watching the two demons. "There is one way that mages can control demons, but it was an art that was forbidden, taught only by those who were consumed with desire."

"Demonology," Seamus continued. "Basically, a mage would devote all of his or her time to learning how to summon and control demons. By the looks of our new friend here, I'd say that he's gotten quiet a good grip on it."

Aiden glanced to Raven. He hadn't moved since the fight began. It made Aiden uneasy that he stood there silently, like he was waiting for something. Zantul and Zeratar prepared to charge once again.

"Enough," Raven commanded, his demons stopping the moment he spoke. Aiden clenched Warfang tighter as he watched Raven closely. For all he knew, their new 'friend' could be planning a surprise attack.

"Not bad, for a near-dead race." Raven walked into the space between his two demons. "It appears the legends were true about how dragons fight. I must say I was not expecting you to live up to it."

Theresa growled. Her wings expanded out from behind her.

"Careful what you say, mage," she threatened. "I haven't even begun to use my power."

"Oh, peace now," Raven said, holding up a hand. "You should really watch that temper of yours, dragoness. Especially with someone who paid you a compliment."

"If that was a compliment, then you really need to work on your manners," Seamus said, pointing his staff at him.

"Answer our questions," Aiden said finally. "We've played your game, now quit hiding what you know!"

Raven's smile faded away as he glared at Aiden. There was a tense silence as they continued to stare each other down. Finally, Raven gave a slight nod of his head.

"You believe you're important, do you?" he asked. "You're not a dragon, boy. Don't think that wielding that sword makes you one of them."

"I might not be a dragon," Aiden said, holding back his anger as best as he could, "but I can still cut your throat if you push me."

Raven laughed.

"You have spirit, threatening someone who has much more training than you. I like that," he said, folding his arms across his chest. "I did say I would tell you what I know."

"Good," Theresa said, her nostrils flared small flares. "I'm growing tired of your games. How did you know we were dragons?"

Raven smiled at Theresa's question.

"That's easy. I was trained by one of the best mages of the Order to summon and control demons. During that training, I was taught how to identify creatures with strong powers from ordinary humans."

"Well that's one answer," Seamus said, but he kept his position ready. "But who the hell taught you to summon demons? Mages have been in hiding since they began burning so-called 'witches'!"

"I'm afraid I can't reveal that to you," Raven answered. "My master isn't keen on letting just anyone know his name."

"Make an exception," Theresa threatened. "Or you'll end up with a sword in your chest."

"Temper, temper." Raven said. "I'm telling you the truth: I can't reveal his name to you. That you can figure out yourself."

Theresa looked like she was about to rip his head off with her own hands. Aiden placed a hand on her shoulder, hoping that she would keep her restraint. Theresa glanced back at him, her eyes like daggers.

"Now it's my turn," Aiden said. "You said that you were taught to identify creatures from normal humans, but you said that you didn't expect dragons to still be around. Who told you that they weren't extinct?"

Raven's smile faded as he turned, taking a few steps away from the group. Zeratar and Zantul followed their master, ready to attack if given a reason.

"That's actually an interesting story," Raven said. "A while back, I was in the midst of training with my demons when I felt this incredibly strong power nearby. Naturally, I was drawn to it. If it was a demon, it could become a new minion to my arsenal."

"So you're greedy for power," Seamus spat, "just like all the other mages that turn to demonology."

"I don't think you should judge me on that," Raven advised. "If one is presented with a chance for power, one should gladly take the chance to seize it." He turned back to them.

"But I'm getting off track. I found the source of the strong power, but it was no demon. No…it was a large, brown dragon."

Theresa and Seamus' eyes grew wide at those words. It didn't take much for Aiden to figure out that the dragon Raven was talking about was the third member of their group, *Aba Itoa Eltragas*. Theresa was the first to speak.

"You...you found him?" she asked.

"Oh yes, I did," Raven answered her, his smile disappearing. "Truth be told, I was terrified at his presence. He was much larger than I thought a dragon would be. I tried to stay hidden from his view, but he saw me and my demons. Unlike you two, he was more than ready to strike out the moment we came into view."

Theresa lowered her weapons as he continued. Aiden was surprised to see that even Seamus gently lowered his staff.

"I thought that if I forced him into his human disguise, that the fight would be a lot easier. Turns out that even when he's not in his true form, the bastard is no easy opponent. His axe damn near took off my head. I had to retreat; I wasn't going to risk my life against an opponent that obviously wasn't going to back down easily."

"Where was he?" Theresa asked quickly. "If you're telling the truth, I want to know if he's still there!"

"Who knows?" Raven shrugged. "It was a while ago; odds are he's not there anymore. Though I'm sure that since you found your friend here," he gestured to Seamus, "you'll be able to find him."

Raven answered, "Who knows? You might even come across your long lost King too! Especially if the stories my master told me of how you felt for him are true."

Theresa snapped at that comment. She lunged towards Raven with both swords, ready to strike him down. Raven snapped his fingers, teleporting himself and his demons away from her attack. Theresa spun to where Raven now stood, a cliff twenty feet above them.

"If our business is done here, I believe I'll take my leave," he said. "And don't worry, I won't reveal your location to my master and his minions. If you haven't noticed, I keep my word."

Aiden snarled as he glared at Raven. Quickly stabbing his

sword into the ground, he aimed his hands at their enemy. A fire-ball came from his palms as he focused on his target.

"*Flarnea!*"

The fireball flew from his hands right at Raven, this time it wasn't dying down as it gained momentum. Aiden hoped it would hit Raven in his face, but Zeratar saw the approaching fireball. The demon fired its own fireball at Aiden's, the two colliding in a small explosion. Its master glanced at Aiden, sneering.

"Not bad for a beginner," he said. "I have a feeling that we'll be meeting again soon. Do keep training; I'd hate for our next battle to be easy."

"Big talk for someone who lets his demons do all his fighting for him!" Aiden shouted, but Raven had already disappeared with his magic.

"Loud mouth punk doesn't know when to shut up, does he?" Seamus asked, stabbing his staff into the ground.

Aiden turned back to Theresa and couldn't believe what he saw. She looked like she was about to cry. Seamus noticed as well, slowly reaching out to put his hand on her shoulder.

"Don't let his words get to you, sister," he said softly. "You're stronger than that."

Aiden walked to them, not used to seeing Theresa so close to tears. She glanced up at him, wiping her arm across her eyes quickly.

"I-I'm sorry...," she apologized. "I let his words affect me when I shouldn't have."

"You've got nothing to be sorry about," Aiden said. "Raven's nothing but an asshole who thinks he knows everything."

Theresa smiled at Aiden as she lightly punched him in the shoulder.

"Thanks, Aiden," she said. "By the way, congratulations on finally performing the spell."

Aiden was too caught up in his adrenaline to realize that he had cast the *Flarnea* spell successfully. A smile crept to his face when he realized his accomplishment. Seamus even smiled as he swatting him hard on the back.

"Excellent job, kiddo!" he said. "I had absolute faith in you the entire time!"

"*Sure you did...,*" Aiden thought darkly. Theresa giggled a little before shaking her head.

"I'll go get some water. You two stay here, all right? Oh and Seamus? Aiden's arm sustained a serious wound. Treat it for me, would you?"

Before Seamus could argue, Theresa was gone. Seamus groaned as he glanced to Aiden, pointing to the cloth that covered his wound.

"All right, kiddo, let's see that cut," he said.

Aiden hesitated at first, knowing that he and Seamus were still at odds with each other. But if Theresa told him to check his wound, he would have to trust her. He removed the cloth covering his cut; the claw marks were still there, but didn't surge with pain like before. Seamus whistled.

"Damn, you got real lucky there," he said, cracking his fingers loudly. "Most humans would have lost an arm from that kind of cut."

"So I was told," Aiden mumbled as Seamus put his hands over the cut.

"*Emalla.*"

Seamus' hands glowed the same peach color as Theresa's had before. The healing magic flowed from Seamus' palms into the wound. Aiden flinched somewhat before the pain died off, the wound itself slowly healing up.

"Oh, relax," Seamus said. "It's just like what you humans use whenever you get an infected cut. What's it called? Neosporin?"

"Yeah, but it still stings," Aiden said, swallowing the pain he felt as the wound sealed up.

"Say, Seamus?"

146

"Yeah, kiddo?"

"What did Raven mean by how Theresa felt for the Dragon King?"

Seamus sighed as the peach glow around his hands slowly faded. A frown replaced his usual cocky grin.

"Kiddo, let's just say that there are some things that I can't talk to you about. That's a story that only Theresa can tell you, but I advise you not to ask her about it unless you're absolutely certain you want to hear the truth," Seamus said, showing a rare moment of wisdom.

"Is...is it something that really bothers her?" he asked.

"Yeah, we didn't talk to her about it back then and I'd rather not bring it up with her now. But let's just say that the bond between Theresa and our King was one that not even the destruction of our race could break."

Seamus took a new cloth and wiped some of the dried blood off of Aiden's arm, smiling at his job.

"And that is how you treat wound. This time it's on the house, kiddo."

"Seamus, if what Raven said about the dragon was true, what is his name? Who is the third warrior?"

Seamus said nothing at first to Aiden's request. His eyes seemed to darken before Theresa's return. He glanced back to her with a frown.

"*Rexkin, shumbel tolua kidon go?*" he asked. Theresa blinked at his question.

"*Kidon go bouk?*" she asked in return.

"*Aba cert ewra zo stragna,*" Seamus answered.

Theresa turned to Aiden. She sighed and nodded her head at Seamus.

"*Seah, xou O'll kidon go.*"

Seamus nodded in agreement. Aiden raised an eyebrow at their conversation, annoyed at not knowing what they had said.

"Well?" he asked. "What was that about?"

"Aiden," Theresa said, "the third dragon that fought alongside Seamus and I is not a dragon you want to have against you."

"What do you mean?"

"What she means is that you don't want to piss off our brother if or when you meet him. And knowing him, he'll keep himself hidden well unless he wants to be found," Seamus said.

"His name is Garrett," Theresa interrupted. "And there's a reason why he's part of our group. We'll find him, but I want you to bear in mind one thing, Aiden: he has short patience for humans. If we find him, do not upset him."

Aiden's face faltered at what she said. Fighting Raven and his demons suddenly susounded much more welcoming than meeting the third dragon.

CHAPTER 12 - THERESA'S TALE

Once Theresa and Seamus learned that Garrett was alive, they cancelled the training session. The chance to find the third member of their team, their ancient friend, could not be ignored, no matter how slight it might be.

Aiden had never seen Theresa like this before. Not that he could blame her. She and Seamus had known each other, as well as this Garrett character, for possibly thousands, if not millions of years He made a mental note to ask her how old they truly were. Although come to think of it he was a bit afraid of what her answer might be.

If he had to be honest, Aiden felt a little left out. True, he had known Theresa all of his life, but in the scheme of things, he was beginning to realize that to her, this was not much more than the blink of an eye. While that couldn't be changed, now he also had to watch while she reunited with old friends. He wasn't stupid; he saw how comfortable she was around Seamus, even if his attitude got on everyone's nerves.

Aiden also noticed how serious Seamus suddenly seemed to be. His cocky attitude had been replaced by a more somber tone, something Aiden would have never believed possible. Seamus truly seemed dedicated to finding their long lost teammate. Aiden didn't expect that from Seamus; he had grown used to Theresa being the only one who took things seriously.

"All right, since our parents know that we're going to be gone until nine, that gives us about seven hours to search," Theresa said as she set a timer on the watch her father had given her.

"How do you guys intend to find him?" Aiden asked, swallowing some water.

"Well, if I know Garrett, he'll either be deep into the woods of a big ass forest, or he'll be in a place where so-called 'gangs' hang out, kicking the crap out of them," Seamus said, cracking his knuckles.

"Wait, why would he be fighting gang members?"

"Garrett's never been one to ignore those who cause trouble, particularly those who pick on others," Theresa explained, placing the watch in Aiden's hand. "Hold this. You're going to have to keep it for me while we travel."

"Travel? Just how far do you think we'll need to go?"

"Kiddo, do yourself a favor: don't ask questions we can't answer," Seamus said, dismissing his staff easily. "I'll go look through the deepest forests I can find. Travel well, *Rexkin*."

Theresa nodded to Seamus.

"*Yokee ter*, Seamus," she said.

With a flash, Seamus morphed into his dragon form and took off into the sky. They watched as he became a small spec, well out of viewing range for anyone on the ground and to avoid being seen by a passing airplane.

"I have a feeling that his chances of finding Garrett are not that great," Aiden said, folding his arms across his chest.

"Focus, Aiden," Theresa said, handing him the backpack. "Put it on, and make sure it's secure."

Aiden did as he was told and wrapped the backpack around himself tightly. Theresa took a few steps away from him, standing in an open area where the sun shown the brightest. She took a deep breath before closing her eyes.

"Aiden," her voice rolled like thunder, "do not come close to me until I say so."

Those were the last words she said before two white wings rose from her back. Aiden watched in awe as Theresa's body began to undergo a transformation he had never seen before. It was something he had wanted to see since she revealed to him that she was a dragoness, but at the same time, he worried about what the transformation was doing to her. It just didn't look the same as when Seamus changed.

Theresa's eyes snapped open. Her pupils were now nothing but long slits in her emerald green eyes. Her body began to grow noticeably larger, as did her wings, as her transformation continued. Aiden fell back in shock as a long white tail appeared from her changing body. Next, her fingers came together to form three claws on each hand. The same process must have happened to her feet; Aiden watched in wonder as her shoes burst apart revealing large, three-toed claws.

Aiden only blinked for a second before another change happened. Theresa's neck and face grew longer, and sharp fangs replaced her human teeth. She reared her head back, letting out a roar that echoed throughout the forest. It wasn't the kind of roar that terrified; it was graceful, melodic, even, and Aiden thought it must be filled with defiance and heart-aching loss.

A pure, white light flashed, surrounding Theresa, forcing Aiden to cover his eyes. It lasted only a few seconds before dying out, allowing Aiden to open his eyes once more. Of all the things he had ever seen or been taught, he was not prepared for what was now standing in front of him.

While Theresa's dragon form seemed to be the same height as Seamus', otherwise it was the total opposite of the only other dragon Aiden had ever seen. How could something so large, so deadly, be so beautiful? Aiden was stunned by her beauty. No horns, no spikes, no roughness to her at all. She was sleek, powerful, and deadly. Her wings were larger now, and looked like they could easily carry her across the sky. Her scales were white as snow, and they shined in the bright sun.

Adding to the beauty of her dragon form were extended translucent white scales that hung off the sides of her head, each one looking like an angel wing. Along with scales that looked like they were crystal clear ribbons hanging under them.

In Aiden's honest opinion, there was absolutely no flaw to Theresa in her dragon form.

As she spun her head back to him, it was then Aiden realized that she was standing on all four of her legs. Even though she was now much larger in her true form, Theresa still gave him a soft smile.

"Are you ready for your first flight, Aiden?" she asked, lowering her neck down to the ground.

"You," Aiden started to say, snapping out of his dream-like state, "you want me to ride on your neck?"

"If I didn't, I wouldn't have lowered my neck," Theresa said in a voice that Aiden suddenly realized was not exactly what he was used to hearing. Sure, he knew it was Theresa, but it sounded like a Theresa filled with ancient wisdom. It was like all of the experiences from her long life could be heard in the music of her voice.

"We're wasting time, Aiden. The fastest way to find Garrett is to fly. I'm not going to let you stay behind while our search goes on."

Aiden didn't argue. His heart felt like it would explode from the sheer excitement. He was going to fly on a *dragon*? Something he had always dreamed about since he was little boy. He climbed onto her neck looking down in confusion for some place to hold on to. Suddenly, small ridges formed on her neck, almost as though his thoughts had caused them to appear. Grateful, her grabbed two of them and held on for dear life.

"Whatever happens, do not let go," Theresa rumbled, a hint of laughter in her voice.

Theresa's large wings opened. Aiden held onto the ridges tightly as he wrapped his legs around her neck. He worried that his legs might bother her throat, but Theresa showed no signs of noticing. Wings flapping, Theresa lifted off the ground, each flap sending them higher and higher.

Aiden watched as the ground grew smaller and smaller beneath them. With each flap of Theresa's wings they drew further away from the solid earth. His heart raced and his nerves began to shake as they reached the top of the trees.

Theresa stopped and hovered above the trees for a few short seconds. Aiden couldn't see it, but she had a slight smile on her face.

"Now, the fun begins."

Without warning, Theresa reared and sped upwards so quickly that Aiden was forced to lean back. His hands clutched Theresa, his legs wrapped ever tighter around her neck as the white dragon flew higher and higher into the sky.

The force of the wind grew stronger as Theresa continued her ascent. Aiden's eyes watered from the wind in his face. So far, his dream of flying on the back of a dragon were not exactly meeting expectations.

He noticed the wind slowly weaken as Theresa's large wings settled into an easy rhythm. Aiden let out a sigh of relief as she finally set a steady speed above the clouds, and the sound of her beating wings seemed to echo all around them.

"Don't look now, Aiden," Theresa shouted as she flew forward, "but you're flying on the back of a dragoness!"

Aiden's blinked hard. In the time it had taken them to ascend, he hadn't really considered what was truly happening. It took Theresa's voice to remind him.

He was flying on the back of a dragoness.

The reality of it spread a huge grin across his face. The feeling was intoxicating as he took the time to look all around. They were hundreds, possibly thousands, of feet above the ground, completely free from anyone or anything below them. Aiden couldn't help but let out a cry of joy as Theresa flew on.

Theresa pulled some quick flying tricks for Aiden. She rolled to the left and right once, then did a fast loop de loop. He almost lost his grip around her neck, but Theresa was faster than she looked. Aiden might have broken some sort of smile record.

"This is incredible!" he shouted, the wind making it impossible to talk normally.

Theresa made a sound in the back of her throat. It took Aiden awhile to figure it out, but it sure sounded like she was laughing at him.

"I'm glad you're enjoying this," she said, "because when we fly into battle, things are never this smooth."

Aiden's face paled at those words.

"Wait a minute, 'fly into battle'?" he asked.

"Correct," Theresa said, separating clouds with each stroke of her wings. "In an aerial fight, there is no time to enjoy sightseeing. You have to be focused on the enemy, just like in regular combat."

"But I can't even fly…," Aiden pointed out.

"True; humans never could get flight down properly. Don't worry though, you'll be taught how to fight on the back of either Seamus or myself. That way you're not completely defenseless if we're attacked in midair."

"And what about you? How do you fight in midair?"

Theresa turned her head back at him, giving him a look that said, "You're joking, right?" He scratched the back of his head, embarrassed at the question.

"S-Sorry, stupid question to ask," he admitted.

"Stupid questions deserve only stupid answers, so I'll let that one pass." Theresa laughed again.

Aiden could only wonder what she meant. He noticed that the

two of them were slowly descending towards the ground. In the few short minutes they had been flying, he had almost forgotten they were traveling far faster than people could drive. Theresa continued to descend towards a forest, one just outside the view of a nearby city. Eventually, she settled onto the ground.

"So, we've just got to find this Garrett guy," Aiden mused as slid from Theresa's neck. "It shouldn't be that hard to do."

"This won't be as simple as it seems, Aiden," Theresa said as she reared back. "Garrett does not make himself easily known to those he does not wish to find him."

"So you have a feeling that he might be hiding from you and Seamus," Aiden concluded, not noticing as Theresa transformed back to her human shape.

"Exactly," Theresa's voice was once again the familiar sound Aiden knew. "Garrett is a big target, but he's not a lumbering fool who makes himself known by staggering around."

"Yet you and Seamus said he likes to pick fights with those he dislikes," Aiden pointed out.

"That is probably the only way we'll be able to tell him apart from anyone else," Theresa admitted, "but he's damn good at keeping himself hidden. You'd be surprised how long he'll stay put before picking a fight."

Theresa easily grabbed the backpack from Aiden's back. She began looking through it, determined to find something.

"What are you looking for?" Aiden asked, but his question was answered as Theresa pulled out a small green orb.

"This, Aiden, is the Soul of Dragons," she said. "All dragons are connected to it."

"They're connected?"

"Yes. While it doesn't exactly locate where a dragon is, it will glow when we are close. When it is at its brightest, it means a dragon is nearby."

"So it's like radar," Aiden said, gently taking the orb from her hands.

"In a way, yes. Only radar works from a distance; the orb only lets us know if another of my kind is close," Theresa lectured, taking the orb from him. "Come on, we have to get moving."

Theresa put the orb her pocket and began to walk away from Aiden. In all the time he had known her, Aiden had never seen her so serious, so determined. It was almost like she was someone else, someone he didn't really know. If they were going to find this Garrett, he hoped it happened soon. This new side of Theresa was unsettling. He checked the watch she had lent him.

It read twelve o'clock. Their fight with Raven and his two demons happened at ten, so two hours had passed. He still couldn't believe how powerful Raven was, even if it was just by using demons to do his fighting. He had to have a lot of power to control them. What really bothered Aiden, though, were the last words he said to Theresa before he vanished. No matter how hard he tried to ignore it, Raven's voice echoed in his head.

"Who knows? You might even come across your long lost King too, especially if the stories that my master told me of how you felt for him are true."

The way Theresa reacted to that really bothered Aiden. And he wasn't the only one. Seamus had shown great concern for her as well, and he refused to tell Aiden what Raven meant.

"Whatever it was, it couldn't have been that sensitive to talk about, right?" Aiden asked himself, but him couldn't bring it up with her.

Theresa continued to walk ahead of them, keeping an eye out for the nearest town or city. For some time, Aiden couldn't start a conversation or even attempt to ask the question. How could he ever ask her how she felt for the Dragon King when it was obviously a very sensitive subject? The question made his head hurt more than any math test.

Finally one of them spoke, filling a silence that had become uncomfortable.

"Listen Aiden, about what happened back there...," Theresa said, catching him off guard. "I owe you an explanation."

"I told you that you didn't need to apologize for what happened...," he started, but she didn't let him finish.

"This isn't an apology, it's an explanation," she continued. "You have to hear this, understand?"

She stopped walking and turned to him, a sad look on her face. Aiden felt a sharp jolt somewhere in his chest at the sadness in her. He wanted to tell her that she did not need to tell him anything, but when Theresa wanted to explain something, nothing could stop her.

"When Raven said those hateful words, they cut me deeply. One of the most important parts of our training was to never let the words of the enemy have power over us. Still, some words they...cut deeper than most." She hung her head, "Those words... they cut me to the heart."

She stopped for a moment to collect her thoughts. She forced a painfully small smile.

"The Dragon King was more than just my leader and king. He was my best friend." Aiden could hear how her voice strained at that last word. "At first the great king had an iron will. He refused to let anyone close to him, speaking only a few words every now and then."

Aiden didn't say anything as she took a deep breath. Talking about it obviously was not easy for her. He wanted to tell her to stop, to not torment herself. But he couldn't find the right way to say it.

"One day, however, his first right hand died from a battle wound delivered by a demon's weapon. The King had to choose a new commander. It was an event I remember well. He came to the training grounds, to decide which one of his warriors was best suited to succeed."

Theresa closed her eyes, folding her arms across her chest. "There were hundreds, if not thousands of us, who were more than qualified for the position. But for some reason he chose me. I became his second. The leader of his armies. To have such a position was a great honor. And I failed him."

She summoned her twin short swords again, glancing down to them.

"My faithful blades, Snow and Fire. These swords were a gift from the King as his newest commander. The position brought me great honor, but I would be lying if I said that was all."

Aiden finally found his voice again.

"What else?" he asked, mentally beating himself up for not saying something better.

"Oh yes, everything has its pluses and minuses. The good thing was that I was the second highest rank in the Kingdom; I answered to no one but the King himself. The bad thing was the King was stubborn, and often refused to relent on changing a plan when he believed it to be fit."

Her eyes narrowed in anger as she clenched her hands around the hilts of her swords. Aiden noticed that her emerald green eyes turned dark as the memories came back to her.

"He could be ill tempered, impatient, irrational, arrogant, and it was almost impossible to force him to see reason when he made his mind up; if that happened, he refused to listen to anyone." She growled darkly. Aiden could have sworn that she was about to spit fire. Theresa's eyes returned to normal as she finished speaking, her two swords disappearing.

"Though as time went on...we became close to one another. He began to see reason, allowing himself to be friendlier with me and with his troops. He became the king our kind needed, the King I told you about, and I was proud to be his closest friend."

Aiden could see that the bond Theresa spoke of between her and the King was like nothing he had ever experienced. A new feeling washed over him: Envy. His friendship with her was nothing more than a miniature version, a pale copy compared to the bond she had shared with the King. His face must have made clear what he was feeling. Theresa placed a gentle hand on his shoulder.

"Aiden, do not think that I don't value your friendship. The friendship I had with the Dragon King was one of the dearest in my long life, but it does not make our friendship any less valuable." Her smile returned. "After being locked away for countless years, you filled the void created as I witnessed the King that last time…"

Theresa once again gave him her signature smile. The envy Aiden was experiencing fell away, or at least in to the background of his mind. It was good to see her happy expression again. He hoped he would never have to see her in pain like that from anything that he did.

She turned, taking the small orb from her pocket, clenching it tightly.

"We've got a long way to go if we're to find Garrett; we've wasted enough time as it is," she said.

"Theresa," Aiden quickly said, stopping her. "Thank you…for telling me all this."

He couldn't see it in the shadowed forest, but single tear slowly traveled down Theresa's cheek.

CHAPTER 13 - THE SEARCH FOR THE FINAL DRAGON

It took them a few minutes to find their way out of the forest. The strong wind took Aiden by surprise when they left the cover of the woods. The wind was so strong, it forced Theresa to tie her long white hair into a ponytail. Theresa led him down a path that became a sidewalk, distancing themselves from the forest as quickly as they could.

Ahead of them was a city next to a large body of water. Aiden could see what looked like an incredibly large stadium in the distance. The strong wind was still blowing against them, forcing Aiden to squint his eyes as they reached the downtown area by the large lake.

"Where are we anyway?" Aiden asked, raising his voice in order to be heard over the strong wind. Theresa turned to him. He noticed that she too had to squint her eyes from the force of the wind.

"This, my dear friend, is a city that you've read about in our history class together," Theresa said, tightly clenching the small orb in her hand. "It's famous for a football team that uses a bear as a mascot."

"Wait, so we're in…." A smile came to his face. "Chicago?"

Theresa nodded. If there was one city that he wanted to go all his life, it was Chicago, Illinois. The one thing that he and his father really had in common was that they were big Chicago Bears fans. As such, neither one of them could stand the Green Bay Packers.

"Wait, why are we in Chicago? How did we get here from Virginia?"

Theresa sighed as they moved down the sidewalk.

"We flew. Don't you remember?" Theresa continued before Aiden could interrupt. "The strength of our wings, and the magic in our bones allows us to travel an incredible distance in a very short period of time. We were so high up that you couldn't see the ground as we flew. It might take an hour or so to get to Chicago in a human jet, but a dragon or dragoness can make the flight in fifteen to thirty minutes."

"Well that answers one question," Aiden said through a mouthful of blustery wind.

"As for why we're here in Chicago, I've been reading online lately that this city has been seeing a huge increase in street crimes the local police have had a hard time pinpointing," Theresa explained, pulling the orb out of her pocket. "If I know Garrett, he'll be attracted to street gangs and their crimes like a moth to a flame."

He remembered what Theresa had said about Garrett after their fight with Raven and his demons. His spine still shivered at the power Raven claimed the third dragon possessed. If he could give this new enemy so much trouble in both his human and dragon form, he had to be extremely powerful. Aiden was still curious, though, about why Garrett had such a short fuse when it came to humans.

"How come he has so little patience with humans?" Aiden asked. "It's kinda odd that someone like him would go and stop street crimes if he's so unimpressed with humans in general."

Theresa gave him a look that said 'Have you seen how some

humans act?' Aiden slapped his forehead when she did so. He made a mental note to not ask stupid questions like that in the future.

"Truth be told, Aiden, I have no idea why Garrett has had so little patience with humanity. Before the King was lost, he cared so little for their actions he acted like they almost didn't exist during the era of the Great Kingdoms."

She paused for a moment, hesitating.

"This is just my own speculation," she continued, "but he probably believes it was humanity that started the Great War all those years ago."

"I thought you said that the harpies started the war by killing the men who came into their territory?" Aiden pointed out, recalling the story she had told him.

"Truthfully, Aiden, it could be viewed from different angles. Some might say that humanity started the Great War while others believe the harpies did. Personally, I think that the harpies started the war."

The small orb in Theresa' hand began to glow a soft white color. Her eyes grew wide in surprise. Aiden blinked; he hadn't expected the orb to be glowing so soon.

"It's glowing already? But we're just walking around...."

"This is the softest glow the orb can emit, Aiden." Theresa clenched her hand around the orb. "Garrett isn't nearby exactly, but he's obviously somewhere in this city. Somewhere relatively close."

"And how do you suggest we find him then?" he asked. She just gave a slight smile.

"Well, I was thinking that maybe we could draw him out by making ourselves look like we're the victims of a crime...," she began, but then started to laugh when she saw Aiden's face falter.

"Not. Funny," he said.

"Oh, lighten up, Aiden," Theresa said through her giggles. "Would I ever put you in danger on purpose?"

"What do you call fighting a bunch of goblins and demons then?" he asked.

"Those were attacks on us," she pointed out. "Besides, I wouldn't have begun your training if I wasn't sure you could handle yourself in battle."

She gave him a smug smile.

"As I remember it, you held your own quite well against the goblins and Raven's ice demon."

"It could be beginner's luck, you know," Aiden said, a sarcastic smile tugging at the corners of his mouth.

"Aiden, I've lived for thousands of years. In my experience there is never such a thing as luck, particularly the beginner's variety."

"Well, all right then all-knowing 'master.' What would you call it if it's not luck?"

Before Theresa could answer his question, a loud shriek startled them. The two turned to look at the entrance to an alley, where two street thugs were trying their best to pry a woman's purse away from her. The woman's boyfriend was trying his best to keep them away. Aiden glanced to Theresa.

"We can't just let them get away with this," he said. "They need help!"

"As much as I want to help them, Aiden, we cannot use our weapons on mere street thugs, particularly human ones."

She glanced around, looking for some sign that the third dragon would arrive to stop the mugging. Unfortunately, there was no sign of anyone stepping up to help. Theresa growled as she turned back to Aiden.

"Dammit, you stay here. I'm getting the police if I can find them."

Before he could argue, Theresa was already off and running. Aiden clenched his fists as he turned back to the thugs. They had nearly succeeded in getting the woman's purse away from her. Aiden saw that her boyfriend was on the ground, clutching his stomach in pain. A part of him wanted more than anything to jump in and stop the thugs, but they were easily taller and more muscular than he was, not to mention much older. Still, why have this power if not to use it? Across the street the woman screamed again, a pitiful sound.

Aiden couldn't take it anymore. He reached for Warfang, slowly taking a step forward. If this Garrett wasn't going to show up and help this couple, he would try his best on his own to stop these muggers. But just as he took a second step towards them, a new voice echoed down the alleyway.

"I suggest you let the purse go and beat it before things get bad for you."

Aiden's entire body shook from the sound of the voice; it was like an earthquake. The two muggers stopped, looking around to find the owner of the deep voice. One of them readied a knife as his partner focused on the purse.

"Who the hell do you think you are?" The thug with the knife asked, spinning around to find the owner of the voice. "Where are you?!"

While Aiden watched, the thug with the knife ran into the shadows. Aiden heard a muffled cry; the second thug looked up as the sound of punches echoed from the darker part of the alley.

Aiden crouched behind a car and watched carefully, curious to see what would happen now that the second thug was on his own.

"Come out here where I can see you!" he shouted. "I know you're back there! If you're so worried about the girl, you better get out here...before it's too late!"

Aiden narrowed his eyes, his grip around Warfang tightening as he watched the scene play out. As if on cue, the stranger stepped from the shadows of the alley. Aiden felt the color drain from his face.

The newcomer looked to be only seventeen or eighteen years old, with dark brown skin, and earthy brown eyes. His hair was pitch black, styled in a short buzz cut. It was his sheer size, however, that would make a grown man shiver. He was incredibly tall; Aiden had to guess he was at least six and a half feet, maybe more. He was built like football player, covered in muscles. His arms were three times the size of Aiden's and they looked capable of punching through solid blocks of concrete.

Not only was his size intimidating, but his clothes made him even scarier. He wore a massive black leather jacket, with three sharp spikes at the top of the shoulders, complete with a row of sharp spines that ran down the arms of said jacket. Adding to the intimidation factor, two chains, one on each part of the studded lapels connected to the sleeves. It seemed to meld perfectly into the darkest parts of the alley. Under the jacket he wore what looked like a dark orange shirt; he also wore black jeans and black combat boots.

He was truly terrifying to look at.

"W-Who the hell are you?" the thug cried out, readying his knife.

"Someone who despises your kind," the dark newcomer said, clenching his fist. "If you want to avoid being knocked out like your idiotic friend back there, I suggest you back off now."

The thug's body quivered with fear as he stared at this large opponent. Aiden watched intently as the stranger continued to walk towards the thug. The situation was getting tenser as the thug haltingly took a step back.

"S-Stay back!" the thug cried. "I'm warning you!"

The intimidating stranger didn't stop. Each step he took made him even more frightening. The thug let out a wordless yell as he swung his knife wildly at his attacker. Aiden's mouth dropped as the dark man just brought up his left arm to block the knife.

"What the hell is he doing?" Aiden thought. "He'll get cut by tha-"

A loud snapping sound rang through the alleyway. Aiden's pupils enlarged in amazement as the blade broke in two, the point flying harmlessly to the ground. The thug looked about to cry as the tall young man grabbed him by the throat.

"Pathetic." he said dryly.

The thug cried out in pain as the unlikely hero slammed a fist into his stomach. He collapsed around the fist planted in his gut, passing out. The young couple turned to the tall dark-skinned man with grateful smiles.

"T-Thank you," the young woman said, grabbing her purse.

"Your thanks are unnecessary," he said, nodding. "The police are most likely on their way by now."

He began to walk away from the young couple. The woman's boyfriend got up from the ground, his eyes full of confusion.

"W-Wait!" he cried out. "Just who are you?"

"...Someone who has no patience for scum" His eyes narrowed. "Folks call me Garrett."

With that the young couple's savior continued to walk away. Aiden clenched his fist tightly. He had no doubt in his mind: this person had to be *the* Garrett. He glanced over his shoulder, hoping that Theresa had returned to see the scene, but she was still gone.

"Dammit!"

He couldn't afford to wait for Theresa and let their target get away.

"She'll kill me for wandering off, but I can't let this guy get away," Aiden mumbled.

Moving as silently as he could, Aiden followed after Garrett. No matter what happened, he had to make sure that he didn't lose this person. It was too important to just let him walk out of sight.

He found that staying quiet while following someone was really hard to do. While he had a lot of cover to use when he was tracking down Seamus, it was not so easy to do now. The real challenge was being able to find cover and not look insane to the passing citizens of Chicago.

"If only Theresa had left the orb with me…," he muttered.

Theresa came back to his mind as he watched Garrett walk. His thoughts wandered back to what she had said in the forest. Try as he might, he couldn't get Theresa's sad face out of his mind. Why did it bother him so much? Everybody, even creatures like dragons, were capable of tears.

"Focus, Aiden," he thought. "You can't let this guy get away from you now."

Forcing his attention back to Garrett, Aiden continued. So far, everything was going all right, if not completely according to plan. But Chicago was a big city; if he lost him now he would not only been separated from Theresa, but lost as well.

The sudden realization came to him as he continued to follow Garrett: what would happen to him if he didn't reunite with Theresa? He was so busy trying to keep up with Garrett he didn't consider that he was at least ten blocks from where she had left him. Having never been to Chicago, he felt incredibly stupid for not thinking ahead as to what it might mean to follow a stranger through a large, unknown city.

"Just great," he grumbled. "Brilliant move, Aiden. Theresa's probably going crazy in the streets looking for you."

Aiden shuddered at the very thought of Theresa in her dragoness form rampaging around Chicago. Why did he have to go and wander after somebody he suspected was the third dragon? Now he just felt foolish. Every building looked exactly like the last. The pounding wind blew into his face and he had to squint his eyes.

Suddenly, Garrett came back into his mind. In the time he spent worrying he was lost, he had forgotten the reason he was willing to separate himself from Theresa in the first place. Aiden looked all around, trying to find Garrett. To his utter despair, he had lost him too.

Aiden felt like a fool. Not only was he lost in one of the

biggest cities in America, but now he had lost the one person he was trying to follow.

Worst. Day. Ever.

The big streets of Chicago were more intimidating than welcoming. Being this far away from his home state made Aiden shudder. He could just imagine his parents raising hell all over his hometown trying to find him. Then the local news would report it, until eventually the entire country would be put on alert searching for him.

What made it even worse was that he was also walking around some dangerous streets now, each looking more dubious than the last. With every turn, Aiden's heart raced as he noticed the large amount of teenagers and young men hanging around every corner watching his every move. They dressed like most street gang members would. Loose clothes, excessive gold necklaces around their necks, and had multiple tattoos on their arms. Odds were he was severely out matched, even by them. True he had a sword, but what good would that do if he wound up in trouble with the police for cutting down gang members?

Eventually, Aiden stopped walking. He could tell that he was in the bad part of Chicago. Garbage cans littered the streets, crude graffiti covered the alleyways, and broken down cars were parked beside often empty houses. He swallowed hard as he began to back away, only to bump into someone.

"Pardon me," he said, turning around to see who he had walked into.

He wished he didn't.

A large street gang member was standing right behind him. Aiden noticed that more of them began to come out from the hidden alleyways. The first gang member grinned wickedly as he cracked his fingers.

"Well, well," he mused, "look at what we have here...a little trespasser."

"By complete accident," Aiden quickly said, taking a few steps back.

"Accident? Listen kid, you just don't wander into Viper territory by accident," the gang member said, advancing on Aiden. "You obviously have a death wish."

Aiden glanced around him, sweating a bit as more and more gang members gathered around. The situation began to look grim as his odds of escaping dwindled away. If he was going to get out of this, he had to make a move now. The leader of the Vipers grinned as he stepped towards him.

"So, ready to die, little man?"

Aiden turned to run as fast as his legs could carry him, but one of the gang members easily grabbed the back of his shirt. He struggled to get free from the gang member's grasp, but his captor had a strong grip on the back of his shirt. Aiden reached to grab Warfang, but another gang member grabbed his arm.

"Dammit, let me go!" he shouted, kicking one of them in the leg.

"Think you're a tough guy, do ya? Let's show this punk what happens when you mess with the Vipers!"

Two gang members walked in front of him with knives in their hands. Aiden scowled at them as they came closer. They pulled their arms back, ready to stab him in the chest.

"I suggest you let the kid go."

Aiden's eyes grew wide when he heard the new voice. The gang members armed with knives turned to see who dared order them around on their own turf. Their faces turned white when they saw Garrett only inches away.

"And just who do you think you are, ordering us around?" the gang member holding Aiden's shirt asked.

"Your better," Garrett said, his hands hiding in his pockets. "I'm not gonna say it again: let the kid go."

"You got some nerve!" a second gang member shouted.

"No one orders the Vipers around, especially in their territory!" the gang leader, the one with the most tattoos and a fairly burly build, spat, his eyes narrowed. "Get him!"

Several gang members surrounded Garrett, each one armed with a switchblade glinting in the sun. Garrett stood his ground, dead calm in the center of the circle. There was no hint of fear on his face as he eyed up each and every one of them.

Garrett then muttered something under his breath. Aiden's excellent hearing was able to pick it up, and his entire body shivered at the thought of what was about to happen.

"Seven thugs. That makes it five broken arms and two broken legs."

The gang members charged all at once. Each of them thrust their knives, hoping to deliver a fatal blow. Garrett was more than ready for them. Aiden watched as the large teen ducked quickly to avoid their weapons. Before two of them knew what was happening, Garrett delivered massive blows to their legs with swift and powerful punches.

Loud cracking sounds echoed through the street. Aiden didn't have to guess at what Garrett had done. The two thugs with broken legs flopped onto the ground, crying out in pain. Garrett held out his hands and caught their falling knives. His eyes glinted as he shot back up from the ground, slicing at the remaining knives with the two he held. The gang members screamed in surprise as they watched their weapons break apart easily.

Garrett threw the knives into the ground with such force that it cracked the pavement. Not wasting any time, he began his offensive attack. Garrett spun, delivering a perfect three-hundred-sixty-degree kick at the attacking thugs. Again, the sounds of cracking bones sang out a painful song.

Aiden watched in amazement as the five remaining gang members clutched their arms in agony. Garrett didn't seem fazed by their cries. His dark brown eyes turned to the gang leader who was still holding Aiden. There was no hint of fear in them as he took a step towards them.

"Your men are down for the count," Garrett said, his fists clenched tightly. "Unless you want to end up just like them, I suggest you let the boy go."

"What...what the hell are you?" the gang leader asked, pushing Aiden aside as he reached for the gun in his pocket.

Garrett stopped once the gun was aimed at him. The gang leader's grip shook from fear, and as he tried to keep his aim, Aiden reached for Warfang. If he was going to summon his sword, it had to be soon.

"Not another step, or I'll shoot!" The Viper gang leader yelled. "I'm warning you, ya freak!"

"So, you resort to a coward's weapon," Garrett scoffed, shaking his head as he took another step closer. "Your kind are all the same."

"I said stay back! I will shoot you!"

Aiden whispered, *"Ladbe."* The gold and silver sword emerged from the figurine just in time. As the gang leader readied his gun to fire, Aiden quickly put the blade under his chin. Even Garrett stopped moving as the sword gently pressed against the leader's neck. Aiden's eyes narrowed as his grip on Warfang tightened.

"Drop it," he said, a hint of danger in his voice, "or I'll cut your throat."

The gang leader needed no further convincing as he instantly dropped the gun. Garrett only had to give him one glare to set him running away as fast as his legs could carry him. Aiden smiled as he dismissed the blade.

"Phew, I owe you my life," said Aiden, turning to face Garrett. "You're a life saver you know...."

Aiden stopped. Garrett was walking away without a word. Determined not to lose Garrett, Aiden ran after him.

"Hey!" he called out. "Where do you think you're going?"

Garrett didn't respond. Aiden groaned in annoyance as he ran after Garrett. He had already lost him once today.

"You're not losing me that easily!" Aiden cried out, eventually catching up to Garrett.

Garrett glared darkly at Aiden before turning away. He continued to move quickly, forcing Aiden to speed up after Garrett, or run the risk of repeatedly losing contact with Garrett every few moments. This went on for what seemed like an eternity to Aiden. Eventually, the dangerous streets Aiden had ventured into began to slowly disappear. Soon he found himself on the more brightly lit streets of Chicago, eventually arriving back at the spot where he had seen Garrett in action for the first time. It seemed hours since he had last been there.

"This is where you spied on me, wasn't it?" Garrett finally spoke. Aiden's mouth almost fell off its hinges.

"How did you...?"

"Please, I could smell you from where you were hiding." Garrett glanced back to him. "You were easy to track down when you got cornered by those thugs."

Aiden blinked. Did he just say *smell*? There was no way a normal human could smell out another human so well. Garrett just stood, hands in his pockets as he eyed up Aiden.

"You could smell me?" he asked. His grip around Warfang tightened. "So then I was right...."

"Hm?"

"You're him, aren't you? I believe you are," Aiden mused. "You even recognize this sword I have in my hand, don't you?"

Garrett's eyes narrowed as there was a dangerous glare within his pupils. He slowly pulled his hands out of his pockets, both of them balled into fists. The two of them stood in silence; the tension was so thick that it could be cut with a knife.

"I don't know who you are," Garrett finally said, taking a step forward, "or how you came across that blade, but let me make one thing clear to you."

Danger radiated in his dark brown eyes and they glinted when he pulled back his right arm.

"I don't like humans who know too much for their own good."

Aiden readied himself to dodge the punch Garrett was about to throw. He couldn't believe the string of bad luck he was having today. Out of the frying pan with the Viper gang and into the fire with the Third Dragon. Before either of them could make a move, though, a sudden pair of arms grabbed Aiden from behind.

"Aiden!" Theresa's voice rang out. "Oh thank goodness I found you!"

"T-Theresa?" Aiden asked. A slight blush of embarrassment grew across his cheeks.

"Do you know how freaking worried I've been?" she asked, turning him towards her. "I thought you had gotten killed! I told you not to move...a...muscle..."

Theresa glanced over his shoulder at Garrett. Aiden swallowed hard, remembering that the two of them had come to Chicago to find the final member of her team. No one made a move as she stared down the much taller Garrett. Theresa gasped in realization before turning to Aiden once again.

"You...you found him?" she asked.

Garrett's eyes narrowed.

"Theresa...it's been far too long, *Rexkin*."

"Indeed, my friend, indeed."

Aiden could not tell for sure exactly what Theresa meant by those words. He heard happiness, sorrow and something more.

Things were sure getting complicated.

"*G*arrett...it's really you, isn't it?" Theresa asked, taking a step towards him.

"Yes, it's me, dear sister," Garrett answered, folding his arms across his chest. "How long has it been? Fifteen hundred thousand years now?"

"You exaggerate, as always." Theresa frowned. "Why do you say such a thing, brother? Are you not happy to see me?"

"You misunderstand me," Garrett sighed, glancing back to Aiden. "I take it that this whelp is your newest student?"

"Whelp?" Aiden asked.

"Yes, whelp," Garrett echoed. "It's what we always call our newest trainees. I'm surprised to see that she found a dragon who can wield the king's sword."

"Uh, Garrett..." Theresa hesitated, "Your senses must have dulled over the years. Aiden is not one of us."

Garrett blinked at her words. His attention turned back to her, a dark glare in his eyes. Aiden swallowed a lump in his throat as Theresa stood her ground.

"He's human."

Aiden watched Garrett carefully as he stood there. The third dragon clenched his fists tightly before baring his teeth. Even though he was in his human form, Aiden could see that his teeth had become sharp. Theresa, however, didn't seem fazed by Garrett.

"You MUST be joking," Garrett growled through his clenched his teeth. "You are training a HUMAN to wield the King's trusted blade?"

"Yes, Garrett," Theresa said, standing her ground. "Is that a problem?"

"Yes, it is a problem," Garrett said. "Where is your draconic honor, sister?"

"Hey," Aiden interrupted, "I may not be a dragon, but I'll have you know that I've taken on goblins and cut off a demon's arm."

Garrett glared at Aiden. It seemed to insult him that Aiden would even dare brag about his victories over the past few days. Theresa put her arm in front of Aiden defensively as she began to growl.

"*Aimabel*, Garrett! *Nomaran yokeer onergall!*" she spat in their language. Garrett glared at Theresa now.

"*Rexkin, tyan toa spenzer go ter titoa aba labe*?!" he retorted. Again, Theresa did not flinch.

"*Lokhan gan os denengar heel aba ladbe guto ots kinsaur!*" she said, standing in front of Aiden now.

Garrett turned his head towards Aiden once again. His dark brown eyes examined him carefully. Theresa, however, stayed between the two of them. Aiden's heart began to race as the largest member of Theresa's team cracked his neck loudly.

"So...the sword has chosen you as its master...has it?" he asked finally.

"Uh...well I guess you could say tha-"

"Did it, or did it not?" Garrett asked. A rumbling sound came from somewhere deep in his chest.

"Yes," Aiden answered hastily, remembering what Theresa told him back at their training grounds.

Garrett scoffed at his answer before turning back to Theresa once again.

"You cannot be serious," he said.

"I am dead serious," Theresa answered him. "You are not going to get me to change my mind, Garrett."

"Theresa..."

"Do not argue with me, Garrett," Theresa said. "Aiden is no mere human being. The King's sword has chosen him as its master for one reason or another."

She turned her back to him.

"Aiden has shown great promise in the training sessions I have been going through with him. Not only that, but our brother has also agreed to help train him."

"Seamus?" Garrett asked in surprise. "He agreed to help train a whelp like him?"

"Believe me; I'm not thrilled about him either," Aiden grumbled.

"Enough, both of you." Theresa turned back to Garrett, a fire in her eyes. "We are heading back to the forest that separates Chicago from Wisconsin. Meet us there soon."

"Is that a request?" Garrett asked.

"No. It's an order."

Theresa began to walk away from Garrett. She tugged Aiden by his collar. He could tell that the final dragon warrior was seething with anger. Now he had two dragons with something against him. Just great.

Slowly, but surely, the windiest city in America gave way to the forest where they arrived. To Aiden, it was so good to see the forest once again after being in the worst streets in Chicago. They took a moment to catch their breath as they arrived at the spot where Theresa landed. This would be the spot where they would wait for Garrett to arrive. He felt a light tap on his shoulder and glanced at her.

SMACK!

Aiden's left cheek burned with sudden pain from Theresa's slap. At first he wanted to cry out, but he restrained himself when he saw the fire in her eyes. They were so full of anger that he couldn't say a word. Theresa's nostrils flared briefly with actual white fire.

"Don't you EVER leave a spot where I've told you to wait! EVER!" she roared. "Do you understand me?!"

"Y-Yes, Theresa," Aiden said meekly, wanting to shrink from her sudden anger.

"What were you thinking?" Theresa asked. "You just wandered off into one of the most dangerous cities in the world by yourself! You could have been killed, Aiden!"

"But I...," he started, but stopped himself when he couldn't find an excuse.

Theresa had been upset with him before; that was natural for friends. But he had never seen her so angry with him. Looking back, he shouldn't have left the spot without Theresa in the first place. He could not imagine feeling worse than he did right now.

The two sat in uncomfortable silence. Theresa didn't attempt a conversation; Aiden was too intimidated and guilt-ridden. He couldn't even try to talk to her. It was almost unbearable to sit in utter silence.

They did not look at each other as they waited for Garrett. Suddenly, a chill blew past, making Aiden shiver from the cold. But just as soon as that cold came it disappeared when he felt warmth wrap around him softly after his body shivered. He blinked at the new feeling and hung his head low as the warmth spread through his body.

Theresa was hugging him.

"I...I was so scared...," she said, tightening her embrace. "I thought that I had lost you like I...like I lost the Dragon King."

Aiden frowned as he closed his eyes. Now he felt even worse. She had told him about how close she and the King once were.

He put himself in danger, without a sure chance of survival, and he didn't even think about how she would feel.

"Theresa," he finally said, "I know that you probably won't accept this...but I am sorry."

He didn't bring his head up.

"I was being idiotic looking for Garrett on my own. I was too busy thinking that I could impress you; I didn't think about how it would make you feel." Aiden continued, "I feel absolutely terrible for making you worry like that."

"Aiden," Theresa hugged him even tighter, "while I am glad that you learned from your little adventure, I'm more relieved that you're still alive."

He felt her head against his shoulder.

"I thought for sure you were lost, kidnapped, or worse," she said, closing her eyes tightly. "If you hadn't found Garrett I...I would have lost you."

Aiden said nothing as he let her hug him. What could he say to make it better?

"Theresa, I...."

"Shh" She shushed him, her gentle smile finally returning. "You don't need to explain. Just promise me that you'll never do something like that again."

Eventually a smile found its way to his face.

"Yeah, I think I learned my lesson."

They shared a quiet laugh, and Theresa pulled away from him. It was nice to know that despite his bad decision she was still his friend. He glanced at Warfang, rubbing his thumb over the hilt of the sword.

"Theresa, how come Garrett got so upset about me wielding Warfang?" he asked.

Theresa sighed.

"Garrett is somewhat of an extremist, Aiden," she explained. "Back in the old days, he believed humans were not equal to our kind. He was one of few who felt that way."

"But why?"

"I'm sure you're aware how greedy humans can be," Theresa said. "Back then, after the Great War, they were no different. Whenever they had a chance to seize power, they would take it. Were it not for the respect the human leader had for our King, there might have been open war between our two races."

Aiden sighed as she shook his head.

"And I thought Seamus was bad."

Theresa laughed slightly as she stood up. Dusting her hands off on her pants, she turned back to Aiden and offered him a hand to help him up.

"No thanks," he said, pushing himself up. "I'm good."

"After what happened, Aiden, I don't think 'good' fits."

"Okay then, what do you think would fit?"

"Scared out of your pants?" she suggested, giving him a smug smile.

"Oh, I was not!" Aiden said, gently pushing her. "Nervous, yes. Scared? No."

Theresa just laughed. As the two of them waited for Garrett, Aiden summoned his sword to practice. Theresa watched from the sidelines as Aiden swung his blade in boredom, reliving the fight with Raven's demons. With each movement, he thought about what he could have done to avoid being wounded.

Though the pain was long gone, Aiden still could feel Zantul's icy claw slash into his skin. If he was going to face creatures like that again, he had to make sure that he was a lot faster. Perhaps with Garrett's help in training, he would gain enough speed to counter such an attack.

As Aiden slashed a branch off a tree, he wondered what kind of skill Garrett specialized in. Theresa mastered the art of combat with the sword; Seamus specialized in magic. Aiden wondered if there was a reason for their skills, how they complimented each other. Almost like a trinity of sorts.

While he was busy slashing off tree branches, Theresa

watched him. Often she would say something about his posture, or how he wasn't holding his blade properly. Aiden couldn't help but feel a little annoyed. Even though they weren't in their forest, she was still tutoring him. Not that he was complaining, really.

Minutes passed as he continued to practice. Aiden didn't know if Garrett was taking his time reaching the forest, or if he wasn't coming at all. Sure, Theresa had given him and order, but they had been waiting at least an hour Maybe Garrett was taking his anger out on any thugs left in Chicago before coming to the forest.

Aiden began to sweat as he practiced with Warfang. He was breathed heavily he pulled away from the tree he was hacking at. He had sliced through dozens of branches; only a few remained.

Suddenly, Theresa turned to her left. Aiden turned as well. From across the clearing, Garrett was approaching them slowly.

Aiden swallowed hard as the tall warrior came closer. The same dangerous look lingered in Garrett's eyes. Theresa quickly stood up beside Aiden.

The final member of the team stopped just short of them, his dark brown eyes studying Aiden once more. Theresa's body seemed to tense as she watched Garrett carefully.

"Let me make one thing clear," Garrett said finally. "I'll come, but before we leave I have to evaluate something."

"Evaluate?" Aiden asked.

"Yes, to see where you are exactly, whelp."

Garrett took off his leather jacket and threw it to the ground. He raised his left arm and Aiden blinked in confusion.

"Take your sword, and strike my skin," Garrett said.

"Are you nuts?" Aiden asked. "I'll cut you."

"At the very least, whelp, you should know by now that you do what your instructors tell you to do." Garrett's eyes narrowed. "Now strike me."

Aiden glanced to Theresa, unsure if he should do what Garrett requested. Reluctantly, she nodded. Aiden sighed and tightened his grip on the hilt of Warfang. He had no idea what Garrett was trying to accomplish.

Aiden's body ached as he began ran towards Garrett. The action of the day was taking its toll on him, but his mind told him to ignore the feeling in his muscles. Aiden pulled his sword back and swung for Garrett's arm.

Of course, Aiden expected his blade to slice deep into Garrett's arm. But that didn't happen. Instead, the blade bounced off, as if he'd struck a pillar of steel. Aiden's arms vibrated from the collision, so badly he was forced to let go of Warfang.

"W-What the hell?" Aiden finally managed to ask as the vibration in his arms faded.

"Is that the extent of your strength?" Garrett asked dryly, the expression on his face showing boredom.

"My strength?"

"Yes. Your strength," Garrett answered. Aiden's attack hadn't left a scratch on his arm. "For some reason, whelp, the sword has chosen you as its master. In the right hands, it is an unstoppable weapon." Garrett's eyes narrowed. "But I do not see why it thinks you can wield it."

Theresa stepped forward.

"Garrett," she said, "remember, he is just starting out."

"That does not mean anything to me," Garrett said as blunt as he could say. "If the sword chose him, it must have a reason. You know that there are far stronger enemies than just goblins and ogres, Theresa. Some of them with skin so rough that it makes the very steel of many weapons break."

Garrett turned to a large tree that was tall, vibrant, and without a doubt incredibly strong.

"Watch carefully, whelp," he said, holding his hand out. "This tree might be old, but its bark is hard. In order to cut it..."

Aiden watched carefully as the ground in front of Garrett trembled violently. The ground soon erupted, the cause of the disturbance rising from the very earth itself. A large, double-bladed axe, easily half again as tall as Garrett, appeared in front of him.

The axe was beautiful, its hilt as dark as the coal that lies beneath the mountains of the world. A strangely shaped bronze metal head held the double blades in place. The blades themselves sparkled like diamonds in the light.

Aiden had never seen anything like it.

Garrett took his axe with only one hand and lifted the mighty weapon easily. Aiden watched in amazement as Garrett swung the massive weapon over his shoulders. The axe must have weighed more than five strong men could carry.

"You must be stronger than your weapon!"

Garrett pulled his axe up and with a mighty yell, sliced into the base of the old tree. Aiden watched the tree intensely. Garrett said nothing as he straightened himself up, eyes closed as he waited.

A loud creaking came from the heart from the tree. The slash from Garrett's axe had left a huge gash in the bark. The old tree continued to creak as it leaned backwards, falling to the ground with a boom as it met the earth below it.

"Without strength, true strength, you are weak," Garrett said, his axe disappearing. "This tree was incredibly strong despite its old age. But for its incredibly strong outer layer, there are monsters that possess skin just as tough."

Garrett turned back to Aiden, gesturing him to pick up Warfang from the ground.

"It seems that you have been trained in sword skill by Theresa. And, if I know her like I do, she has Seamus teaching you how to use magic."

"That is correct," Theresa said. "Aiden has shown amazing progress since I started his training. With your help, Garrett, I believe he will become strong enough to fight on his own."

Garrett remained silent for a very long time. His eyes studied Aiden. Whatever he was thinking, Aiden did not want to know it.

He had seen the raw brute strength behind those muscles. Honestly, it terrified him.

"Garrett?" Theresa asked.

"If I help you train this whelp, I want to make one thing very clear," Garrett said.

"What is that?"

"He does not make any attempt to 'socialize' with me, as humans would call it. And when I judge him ready, I will leave."

"But...," Aiden started. Theresa placed a hand over his mouth.

"I understand," she said. "But give it time, brother. I think you'll come to understand why our King's sword has chosen him."

Garrett said nothing as he grabbed his jacket. Aiden turned to her, quirking an eyebrow at her decision.

"I thought we wanted him to stay with us?" he whispered.

"Just leave this to me, Aiden," Theresa whispered back. "Garrett will relent. I know him too well."

"He has no patience for humans," Aiden argued.

"Remember, Aiden, I'm his commander," Theresa said. "He'll do what I tell him to do."

Aiden sighed, deciding not to push the issue. Theresa turned to Garrett, who was standing about thirty yards away. She sighed as she shook her head at him.

"Aiden, remember: do not come near us when we transform."

He didn't need to be reminded as he turned his attention to Garrett. The large warrior growled low as rocks tumbled and cracked apart around him. Even Theresa watched carefully as her comrade stood alone. Rocks and rubble continued to rise around Garrett, shattering as they drew closer to his head.

Garrett's back sprouted large, dark brown wings. His pupils turned to slits, much like Theresa's. Aiden watched in awe from the sidelines; this was the third time he had witnessed a dragon transformation.

Unlike Theresa's transformation, however, Garrett's was violent and dark. The very ground he stood on collapsed, like someone had taken a large bowl and pressed it down hard into the earth. Garrett let out a loud and powerful roar, a combination of anger, hatred, and determination. A bright flash of brown light consumed Garrett's body, forcing Aiden to once again cover his eyes.

When he uncovered them, what he saw numbed him to the core.

Garrett's dragon form was MASSIVE. He was much taller than Theresa and Seamus in their dragon forms. His scales were dark brown, like the rich soil under their feet. Multiple scars covered his chest and underbelly. Also, unlike Theresa's or Seamus' forms, Garrett had three large horns on his huge skull. A large curved one on the tip of his snout and two extremely tall ones evenly placed on his forehead, like a triceratops. Sharp spines sprouted from the tip of his neck to his spiked tail.

Theresa kept quiet as Garrett turned. His eyes narrowed dangerously as he looked at them.

"If we're going to wherever the hell you're training this whelp, then let's go." Aiden took notice of how his voice echoed and rumbled at once. "I don't want this to be a waste of my time."

"Of course, brother," Theresa said, stepping away from Aiden.

Her wings sprouted first as she changed. After seeing Garrett's horrific transformation and beastly form, it was a relief to watch Theresa's elegant dragon again take shape. She lowered her neck to let him.

"Are you ready?" she asked.

"I'm good to go," Aiden said, getting a firm grip around her neck with his legs.

"Good." Theresa turned back to Garrett. "Stay close, brother, and remember: do not let any human see you."

Garrett nodded slightly at her order. Theresa was the first to take off, entering the clouds and sky before Garrett. Aiden glanced back to watch him take off from the ground. It amazed him that, despite his large size, Garrett was capable of keeping up with Theresa in the air.

Aiden shook his head, dismissing the thought of how powerful Garrett could really be. He glanced down to Theresa's, a soft smile on his face as they flew.

"Theresa," he said, "what if Garrett tries to…"

"He won't, Aiden," Theresa said, as if she knew what he was going to say. A soft growl could be heard in her words. "If he even tries to hurt you, I'll stop him myself."

Aiden sighed. He closed his eyes briefly and enjoyed the soft wind blowing against them. It felt like true freedom as they flew above the world below. The life's heavy burdens drifted away with each flap of Theresa's wings.

The effect was almost intoxicating.

Sure, the flight was brief and would only last fifteen minutes. But he didn't care. As far as he was concerned, he could fly free forever. The beating of Theresa's wings died down as she descended.

The must be back in Virginia, Aiden thought. A shame.

"Well, look who's back!" Seamus' familiar voice said. "How was your first flight, kiddo?"

"All things considered?" Aiden reflected. "Probably the best part of the day."

"Heh, I bet." Seamus glanced at Theresa. "Sorry, sis, but I looked all over this state. I couldn't find him. Odds are he's not even on the same continent."

Suddenly, a loud thud echoed from behind a three. Seamus blinked at the shockwave of vibrations.

"You found him, didn't you?"

"Yup," Aiden and Theresa said together, the latter transforming back into her human form.

"Typical," Seamus grumbled, folding his arms across his chest. "I end up with a dead end, and Theresa finds him."

"Actually," Theresa said, a slight smile on her face, "Aiden was the one who found him."

"Really now?" Seamus turned to Aiden, and for the first time gave him a kind smile. "Not bad, kiddo. Maybe you are learning after all."

Aiden didn't have time to say thanks. Garrett had transformed back into his human form once more. He joined the three of them, a small smile on his face as he saw Seamus.

"I see you were dragged into training this whelp as well, Seamus," he said.

"Eh, what can I say?" Seamus shrugged. "You know I can't resist a lady's request, Garrett."

"Watch it, Seamus," Theresa threatened. "You know what I said about flirting."

"Oh now, now, sister." Seamus grinned. "I'm allowed some fun, aren't I?"

One glare from her was enough for him to drop the subject. Garrett gave a half-hearted laugh, something Aiden did not expect.

Garrett's dark brown eyes were evaluating him once again.

"Well, whelp," Garrett said, "you've had a good little break on our way back here."

Aiden's gut twisted in a knot as Garrett cracked his large hands. Seamus blinked in surprise as his brother smiled darkly.

"Welcome to hell," Garrett said. "When I'm done with you, your muscles and bones will feel like they're nothing but dust."

Aiden's face paled. As if training hadn't been hard enough, now he was going to have to learn another skill under a third teacher. A massive, terrifying teacher. Theresa frowned as she placed a hand on Garrett's shoulder.

"Garrett, remember: he is human," she said. "We don't want him to feel like he's dying."

"Theresa," Garrett said, "he is going to learn that when you train with our kind, you have to keep up."

His eyes narrowed dangerously at Aiden as he glanced to the pocket that kept Warfang.

"Especially if he wields our King's ancient and powerful weapon," Garrett mused. "Let's discover what it is that Warfang has seen in you, whelp."

From two tough trainers to three; Aiden's luck was getting really bad, as of late. Still, he would be lying if he said it wasn't cool. He had three mentors, each of them a member of a powerful race: Theresa, skilled in sword combat; Seamus, skilled in the magical arts; and Garrett, blessed with incredible, but terrible, strength.

Like a perfect Trinity.

CHAPTER 15 - TENSIONS BUILD

Another week had passed since Raven's attack and locating Garrett. School hadn't really changed that much since Patrick attacked Aiden. He soon found that training with all three of his mentors was incredibly challenging. Theresa still managed his combat training, in which he began to show slight improvements, while Seamus continued to mentor him in magic training. As such, Garrett was in charge of building up Aiden's muscle strength.

But as much as he enjoyed time with the dragons, Aiden wondered why they were training. While it was in a way to learn self defense, he couldn't help but feel curious about why Theresa saw fit to train him out of all people. Her answer, for the most part, did bring some light to it.

"Aiden, before we were sealed the Dragon King told us that even with his great power his seal would not last forever. Ordering us to only awaken when we sensed a power similar to his." She told him. "While Garrett and Seamus grew tired of waiting, I waited. Waited for you. The Great Evil that destroyed the Kingdoms of Old will return. By the time it does, we will be ready. And so will you."

That was the closest answer that Aiden would get from her about the subject. Now it made sense why they were training him. To make sure they were ready when the Great Evil returned.

No pressure, right? The worry was something that Aiden had learned to actively dislike, if not hate.

Saturday, though, they would begin his magic training again. Seamus, who had begun to slowly lighten up, took great interest in improving Aiden's magical skills. That was something that Aiden did not expect from the second warrior. Still, Seamus made his sarcastic comments and would often flirt with every girl he came across.

After his magic training, combat training would resume between him and Theresa. This was his best skill. He didn't know why, exactly, but the more he practiced using a sword, the better he became. It just felt natural to him. Theresa was also the kindest of the three, somewhat expected since she was his best friend, but she still lectured him when he made a mistake.

After combat training, Garrett would begin strength training. Aiden shivered at the thought of it.

Still, it was nice to know that the easier training sessions would be first. Seamus stepped forward, staff in hand once again.

"All right, kiddo. Since you were able to cast *Flarnea* with Raven, we'll give it some more practice today," Seamus said, pointing his staff at the old pile of tree branches. "Think you'll be able to hit 'em?

"Honestly, I don't know," Aiden admitted. "When I cast the spell before, it was more on the spur of the moment."

"Hmph," Garrett scoffed. "You mean to tell me that you cast a basic spell, one that any mere whelp could cast, only when you were upset?"

Aiden glanced at Garrett. Last weekend had been rough on him since Garrett joined their little group. His training beliefs were so tough that the strongest man in the world might cry uncle. There was absolutely no love from Garrett when it came to Aiden's training.

But what it really boiled down to here was that Theresa was still the leader of the group. Even Garrett did not question her when she made it an order. In a way, it was sort of ironic. Garrett was vastly taller than any of them, but he dared not disobey any orders from Theresa.

Still there was a part of Aiden that did respect Garrett. No one could argue that when it came to physical strength no one could beat him in it. But despite Garrett's incredible strength, Theresa was still his superior. Aiden had learned quickly how skilled Theresa truly was. Garrett had a lot of power behind him, there was no denying that. Though when he was pitted against Theresa's skill and speed, he couldn't touch her.

That didn't mean that Aiden had to like Garrett, though. It seemed that everything he did, Garrett criticized. He hated to admit it, but as much as he disliked Seamus and his smart comments, Aiden gladly preferred him to Garrett. At least when he accomplished something, Seamus gave positive feedback.

Garrett was a completely different story. His belief was that if you didn't get it right the first time, you weren't worth his time. Aiden knew that if it weren't for Theresa's rank and superior skill, Garrett would have left the moment he met Aiden.

But how could a mere human possess the awesome strength he witnessed from Garrett?

"Oi, kiddo," Seamus said, catching his attention again, "focus on the task at hand."

"Huh? Oh, right. S-Sorry," Aiden said hastily.

Garrett rolled his eyes as he watched Aiden. Seamus repositioned him into the same spot as before. Lifting his arm up slightly so that Aiden could aim at the branches.

"Remember what I told you: concentrate, but don't overdo it," he instructed.

Aiden nodded as he focused on the branches.

Slowly but surely, he felt the prickling heat. The sensation ran from his arm to his hand, creating flames that danced around his palm. He smiled as he held the fire.

He couldn't afford to stare at it for long, though. Every second he delayed, the weaker the spell would become. Aiden took careful aim at the pile of dead branches, determined to hit his targets. He had pulled the spell off before, but could he do it again?

"*Flarnea!*"

Just like before, a fireball leapt from Aiden's hand. This time, however, it was much bigger and moved faster than his previous attempts. Biting his lip, he watched the spell carefully. If he didn't have mastery over this spell by now, his magic training might be put to an end before it really began.

"Come on," he thought, swallowing hard.

Just as it looked like the fireball was about to die out, it reached its target. The tree branches went up in flames. A grateful smile grew across Aiden's lips. After what felt like endless attempts, it was rewarding to see that the spell did not fail. Seamus slapped him hard on the back.

"Well, I'll be the son of an ugly demon's mother!" he said. "Am I a great teacher or what?"

Aiden rubbed the spore spot on his back where Seamus hit him.

"Good job, Aiden," Theresa said. "Just remember, when you're casting a spell in the middle of combat, you have to cast it quickly."

"Theresa is right," Seamus said. "See, magic has a lot of power behind it. If there's one thing the enemy fears, it's power. They will want to take it out before that power becomes a true threat."

"In other words," Garrett said from the sidelines, "you're a sitting duck when you're just standing there."

Garrett gave a dark grin as he noticed Aiden turned back to face him.

"But then again, humans have always stood around and made themselves sitting ducks."

Aiden gave the much taller dragon warrior a dark glare.

"Yeah, well for sitting ducks we've progressed pretty far, if you ask me," he said.

Theresa quickly stepped between them, just as she had done whenever he and Seamus would go at it. Garrett just snorted a bit before turning away. Theresa gave Aiden a look.

"Keep your cool," she instructed. "If you and he can't get along, things will never work out properly."

"He doesn't want to work with me at all," Aiden mumbled.

"Hey now," Seamus interrupted, stabbing his staff into the ground. "Don't get distracted kiddo! You still have magic training to do!"

Aiden frowned as he turned back to Seamus. Garrett still had his back to them.

"All right, kiddo," Seamus said. "Now that you've mastered one spell, it's time for us to see how many fireballs you can cast rapidly."

Aiden's face faltered at the word 'rapidly.' Theresa narrowed her eyes at Seamus. He just smiled at their expressions.

"Just kidding!" he said, laughing. "He's nowhere near good enough to do that many yet!"

Theresa slammed her fist down onto his head. Seamus rubbed the top of his head in pain.

"Not. Funny," she said dryly.

"You didn't have to hit so hard, you know!" Seamus groaned.

"It's you, Seamus," Theresa said dryly. "I always have to hit hard."

Aiden chuckled. He glanced to Garrett, who had kept silent.

"Don't get over-confident, whelp," Garrett said now. "Casting a basic spell proves nothing."

Once again, the good feeling Aiden had was washed away. Try as he might, he couldn't help but be increasingly annoyed by the

unimpressed comments. And Garrett had a comment for everything that Aiden did.

Theresa placed a hand on his shoulder.

"Anyway, it's time for combat training," she said. "Take up
your sword and let's begin. You'll face me today while Seamus
and Garrett face each other."

"Oh that is NOT fair!" Seamus complained.

"What's the matter, brother?" Garrett asked, a dark smile on
his face. "Afraid to face me head on?

"Don't ask me that question, Garrett! Everyone knows that
you don't give anybody a chance to counterattack!"

Theresa just smiled as she summoned her two short swords.
Aiden responded by taking Warfang and summoning his weapon.
It was nice not to have to listen to Garrett as they focused on
combat. He felt somewhat bad for Seamus though. Even though
they often had their spats, he wouldn't wish pain on him. Well, at
least from Garrett.

Aiden cleared his mind of the large warrior and refocused on
combat training. Theresa was already on the move as she swung
Fire at him. He quickly blocked her sword with his own then
ducked as she swung her second. He had learned that Theresa
had a pattern to her attacks.

Often, she would distract her opponent with one blade, then
attack with the second. It took him a while to figure out that
pattern, but she did it so often that forced himself to
remember.

Theresa smiled as she drew her blades back. Taking a new
stance, she held one sword high above her head and the other
close to her hip, a stance Aiden believed to be a mix of both
attacking and defending positions. He placed both hands around
the hilt of Warfang, ready for anything that she might throw
at him.

Theresa immediately charged him with quick thrusts and
slashes. Aiden blocked each slash that he could and barely

dodged her thrusts, the tip of one of her swords cutting through the fabric of his shirt.

He had to get on the offensive. It was the number one thing that he had learned in combat training. If you were on the defensive for too long, your opponent would eventually find a weak point and exploit it. Theresa continued her assault, each blade coming closer to cutting him.

Finally getting a strong foothold, Aiden pulled Warfang back and swung it in a arc. His sword clashed against her two blades just as she swung them. Theresa narrowed her eyes as pushed back his sword. Aiden didn't relent, however; he pushed back against her blades just as hard.

Theresa looked like she was about to lose her footing, and an idea came to him. He pulled back Warfang quickly, hoping his plan would work.

His heart beat with joy as he saw Theresa stumble. Now was his chance to attack! Aiden swung Warfang again, hoping for once to land a decent blow. But of course, this was Theresa; she wouldn't be down for long.

As quickly as she had stumbled, she recovered, blocking his attack with Snow. Aiden continued to swing Warfang. Theresa blocked each blade skillfully, as expected, but Aiden's constant attacks didn't allow her any chance to counter. Each hit sent sparks flying from their swords as the strong metals clashed against each other.

Aiden pulled back his sword, then quickly thrust forward. Theresa blocked the tip of his sword with both of her blades. She then employed the holding technique she used with her two swords before, keeping Warfang in place. Gritting his teeth, Aiden tried to twist his sword out of the hold.

"Not bad, Aiden," Theresa said, a proud smile breaking across her face. "You're learning to exploit weaknesses."

Aiden gave her a smug smile. Putting all his strength into his arm, he managed to wiggle his sword away from the hold. Once again, his blade was free.

"Took you long enough, whelp," Garrett said from the sidelines. "You finally showed what kind of strength you have: minute."

That was the final straw. Aiden turned to Garrett and gave the taller warrior an angry stare. Theresa immediately got between the two of them, her own eyes full of anger.

"That's enough, both of you!" she snapped.

"Letting her defend you, whelp?" Garrett asked. "What kind of warrior do you think you are?"

Aiden's eyes were beginning to see red. He had just about had enough of Garrett's retorts and comments. His blood boiled as he took a step towards Garrett. Theresa kept him away easily, despite being somewhat shorter than he was.

"What the hell is your problem?!" Aiden asked. "I've done nothing to you since the day we've met!"

"Oh ho, look at this. How cute," Garrett sneered. "He's getting angry."

"Come on, Garrett," Seamus stepped in. "Let's not fight with each other here…"

"Stay out of this, Seamus!" Theresa snapped again. "The last thing we need is your input!"

Garrett continued to sneer at Aiden, with Theresa trying her best to keep the two from ripping each other apart. Aiden clenched his fist tightly.

"What's the matter, whelp?" Garrett crossed his arms. "You can't fight your own battles?"

"I'm warning you, Garrett," Aiden threatened, "don't push me!"

"Oh, I'm shaking," Garrett scoffed. "If you're serious, then show me that you are."

Aiden thrust his sword into the air. With a wordless yell, he swung it at Garrett. The larger warrior just sneered as he readied himself to block the attack. But one of Theresa's swords blocked Aiden's weapon easily.

Her nostrils flared dangerously as she glanced between them.

"Enough!" she shouted, a roar hiding somewhere in her voice. "You two are going to learn to respect one another, even if it kills me!"

"Why should I respect someone who hates me for being a human?" Aiden asked. "I did nothing to him since the day we met and he's been giving me crap!"

"You think you're different from all the others?" Garrett scoffed. "You're just like every other damn human I've ever had the displeasure of knowing."

"Who do you think you are to judge me? You don't even know the first thing about me!"

"And I don't WANT to know the first thing about you." Garrett's voice began to rumble. "Do not push your luck, whelp."

Never in his life has Aiden been so enraged. Garrett didn't even know him, but he was dead set on not getting along. Not that Aiden would even want to be friends with him. He glanced back at Theresa. The message in her eyes was simple enough to read: *Do not engage.*

It took every ounce of restraint not to attack. Aiden wanted nothing more than to slash his sword into Garrett's chest. Theresa's sword still blocked Warfang. Seamus began to sweat as he watched from the sidelines.

"Are you done?" he asked. "We've been reunited for only a week; let's not spoil this moment with a fight."

"I'm surprised to even hear you say that," Aiden admitted. "You and I were at each other's throats when we met."

"Kiddo, when it comes to very old battle comrades, there's an exception."

Garrett scoffed as he turned away from them.

"Whelp, if you want to show any true sign of strength,

channel that anger into your muscles," he said. "I'll make you see what I mean when our training begins."

With that, Garrett walked away. Slowly Theresa turned to Aiden. His body tensed, expecting her to smack him across his face. But as he noticed her eyes, his body relaxed. They were full of relief.

"Aiden," she said softly, "I know he's hard to understand…but please, do not let your temper blind you."

"But…," he started, stopping when she gave him a quick hug.

"He could have killed you," she said breathlessly. "Do not let him pull you into a trap."

Those words made his spine shiver. Garrett tried to pull him into a trap? He didn't understand why he would do such a thing. He glanced back to Garrett, still walking away. Seamus sighed.

"What she means, kiddo, was that Garrett was egging you on intentionally," he explained. "It's a ploy that he's used since the old days. And the weak ones usually end up attacking him in blind rage."

Aiden stood dumbfounded. He watched the tall warrior, now a hundred yards away from them.

"It's sort of his own way of testing you, Aiden," she said, "to see if you are worthy enough to train."

"And kiddo, I think you passed." Seamus said.

Aiden didn't know if he should be honored or terrified. What horrors did Garrett have waiting for him now?

CHAPTER 16 - THE DRAGON'S STARE

$\mathcal{T}$he rest of the day did not pass as quickly. After the confrontation with Garrett, combat training resumed. Aiden could barely focus. If it weren't for Theresa's intervention, he would have made a terrible mistake.

Deep down, he wanted to stab Garrett in the heart for his insults and constant berating. Who wouldn't want to? Garrett would say things that would make even the rudest person blush. No matter what small achievement he made, Garrett would say something to rattle his cage.

Combat training helped take his mind off of the event.

A nice benefit from the training now though was that Seamus was starting to ease up on his insults.

No matter how hard he tried, he couldn't get Garrett's anger off his mind. Maybe the third dragon had a deeper reason for hating humans.

Aiden groaned in annoyance. Now he knew why people often said that they felt like their minds were frying when they got upset. The more he thought about it the more it pissed him off. It was just too much!

He couldn't take it anymore. He blocked Theresa's blades one last time before throwing the tip of his sword into the ground. Theresa looked confused as he walked away.

"What's wrong, Aiden?" she asked.

"I can't focus, Theresa," he said. "Garrett's little 'test' is still rattling me."

"You still going on about that, kiddo?" Seamus asked as he leaned against a tree.

"Oh and I suppose I should just let it go?" Aiden scowled.

"Believe it or not, yes. You should." Seamus gave a coy smile. "No good comes from holding on to past events."

"That's not what I've seen from Garrett."

Theresa sighed as she dismissed her two swords. She motioned Aiden to take a seat on a log.

"You have to understand something, Aiden," she said. "While Seamus has a point about holding on to the past, there are some things that take longer to get over."

He quirked an eyebrow at her.

"I'm confused," Aiden admitted. "What could have happened to make him act like such…."

"A jackass?" Seamus finished for him. Aiden noticed he was spinning his staff again.

"Honestly, kiddo, it could be for a number of reasons," Seamus said. "Sore battle with a human, humans taking advantage of every resource they have, how greedy they became during the Dark Ages."

"I'm sitting right here, you know."

"What? I'm not saying that YOU were like any of those humans." Seamus grinned. "Nah, you're more like the rioting kind if you ask me."

"Seamus," Theresa growled, "that is not helping."

"My point is, ol' Garrett has always had something bugging him since the old days. It varied time from time, but he always found a topic to gripe about."

The more he heard about Garrett's past, the more curious

Aiden became. He knew that he was stepping into deeper waters, but he had to know more. It was a trait he inherited from his mother: every little detail he had to know. Something could come in very handy some day.

A new question formed in Aiden's mind now. Seamus and Garrett had been out of their seals for years now. Did the two of them ever see each other over that time?

Aiden hoped he wasn't stepping over any boundaries.

"Say, if you and he broke out of your seals earlier than Theresa, did you guys ever come across each other?"

Seamus was silent for a few moments as his mind worked back to events long before Aiden was born. Seamus spun his staff before dismissing it. The tension built as the silence continued.

Finally, Seamus sighed, but gave a slight nod.

"Occasionally." Seamus' eyes seemed to turn a bit older. "Whenever we did, there was always some new thing that would make him upset. It usually was something that humans had done: Not recognizing that they could have stopped the Black Plague if they had burnt the rats earlier; the endless crusades for the supposed 'Holy Land' that left families ruined; World Wars' I and II. You name it, he was not happy about it."

Seamus shook his head.

"A lot of the fires that burnt many villages infected with the plague were caused by him. I say it was because he was sparing them from a slow and painful death."

Words could not come to Aiden's mouth. Garrett had seen all these infamous events in history? The Black Plague during the Middle Ages, holy crusades for Jerusalem, and the two World Wars?

Dragons just continued to blow his mind!

His imagination soared. Aiden could picture Garrett flying around during the Black Plague, burning those who were too sick to survive. For each crusade for Jerusalem, he could picture Garrett sitting on a large perch, watching as men clashed weapons. He then imagined him being present for the numerous wars between England and France, the French Revolution, the America Revolution, and the American Civil War. He had a harder time seeing him flying around in his dragon form during the World Wars, however. How would the armies react to the sight of his large shadow from the sky, breathing fire on them in rage for having a war?

"Aiden," Theresa scolded, snapping her fingers in front of his face. "Focus, please."

"S-Sorry," he blushed in embarrassment. "I couldn't help myself."

"Got an over-active imagination, don't ya kiddo?"

"Anyway," Theresa said as she drove her blades into the ground, "we'll take a break from training right now. You've been through a lot."

"Theresa?" Aiden asked in confusion.

"Hey kiddo," Seamus interrupted, "when Theresa says to take a break, take it. It's an opportunity that doesn't present itself that often!"

Theresa gave Seamus a glare before walking to the river. Aiden turned back to him, arms across his chest.

"I'd watch what I say if I were you," he said. "I wouldn't want Theresa on me if I kept running my mouth."

"Ah, it's no big deal." Seamus shrugged. "It's my way of letting her know that I mean well."

"By saying that her giving breaks are rare?"

"That?" he scoffed. "She knows that I don't mean any harm."

Aiden rolled his eyes as he picked up Warfang, dismissing the blade before placing its figurine in his pocket.

While he hated to admit it, Seamus had a point. For as long he's known Theresa, she never once allowed a break for anything. From homework, exercise, or even household chores. She viewed breaks as a waste of time. Why? He had no idea.

Seamus stretched a bit as he headed off into one direction,

leaving Aiden to have some quiet time to himself. A past time that was starting to get rarer and rarer that more they trained.

Aiden allowed his aching legs to rest. As much as he enjoyed learning from the Trinity, he was more than willing to take a break. Training almost every weekend with her, Seamus, and now Garrett, made his body ache.

He couldn't argue with the results though. His muscles were slowly starting to build up. Even if they did ache more than ever before. His mind began to wonder how much tougher Garrett's training would become. How much pressure would he have to endure?

A slashing sound to his right caught his attention. Aiden looked over and part of him wished he didn't.

Garrett, with his large, double-bladed axe in hand, was hacking into large dead trees. The sheer force of each hit made thousands of pieces fly into different directions. With a blank expression, he swung his axe through three trees at once, slicing through their middles with no ease.

What kind of being had such power? Not even the strongest human in the world, in his prime, could do what he did. Aiden knew that Garrett was a dragon, but this was insane. He shivered at the thought of what kind of training Garrett would put him through next.

If he could plow his axe through several trees, what else could he demolish?

Garrett reached for the hilt of his massive axe and quite easily pulled his weapon out, mumbling something under his breath as he swung the axe over his shoulder. Aiden tried to make out what he said, but his hearing couldn't pick up anything.

"Oi, kiddo!" Seamus called out. "Come talk with me for a bit!"

Aiden nearly jumped out of his skin. He had been so lost in thought and awe at Garrett's strength that he forgot he wasn't alone. Unfortunately, he wasn't the only one who heard.

Garrett turned his head to Aiden, his eyes full of silent anger as he glared at him. For the slightest moment, Aiden could have sworn he saw an outline of dark colors surrounding him. A new feeling grabbed hold of him now.

True fear.

Aiden would have gladly been anywhere else. The glare from Garrett made his entire body freeze. Never in his life had he felt such fear grab a hold of him. His heart began to race the longer Garrett glared at him. He would have done anything to avoid Garrett's glare of hatred.

"Oi, kiddo!" Seamus shouted again. "Come over here already!"

Relief flowed through Aiden at the sound of Seamus' obnoxious voice. Quickly turning away from Garrett, he headed towards Seamus. The green dragon was already sitting on another log, patting a spot beside him.

"You OK there, kiddo?" Seamus asked.

"Do I look OK to you?" Aiden asked, going from terrified to annoyed at Seamus' question.

"Well, since you asked, you look like you saw a hundred dead men charging at you." Seamus just smiled somewhat as he leaned his back to look at the sky above them.

"Garrett gave you the Dragon Stare, didn't he?"

"Dragon Stare?" Aiden repeated.

"Yup, that's what I said." Seamus grinned again. "I didn't know you were such a good parrot, kiddo."

Aiden just gave him a glare. Seamus sighed as he leaned back up.

"Oh lighten up. Can't you take a joke?" he asked, slighting patting Aiden's back. "I'll let you in on a little secret: you don't want two dragons against you. It doesn't end up well to be outnumbered by fire breathing creatures."

He hated to admit it, but Seamus had a point. It was better to have only one dragon against him rather than two. Even if he had Theresa as his bodyguard, he dreaded the thought of what even one angry dragon would do if she wasn't around.

"Anyway, like I was saying, he gave you the Dragon Stare," Seamus continued. "It's a warning sign from dragons to those they don't like."

"A warning sign?"

"Correct," Seamus said, folding his arms across his chest. "You see, dragons tend to choose their foes carefully. When we find somebody we truly do not like, we give them a stare that has different results for everyone who witnesses it."

"Wait," Aiden interrupted, "what kind of different results?"

"Feelings of anger, hatred, envy, and fear flow through the victim's body," Seamus explained. "See, it's kind of how we let somebody know that we really don't like them. I hardly ever use it, nor does Theresa. But Garrett…oh he'll use it any chance he gets."

The Dragon Stare. Aiden had no doubts now: Garrett must truly hate him. But why? What did Aiden ever do to deserve such hate from the final dragon warrior?

"Why?" he asked. "Why did he give me the stare then?"

"Who knows why?" Seamus shrugged. "With Garrett, it could be he truly doesn't like you at all. Or it could be something he ate. No one can tell with him. Heck, even if you got to know him I doubt he'd like you."

Seamus turned to Aiden, frowning a bit as he saw the fear that on his face.

"Hey, listen kiddo," he said, his tone much kinder than before. "If you ask me, you're not so bad. Garrett's obviously got something against humanity that he won't let go easily. Me? I don't let the little things from the past dictate what I do with my life."

Aiden knew that he had to be on another planet now. Seamus had just given him a compliment. He didn't know how to feel, actually. There was no way this was the same Seamus that Aiden had come to know over the past few weeks.

Then again, a lot of things had happened that he didn't expect. His best friend was a dragoness of great skill, certain humans were actually monsters, and there were apparently other sapient races.

"Anyway, kiddo," Seamus started up again, "if you want my advice, here it is: don't let your mind wander about why Garrett dislikes you. You have more important things to focus on."

"Since when have you ever been so full of wisdom?" Aiden asked, with a cocky grin on his lips.

"Oh I can be wise when I choose to be." Seamus retorted. "It's just I don't give my wisdom to people who I regard as idiots."

Aiden crossed his arms across his chest.

"And where am I then?"

"I gave you some tips, didn't I?"

Seamus jumped up from his spot. Cracking his neck once.

"Anyway, kiddo, just remember that if you want Garrett's respect, you gotta earn it. Don't engage in an argument with him and whatever he tells you to do, just do it," he said.

Before Aiden could continue the conversation, Theresa returned.

"Break's over, guys," she said. "It's time to get back to training."

"Aw, come on Thes," Seamus said in a joking tone. "That was only fifteen minutes."

"That's more than enough time to relax, Seamus." Theresa gave him a grin with her sharp teeth. "Or do I need to whack you hard to convince you to train?"

Seamus immediately summoned his staff. Aiden smiled at how quick he reacted to her little threat.

He glanced over to his left one last time. Just as he thought, Garrett was far from where they were standing. Truthfully, he felt relieved. Especially after he was just given the dragon's version of a death threat.

"One way or another, Garrett, I'll get your respect." He thought. *"Even if it kills me."*

CHAPTER 17 - THE TRINITY IN ACTION

*T*he school year was closely approaching its end, and
Aiden couldn't be more excited. School was boring
and it got in the way of his time training with Theresa, Seamus,
and Garrett.

The latter he could have done without. Garrett's training had
proved to be the hardest out of all three. The third dragon used
extreme measures of training to keep his muscles big. When he
started Aiden's training, he had expected him to lift fifty pounds
with one hand.

That didn't end well. After embarrassing Aiden, Garrett
insulted him in his language, calling him 'Kalen.' Theresa
wouldn't translate it for him.

During their weekends of training, Aiden spent at least three
hours with them back and forth until the sun started to set: one
hour with Theresa while the other two were with Seamus and
Garrett. And with the exams fast approaching, they would have
to cut down on training for studying for the exams.

Building muscle was not as easy as the people in TV commer-
cials made it look. It required constant lifting; and it didn't get
easier. Every time he had a session with Garrett, he would always

have to do a brand new course. It was never the same thing, like it was with Theresa and Seamus.

Aiden's muscles would always tremble when the training was done. He barely had the strength to move after the rigorous training with Garrett. It took every bit of his restraint to not lash out in frustration at Garrett for what he put Aiden through.

Still, Aiden's muscles were slowly starting to build. Every time they trained, he could feel his body go further than he thought it would. He was nowhere near in top shape or 'ripped' with muscles, but he could now lift objects that he couldn't before.

Not that it would impress Garrett, though. The first time Aiden lifted an object that was around twenty-five pounds, he had an insult ready.

"So you managed to lift what an infant dragon could lift with its tail. You're still a weakling."

Aiden noticed that Theresa did not seem pleased with Garrett's sarcastic comment. He was glad she that she didn't seem to be a fan of what some people would call 'tough love' in training sessions.

Despite their disagreements, the two seemed to be quiet close. At least, that's how it looked. If Garrett did smile, it was only when he talked to Seamus and Theresa.

That didn't bug him that much. He certainly didn't prefer Garrett's company.

The rest of the school year was sadly uneventful. Raven had disappeared since his one-week attendance, which was just fine with Aiden and the others. No other creatures had revealed themselves yet. It wasn't exactly exciting to not have anything to fight when he was training till his arms felt like they were about to drop.

Finally, only four days remained until the end of school. Sadly, Theresa decided that training would resume after final exams were over.

If there was a one word that Aiden hated, it was 'exam.' It was his bane. Test anxiety really got to him when it came to finals. They weren't like any other tests. Finals were all back to back and if you were to pass you had to be prepared for all of them. .

He wasn't worried about his history exam, though. That one he could ace easily. While he knew he had to study a little harder on other subjects, like English and Science, the one final he would have to study for like crazy was math.

Aiden wanted to rip his own head off at the mention of the word "exam." Thankfully, his mother was there for support when he was studying. Whenever she helped him, he felt a lot better. She was always his biggest supporter.

As exam days drew closer, Aiden's studying intensified. At times he would see Theresa and the others, but they often had little time to talk. Thankfully, Theresa also helped him study for his math final. When it came to studying, Aiden never once saw her study by herself. After learning that she was an incredibly smart dragoness from ancient times though, he assumed that she had no true reason to study. She too was looking forward to summer, mostly because they could focus on training for more than just two days a week.

A part of him was curious why they hadn't been attacked since Raven's appearance in their training grounds. It had been too quiet since that event. He was beginning to feel anxious. Even a fight against a weak goblin would have been nice.

He couldn't dwell on it for too long, though. He had to focus on finals.

At least after these exams he would forever be done with middle school! The only thing after that was four more years in high school, then he would be done with public schools forever.

Some of the questions that the teachers gave for their study guides didn't help much. If anything they were an even bigger headache. If he got too frustrated with one question, Aiden would take his frustration out by lighting a pile of dead branches on fire in the forest. True, he got lectured by Seamus for a misuse of his magic, but it was worth it to get his frustration out.

It had not been easy coming up with excuses to tell his parents about what he did during the weekends before finals. As the weeks progressed it was getting trickier. Aiden had to be careful with what he said to them; sometimes he could have sworn his father knew Aiden was lying.

At long last, the day for finals came. Aiden's stomach was tied into a knot. All the studying in the world could not make him feel better. He worried if he would even remember what he had studied.

On the morning of the exams, Aiden and Theresa waited at the bus stop together. Garrett and Seamus would be waiting on top of the school as they took their exams. As they waited for the bus, Aiden hands began to shake badly.

"Would you relax?" Theresa looked somewhat annoyed. "These exams are nothing but a joke, really."

"Easy for you to say," Aiden said. "You've got eons of wisdom, you can pass these exams wearing a blindfold."

"Don't give me that." Theresa pursed her lips. "I know you'll do just fine."

"That's what you think," Aiden grumbled. "I felt like I could have done so much more to prepare!"

Theresa rolled her eyes as she leaned against a wall of the bus stop.

"You need to not doubt yourself so much, Aiden," she said.

"What?"

"You doubt yourself, it's that simple." Theresa folded her arms. "It's one of the reasons why your training with Garrett has not gone as well as it should."

Aiden blinked as he turned to her. Was he doubting himself? What did she mean by that?

"When you doubt yourself, Aiden, it takes a toll on your abilities."

"But what does that have to do with my training?" he asked.

Theresa sighed.

"It doesn't matter what you're doing, confidence is always the same. It doesn't matter if it's training or studying: when you doubt yourself, your performance suffers. Your skills will falter. Be it with sword, magic, or knowledge. You must always remember, keep your confidence up. Never let it falter."

Aiden watched Theresa closely. In truth, he had always known she was incredibly smart. Whenever she put herself to a task, she never failed to complete it. For years Aiden thought it was simply intelligence, but now, now it made a lot more sense. She was not only smart, but wise.

It wasn't brainpower that allowed Theresa to succeed; it was her will, confidence, and being a member of an incredibly powerful race. All those years he watched her, now he knew: if she could do it, then he could have done it as well.

The bus slowly drove up to them. Before it stopped, a small smile crept to his face.

"Let's do this." he said.

Theresa's kind smile appeared once again.

Because it was finals day, the normal schedule was completely different. Luckily for him, his last exam would be history, his best subject. Unluckily, his middle exam would be math. But he couldn't doubt himself yet; he had to remember what Theresa told him.

Aiden's first round of exams did seem to go smoothly, with Science, English and PE all a bit easier than he feared. Math taxed his brain to its limits, but at last he made it through to the one-hour break.

"How can they expect most students to even last nearly five hours of exams without a break?" Aiden asked as he sat down with Theresa at their usual table.

"Honestly, Aiden, these exams are nothing," Theresa said.

"The exams dragons took were much longer. Sometimes they lasted for days."

"Days?" His face turned a bit gray. "What kind of exams last for *days*, Theresa?"

"Oh the usual. Fight exams, magic exams, survival exams, physical exams."

Aiden sat in flabbergasted silence.

"Those are the usual?"

"What did you expect?" Theresa asked, taking a sip of milk. "That we just flew around all day and burnt the fields?"

"Now you're sounding like Seamus." Aiden grinned ruefully.

"Oh, you know I'm kidding," Theresa said, giving him a smile. "But seriously, these exams are just child's play, really. Sometimes I wonder if humans have grown soft over the years."

Aiden didn't even want to know what kind of exams humans did in Theresa's time. He was having a hard enough time trying not to get nervous over tests with multiple answers.

"Screw you, Eric!" A loud voice cut out through the lunch hall.

Every student turned to see Liza Hollingsworth, racing out of the room in a huff. A triumphant looking Eric grinned as he watched the popular girl storm out. Once she slammed the door, heading out towards the soccer field. Everyone gave the local bully a dark disapproving glare before they resumed their lunches.

Theresa frowned before looking back over to Aiden.

"Wasn't that Liza Hollingsworth?"

"Yeah it was. And she looked like she was very pissed off by something Eric said to her. What do you think is eating her?" Aiden asked.

"My guess? Probably questioning her tastes in personal matters." Theresa said with a glare over to Eric's table.

Aiden turned to the table and watched in anger with her. Sitting there was Eric, a cruel smile on his face as looked as he leaned back in his chair. Like the smug jerk had just accomplished something great in his life. It made Aiden truthfully sick to his stomach.

"I should break his nose." Aiden mumbled.

"And what good would that do you?" Theresa asked. "You'd get suspended and all your finals would be nullified."

"Still, it would feel really good to do it," he sighed.

Then an idea came to him.

"Say, how long do we have until the last exam?" he asked.

"About half an hour," Theresa answered, wiping her mouth with a napkin. "Why?"

"I'm gonna go talk to Liza," he answered, "see if I can offer any help to make her feel better."

"Aiden…."

"Look, I know that I don't know her that well, but she shouldn't be alone, especially if she's upset."

Before Theresa could argue with him, Aiden walked quickly to the door. He had thirty minutes to find out what was making her so upset. That should be more than enough time to talk.

The moment he stepped outside, he saw Liza alone on the soccer field. She was bouncing a soccer ball on her foot. Aiden always found it to be a very neat talent. He couldn't even bounce a hacky sack.

Liza stopped bouncing the ball and pulled her leg back, waiting for the right moment. When her target landed on the ground, she delivered a swift and powerful kick into the net. Liza no doubt was impressive, when it came to soccer.

Then again, he could use small magic spells and was being trained in the art of swordsmanship. So he had his own merits.

He almost forgot why he came out to check on her. There wasn't any time to be impressed by her talents. Aiden sighed as he walked up to her, wondering what he would say.

"What do you want, Aiden?" she asked. This caught him off guard. He hadn't said anything to let her know that he was there.

"How did you know it was me?"

"I saw you watching me, just like everyone else was." Liza answered. "Shouldn't you be talking with Theresa? Or did you wanna mock me for something like that fatass just did? The entire school probably wants to by this point!"

"W-What?" He stumbled out. "I-I wasn't coming out here to mock you about anything, Liza. I was just concerned. I know Eric's an ass but you seemed to really take what he said to heart." He frowned. "Are you certain you're okay? I mean if you aren't I can-"

"I'm fine," Liza interrupted, obviously not wanting to talk. "You should go back and enjoy what time you have left before the final exam."

"We've got more than enough time before the bell rings," he argued. "Besides, if Ms. MacDonnell doesn't see you in class, she'll send out a search party. And you know that the finals go towards wither you graduate or not."

Liza gave a slight laugh. The two of them knew that their history teacher viewed them each as her own.

"I'm sure Ms. MacDonnell wouldn't do that, Aiden," she said. "She might be protective of her students, but there's no way she would alarm the entire school."

"You wanna bet?"

Aiden blinked as he saw Liza look down in sadness. Truthfully, he expected her laugh again. Whatever Eric had said must have really hurt her.

He reached out a hand to her shoulder. Any form of comfort that he could offer would be nice. But he had no experience comforting anybody other than Theresa. Liza was a completely different girl. How would she react?

"Liza, if you need to talk about what's upsetting you, just know that I'm here."

Liza turned back to him. Now was the moment of truth. Would she accept his offer, or would she reject it completely? Just as she was about to open her mouth, though, a low rumble caught their attention. Aiden and Liza looked around. Aiden's ears picked up where it was coming from: the ground.

Was it an earthquake?

"Did you hear that too?" Liza asked.

"Yeah, I did," Aiden said, glancing around once more. "And I don't like it."

The rumbling continued to grow louder and louder. Whatever it was, it was moving fast, and Aiden couldn't figure out where it was heading. If it was an earthquake, the entire school would have to be evacuated. It didn't sound right.

"W-What's going on?" Liza began to panic.

"I don't know…but the important thing is that we have to…."

Aiden didn't have a chance to finish. The earth behind them erupted, tearing the ground in half. Liza let out an uncharacteristic yelp. Aiden turned quickly.

He hoped his eyes were tricking him.

There, standing before him and Liza was a creature the size of a minivan. It had the body and face of a lion with large, scaly wings. Its tail was a massive scorpion's tail; its eyes were the darkest green Aiden had ever seen. There was one name for this monster.

A manticore.

Liza let out a scream of terror. Aiden's eyes widened in fear and awe. A part of him was fascinated by the creature, how it moved and how strong it was; The other part, if it had a voice, would be screaming at him, 'WHAT ARE YOU DOING? GET OUT OF THE WAY!'

It took a roar in the face from the manticore to snap him out of his trance. The beast's breath smelled like ten garbage cans piled together in one room. Aiden had to fight back a gagging reflex in his throat.

"What is that thing?!?" Liza cried out, hiding behind him.

"A-A manticore!" Aiden stammered.

"A what?!"

"It's a creature from stories and such!" he explained.

She gave him a very confused look. Aiden felt like slapping himself. He had forgotten that Liza was not one to follow up on creatures, magic, or anything fantasy like. Not that he expected her to, of course. If she did, she wouldn't be one of the most popular girls in school.

"Look, just know that it wants to hurt us, all right?!" He shouted, grabbing Warfang from his pocket. "You stay behind me and I'll deal with this.

"W-What are you doing?!" she cried. "That thing will eat you!"

"Don't worry about me," he said, pointing the figurine at the manticore. "You just stand behind me, all right?"

Liza didn't get to argue any further as the manticore's roar muted her voice. Aiden put both hands around the figurine. This would be his first battle without the help of the others. Now if only he had an excuse to explain to Liza what was happening.

"*Ladbe.*"

The golden silver blade emerged from the figurine in all its glory. The manticore hissed at the bright light reflecting off the sword. Liza stood dumbfounded. Aiden didn't blame her; he was just like her before spring break.

His real focus though was the manticore. He had to be careful in this fight. If what the books said were true, this beast had a powerful venom. Aiden positioned himself for combat.

"Come on, ugly," he said. "Show me what you got!"

The manticore growled low as it raised its left claw. Remembering his training, Aiden rolled to avoid the swipe from the beast. Quickly getting back to his feet, Aiden slashed the manticore's front leg. His sword cut easily through the monster's skin, like a knife through butter.

Once more, the beast roared. Its lime green eyes seemed to glow with a dark force.

The manticore's tail suddenly arced up, revealing the large

stinger. Aiden swallowed hard at the sight of it; he had to avoid that stinger at all cost.

With a new burst of speed, the manticore's stinger struck at him. Aiden quickly rolled out of the way once again. Taking his chance to attack, he swung his sword once more. The manticore, however, was more than ready for his attack. The beast let loose another roar and swung its claw.

The sharp end of Aiden's sword sliced against the rough skin of the manticore's paw. He expected the manticore to roar in pain from his slash, but the beast didn't stop. Bracing as best as he could, Aiden took a direct swat from the monster. Aiden felt himself fly into the soccer net behind them, the force of the hit knocking his sword from his hand.

"Aiden!" Liza cried out, running to him.

"D-Dammit!" Aiden cursed, trying to find the hilt of his sword once again. "I let my guard down."

Finding Warfang, Aiden forced himself to stand. Liza bent down to help him and he could tell by the trembling of her hands how terrified she was. She had every right to be. A manticore was twice as scary than an ogre.

"Liza, whatever happens, stay behind me." Aiden managed to gasp out.

"You're hurt, Aiden!" she responded. "You can't fight that thing!"

"If I don't fight it, we'll both end up dead!" he snapped, turning his attention on the glancing beast. "Now stay behind me!"

Liza bit her lip as the giant creature approached them. The manticore's jaws began to drool as it slowly stepped forward, knowing that it had to be careful of Aiden's sword. Still, it had the advantage.

Both Aiden and Liza were cornered into the soccer net. There was nowhere to run and the beast knew it.

Aiden's grip on Warfang was damp with sweat. Was this really how it would end? He and Liza as the next meal for a stupid monster? What was all that training worth if he couldn't stop one beast?

The manticore crouched, then pounced towards them. Liza clenched her eyes tightly as Aiden steadied himself. If he was going down, he would go down fighting.

Suddenly, the creature came to a halt in mid air. It let out a confused cry as it fell onto its belly.

Aiden stared in confusion. He had done nothing. Why did the beast fall?

It was then that he saw that somebody standing behind the fallen manticore. A small smile crept to Aiden's face.

It was Garrett.

Garrett was easily gripping the manticore's tail with just one hand, a bored expression on his face. The weight of the tail must have been massive. Yet Garrett was acting like it was nothing at all.

"Are you that weak, whelp, that you can't even defeat a manticore?"

Aiden didn't get a chance to answer. With one yank of his arm, Garrett ripped off the tail of the manticore completely. The beast roared in pain as its tail was pulled away. Black blood spilled from the severed tail which Garret promptly tossed aside, when it landed onto the ground it soon disintegrated into nothing.

"Yo!" Seamus' voice came from the side. "Send it over here, Garrett!"

Garret rolled his eyes as he grabbed the hind legs of the manticore. Without any effort, the large warrior threw the massive beast to Seamus.

Seamus smiled as he spun his staff. It took Aiden a few seconds to realize what he was doing. A small wind vortex was forming in front of Seamus. The faster he spun his staff, the stronger the vortex became. It was a brilliant strategy.

The manticore was helpless as it was sucked into the vortex. It spun around as it flew up higher and higher into the sky. Just as the vortex died down, Aiden saw a new being was awaiting right above the monster with two large white wings.

Theresa.

With both Snow and Fire in her hands, the leader of the three dragons swung her swords. Her slashes were so fast that Aiden couldn't see them. After possibly twenty slashes, Theresa landed on the ground safely.

The moment her foot touched down, the manticore's body began to fall apart. Hundreds of manticore pieces disintegrated into nothing as the once-proud monster let out a dying roar. The threat had been eliminated.

As the three dragon warriors gathered together, Aiden turned back to Liza.

Just as he expected, she was completely stunned by what she had just seen.

A cheesy smile came to Aiden's face.

"Uh, Liza," he started out, but Theresa placed a hand over his mouth.

"Liza," she said. "Your mind did not trick you."

"W-What are you three?!" Liza asked in shock.

Theresa glanced to Seamus and Garrett. With a heavy sigh, she turned her attention back to Liza.

"We're dragons."

Just like Aiden before her, Liza promptly fainted.

CHAPTER 18 - KEEPING A SECRET

*I*t took five minutes to get Liza to wake up. It took ten to convince her that she was not dreaming. It took even longer to calm her down. Aiden didn't blame her. It was a lot to take in.

Theresa was the one who did the most talking. Liza seemed to listen to her much more than she did to Aiden, Seamus, or Garrett. Aiden would have made things much more confusing; Seamus would have shamelessly hit on her. And the strong voice of Garrett probably would have terrified her even more.

Half of the half hour break was gone when Liza finally began to piece things together. Aiden could tell that she was slowly accepting the information.

"So...let me get this straight," she finally said, "there was an era of time when all the creatures in fairy tales, existed in one world?"

"Yes," Theresa confirmed.

"And around this time, both men and women of all species were allowed to fight and command at the same time as well?"

"Pretty much, yes," Seamus said, spinning his staff around.

A slow grin came to Liza's face.

"So women were equals to their male counterparts then hmm?"

Aiden, Seamus, and Garrett's faces made completely shocked expressions. Theresa burst out laughing at Liza's question.

"Hey!" Seamus said. "That's kind of unfair to say!"

"Well, seeing as how Theresa is your leader and all," Liza said, "I figured that women would have to fight to be viewed as equals."

"In a manner of speaking, yes," Garrett said. "But Theresa is our leader because of her skills and wisdom. Not because of her gender."

"Indeed," Theresa said, drying her eyes after laughing. "But back to my point, Liza, you must understand the reason why we have told you this."

Liza looked confused. Aiden was the next to speak up.

"It's a very big secret. The rest of the world, save for a few beings, don't know about the existence of dragons, mages, demons, and everything else from fantasy tales. No one can ever know."

"But...why?" Liza asked. A question that Aiden mentally slapped himself for not asking before. He always had these questions in his head, but whenever he held Warfang they just seemed to go away. "If you think about it, this is ground breaking! Think of what we could learn from the ages of the past, Aiden. It could be the greatest story in history!"

"It cannot be allowed," Garrett said, his voice booming. "I've seen what human kind has done with knowledge when they were given it or discovered it."

"Garrett, not all humans are ignorant," Theresa said. "You must remember this."

"You were not there when the Americans discovered their most deadly weapon of all time, sister. Their discovery of nuclear power has put the world on edge."

"That's not a fair argument," Seamus said. "Americans aren't the only ones who knew about nuclear power."

"No, but because they used it, the rest of the world has now been addicted to its destructive power."

"Look, we can discuss this subject later," Theresa quickly interrupted, stopping any chance that things could get out of hand. She turned back to Liza, who was still in both awe and shock.

"I know that this must be hard for you to keep to yourself, but you cannot tell anyone about us. If the world was to learn that dragons still existed, the consequences could be drastic."

"But think of what the world could learn!" Liza argued.

"We have," Garrett growled.

"You can't change their minds, Liza," Aiden said. "The one thing you'll learn being around dragons is that when they set their mind on something, they'll be very persistent about it."

Liza was quiet for a moment before asking another question.

"Why can't humans learn about their true ancient past?"

Aiden himself was also wondering why the rest of humanity couldn't learn about their past. He knew that he had to keep the secret quiet and no one could ever learn it. Theresa however never really gave an exact reason as to why it was forbidden to mention it.

As if on cue, Theresa sighed.

"Back in the old days, Liza, humanity shared one view together. There was no fighting amongst them about who was right or who was wrong; they were peaceful to one another. Supportive. They never once blamed one of their own of wrong actions nor did they judge someone by their appearance or preferences."

Aiden noticed that Theresa's voice began to sound a lot older. Whenever Theresa spoke like this it was hard for him to adjust to how wise she really was. He had to remember that she was much older than her human appearance.

"But after those days ended, when the Kingdoms fell and were nearly wiped out, humanity began to crumble. Wars began to break out among them. Slavery, corrupted governments, murders, crime, they erupted afterwards. Then when Rome fell, humanity lost even more knowledge and entered the Dark Ages. Soon, when different religious beliefs sprouted, more wars erupted. And now, humanity is even more divided than it was before."

Theresa's eyes locked with Liza's.

"What do you think would happen if they learned about their true past?"

Liza didn't have to answer the question. The answer was in plain sight. There one thing that could have divided humanity, even more than it already was, if they learned the truth. They would be searching for everything related to their ancient past. They would begin looking for ways to make their nations stronger, and in turn threatening to destroy one another if they got in the way of each other. Innocents would have been killed in the battle for control. The planet would erupt into one thing completely.

Full scale war.

For a few moments the air was filled with tension.

"Do you understand why you can't tell anyone?" Theresa asked.

Liza looked down at her feet in silence. Aiden knew that she was coming to accept how sensitive the information was. He understood why it was such a heavy burden. Something about the excitement of it all had never even made him question it - it just felt right to him.

What made it even heavier was the fact that Theresa, Seamus, and Garrett's very existence was in danger of being exposed. The pressure was intense!

Time seemed to slow down as they awaited her answer. Liza brought her head back up.

"I understand," she said. "I'll keep the secret."

"Swear it," Garrett ordered. "Swear that you will not tell anyone."

"Garrett...," Seamus started to say, but the large warrior spoke out again.

"Swear it!"

"I swear!" Liza said, her voice nearly cracking in fear at Garrett's shout.

Theresa sighed as she gave her fellow warrior a glare. Garrett rolled his eyes as he turned around, opening his wings and flying away from the group. Seamus stayed behind with them. He shrugged his shoulders silently before putting his hands behind his head.

"Don't mind Garret, he's not always in a foul mood like this."

"It certainly seems like he always is...," Liza mumbled.

Theresa chuckled a bit. Aiden and Seamus couldn't help but laugh lightly as well. Liza joined in with them a few seconds later. Despite the high tension a few moments ago, it was good to see that the four of them could laugh at how Garrett always seemed to be in a bad mood.

The school bell rang loudly, signaling the end of the lunch break. Just before they headed back, Theresa turned to Liza once more.

"Listen, if you keep this secret, you have to learn how to properly defend yourself," she said. "Sometime tomorrow tell your parents that you're going to hang out with some friends. Seamus will come pick you up."

"Wait, what?" Seamus asked, looking confused. "Why does she have to learn how to defend herself?"

"You know as well as I do, Seamus, that there are types of magic that can extract information from the mind," Theresa answered. "And the one thing we don't want is our secret being revealed."

"But I can't fight!" Liza said. "I know nothing about how to fight!"

"Neither did the kiddo here." Seamus laughed. "But after a few months, he's gotten the hang of it. Though his magic is still a bit rusty."

Aiden shot him a look, but Seamus opened his wings. After seeing Garrett take off with his own wings Liza didn't react badly to seeing Seamus' wings. He gave a slight nod to Theresa before turning his attention back to Liza.

"Don't worry. I'll pick you up for training in the morning. *Catch* you tomorrow, Liz!"

With a quick wink, and a flap of his wings, he took off into the air. Theresa sighed as Seamus flew off. Without saying a word she grabbed Aiden's wrist.

"Come on," she said. "We need to get to class."

Aiden didn't have time to argue as she dragged him.

"Hey, wait up!" Liza called after them, jogging to keep up.

Aiden was more than happy to stop and wait for his friend.

CHAPTER 19 - RAVEN'S MASTER

The final exam felt like it was going to take forever to Aiden. Not that the exam was hard. He could easily ace it in his sleep. But summer just a half an hour away....

It was no surprise to him that he was the first to finish the history exam. A couple of his fellow students gave him some annoyed glares at his accomplishment, save for Theresa and Liza.

The rest of Aiden's time in class was spent recounting all the events of the past few months. All of it started thanks to a simple gift from his father. Since then, he'd experienced what most people could only dream of.

One thing kept coming back to him: Raven. Out of all the confrontations that he had faced in the past few months, the one with Raven was the toughest and most dangerous. Even with both Theresa and Seamus' help, they had barely managed to win the fight.

His arm began to tense up in pain, almost as if it was remembering the slash from the encounter. His first battle wound. The more he thought about it, the more he began to realize why the battle was such memorable thing. It made you feel alive and completely in the moment, in a way nothing else ever had.

The demons he had fought were not wild and disorganized like the goblins. They thought ahead, planned out attacks, knew how to counter attacks, and could calculate their opponent's next moves. He wouldn't have been surprised if the demon that slashed his arm planned on him lowering his guard to get a good swipe at him.

The very thought that Raven and his demons could be planning their next attack bugged him. It was obvious that Raven was incredibly skilled. How skilled, he did not know. But there was no doubt that Raven was more skilled than Aiden.

There was a silver lining, though. He remembered how Raven talked about how he had trouble facing off with Garrett in both of his forms. Now that the three dragons were a team once more, there was a chance that they could take on Raven and his demons without much trouble.

Of course, there was the question of whether Garrett would even help if they came across him.

There was no doubt, he was the strongest of the four by far. But from what he's seen, Garrett would only help unless he was ordered to or was forced to step in. Aiden tried to push the issue out of his mind. He couldn't believe that it was so close to summer and he was focusing on things that he didn't want to concentrate on. He would have to force himself to get through the final moments of the exams. After all graduation was on the line, and summer was the time for his mind to be free and not worry about the burdens of the world.

The minutes began to feel like hours as the test took its toll on many of the students. Aiden nearly fell asleep a couple of times as he waited for the day to come to a close. The only thing that kept him awake was the fact that Theresa was sitting behind him. Whenever he began to drift off, she would jab her knee into his back to wake him up.

"Stay awake!" she hissed behind him. "If you fall asleep now you will sleep through the bell!"

"I will not!" Aiden whispered back, slightly annoyed that she would dare accuse him of such a thing.

A soft 'thud' came from the roof above them. Most of the students looked up at the ceiling, but after a few minutes, they shrugged it off. For all they knew, it was just some staff members fixing the roof.

Aiden glanced back to Theresa to see if she was bothered. She just shook her head in annoyance. It wasn't a threat. If anything, the thud came from either Seamus or Garrett landing on top of the building. Aiden sighed as he turned and let his mind wander again.

If it was Seamus, he was doing one of two things: listening into the classroom to hear any conversations, or spying on an attractive woman.

As for Garrett, Aiden could only picture him keeping an eye out for trouble.

His eyes glanced towards the clock. The time was one forty five. Summer was taking its sweet time arriving. It wasn't just the summer he was waiting anxiously for. His birthday was coming up this week. He wanted nothing more than to get out so he could not only relax, but enjoy his birthday with family and friends. The clock turned to the next minute. One forty six. It felt like it was an insanity test for him.

Groaning in annoyance, Aiden laid his head down on his desk. As he expected, Theresa jammed her knee into his back. As if it wasn't annoying enough that she wouldn't let him sleep away the last few minutes of class while the rest of their classmates finished the exam.

Then, a prickling sensation began to run down his neck. Aiden's muscles tensed up briefly. He knew this feeling. It was his magical sense beginning to pick up. He wasn't exactly good with it, like Seamus, but he was beginning to sense the basic magical traces.

The prickling intensified. During training sessions, Seamus

would purposely increase the magical energies around him to help Aiden get used to strong magical pressures in case they ever came across a powerful mage. But there weren't any other mages around the school. Seamus was the only one who could have created such a pressure.

If this was a prank from Seamus, it wasn't a funny one. The prickling sensation began to grow even stronger. It got so strong that there was painful ringing in his ear. Aiden's face scrunched up in pain. He couldn't do anything in the middle of class without the other students noticing him standing up.

Just as it seemed that the pain was about to make him scream out, a new feeling washed over him. Aiden blinked in confusion as the sensation began to overcome the pain. It was a soothing touch, one that healed the prickling pain. He glanced over his shoulder. Theresa had two fingers placed onto his back. A small smile came to his face. She had cast a small healing spell to stop the pain.

"You okay?" she asked in a whisper. "I noticed you were beginning to flinch in pain."

"Yeah, I'm fine now," he whispered back. "Thanks, I thought I was gonna run out screaming."

By this point, there was only one person who was still taking the exam. Most of the students were having side conversations with one another now. Aiden turned to face Theresa.

"Did you sense it too?" he asked.

She gave a nod.

"I did. And I don't like it."

"Do you think it was Seamus?"

"No. Seamus might be a fool at times, but he would never put so much magical pressure that it would physically hurt a being who is sensitive to magic."

Aiden pursed his lips in annoyance.

"You know what I meant." Theresa said, rolling her eyes.

"That depends. Do you mean a being who is just learning how

to sense magical pressure or do you mean a person who is extremely sensitive to magic?"

"Aiden!" she spat. "Don't try to argue with me about this!"

A confident smile grew to his face. It wasn't every day that he was able to annoy Theresa like this.

"Getting back to my point, I don't like this at all," Theresa frowned. "Somebody is waiting for us...."

"You don't think that it's Raven, do you?"

"If it was, I would be able to tell." She frowned. "But this isn't his pressure. It's stronger...deadlier."

The color in Aiden's face faded away.

Raven was the strongest enemy they had faced. His magic and control over his demons were incredible. How could he even think to face somebody even stronger so soon?

It didn't help that even Theresa looked upset about this as well. There was no doubt that she had faced strong enemies before. The tone of her voice made the matter even tenser. Aiden knew whenever Theresa got serious, the threat had to be taken seriously.

He glanced up to the clock on the wall. Watching the hands of the clock slowly tick down. They were so close yet so far from being free. Aiden began to tap his right foot in frustration as he waited patiently.

At long last, the bell rang. Summer vacation was finally here! Aiden was so ecstatic he nearly jumped out of his chair as he got up to to leave the prison that is school. The rest of the class stood up as well, grabbing their backpacks. They said their good byes to Ms. MacDonnell and headed towards the buses.

Aiden and Theresa nearly took a step onto their bus when they heard a voice call out from behind them.

"Wait!"

Both of them turned to see Liza, who looked like she'd run several hundred yards to reach them.

"Tomorrow, you said that this Seamus guy was going to pick me up?" she asked in a whisper.

Theresa glanced around her quickly before answering.

"Yes, but remember, you must keep it to yourself."

She glanced over Liza's shoulder to the roof of the school. Both Seamus and Garrett were waiting patiently. Garrett scoffed slightly before he turned away. Seamus, however, gave a thumbs-up before he walked out of view. Aiden could only presume that he was about to transform into his dragon form.

"Liza, I want you to know how thankful I am for you understanding," Theresa continued. "It means so much to us."

"You're welcome, Theresa. It'll be difficult, but I'll keep quiet about this for as long as I can."

Before either she or Aiden could say another world, Liza ran towards her bus. Both of them gave a short sigh of annoyance as they finally took their seats on their bus. Aiden caught a glance at what the local school bully was doing.

Eric was already at the back of the bus, rolling up some paper balls. Aiden groaned as he turned away from him, knowing what Eric was going to do when he was ready.

"Can't I just set his head on fire just once?" he whispered.

"Oh, don't worry so much," Theresa said in a calm voice. "I already have something in mind for him."

Aiden blinked in confusion. Normally Theresa would be preaching about ignoring everything that Eric did. She was usually the first one to remind everyone not to resort to violence or reacting to any unnecessary acts. Now he was curious about what she was up to.

Behind them, Eric prepared his spit wads and aimed carefully at Aiden's head. A sly smile grew on his face as he fired the spit wad from his straw. Aiden fully expected the spit wad to slam into the back of his head at full force. That's when Theresa made her move.

With almost lighting-like reflexes, Theresa brought her hand to Aiden's head and blocked the spit ward. But the action did not stop there; instead, Theresa turned her hand over, rolling the spit wad onto the palm of her hand easily. Not even looking back to aim, she flung the spit wad at Eric.

The bully had no time to recover as his own spit wad slammed back on his forehead. Eric let out a yelp as his head reared back. Aiden's mouth dropped in amazement. Theresa didn't even look back as a knowing smile grew on her face.

"Let that be a lesson to you, Eric," she said. "Keep spitting those things at us, and I'll fling them right back at you!"

Eric rubbed his forehead, grumbling something under his breath. Aiden tried hard to stifle a laugh, but it was almost irresistible to not to. Seeing the bully being hit by his own spit wad was just too priceless. Theresa turned back to him, giggling a bit herself.

"I told you I had something in mind for him."

The two laughed the entire way back home. The troubles of the dangerous world he would eventually become part of could wait for another day. For now, it was nice that the two of them got to share a laugh at a bully's own folly.

* * * * *

THE NEXT DAY was the official first day of summer vacation. Graduation day would be held on the first Saturday, which was only a few days away for Aiden and Theresa. Both of them had passed, in Theresa's case it was with flying colors. Aiden had managed to pass with varrying Bs and As in his exams. A huge relief off his shoulders at the joy he felt in his chest learning those grades.

To make it even more sweet for him, Aiden's birthday was only a few days away. That made the week even better.

Before he could meet up with Theresa and the others though, he had to do his chores around the house. They ranged from cleaning the kitchen, vacuuming the floors, and dusting off the multiple shelves where his mother had placed her favorite items. He used to get annoyed with doing these chores daily, mostly due to his teenaged mind thinking that adults were more than capable of doing simple house hold chores, but now he didn't complain. Compared to training with dragons and fighting off creatures that wanted to kill him? He was more than glad to do them.

"You've been hanging out with your friends quite a lot lately, Aiden," Helena said.

"That's not a bad thing, is it?" Aiden asked from across the hall, placing Warfang within his pocket so his mother wouldn't notice.

"Oh, of course it isn't." She smiled. "I'm just really glad that you're becoming more open and outgoing. You usually just stay home and stay in your room, surfing the Internet or reading one of your books."

Aiden quirked an eyebrow at his mother's statement. She was obviously trying to prove a point to him about something. Unlike his father, though, she encouraged him to have a free mind and enjoy the things that made him happy.

"I guess the point I'm trying to make here is that your recent change has...caught me off guard." Helena ruffled his hair. "I'm so used to having you at the house that it feels really empty whenever you're not home."

Now he felt bad. He had been spending so much time training with Theresa and the others that he had forgotten that his mother was usually home alone. His father spent long days working, so until he came home, Aiden was the only company she had. Helena noticed his frown at his realization. A soft smile came across her face.

"Don't worry, Aiden. I'm by no means against you being out

of the house at all. It warms my heart to see you growing up and doing new things instead of your usual routine," she said.

"I know, but aren't you lonely, Mom?"

"Aiden Russell," she said firmly. "Do not let your mother's feelings or wishes get in the way of what you want to do. You're a young man. One of these days you won't be living with me or your father anymore. You'll be making your own choices about how you want to live your life. I'll always be your mother, but I cannot stop you from growing up."

Aiden began to feel a bit better after she finished. His mother was so understanding. It made his heart feel so relieved when she said that she had no trouble with him being out of the house.

"Well, how come I have to keep doing house hold chores?" he asked sarcastically. His mother chuckled before nudging him.

"Watch it buster, there's a difference between making your choices and doing what your mother tells you."

Helena ruffled his hair again before gently pushing him towards the door.

"Now get on out of here, I believe somebody's waiting for you."

"Heh, yeah. I'll see you later, Mom."

Aiden jogged out to meet up with Theresa, who was already in front of his house. The two exchanged quick chitchat before heading to the forest. They speculated how long it would take Seamus to start hitting on Liza. Out of the two, Theresa seemed less sure. Aiden would have asked why, but after getting to know the second dragon over the months, he thought he probably knew.

As they arrived, Garrett was already waiting for them. Multiple trees that used to cover one part of the forest had been sliced down, or burnt, by him. Aiden was flabbergasted at what he saw.

"W-Why the hell did you do this?" he asked.

Garrett scoffed as a puff of smock escaped his nostrils.

"Whelping, if you truly have to ask why, then you've learned nothing."

Theresa frowned at his statement.

"If you were bored, Garrett, why didn't you go hunting?"

"Hunt what, Theresa? There's no game in this forest. Those common deer don't count since there is hardly any damn meat on them."

"Did you even bother looking for the Deer?" Theresa pointed out, making it clear by the sound of her voice that she was talking about something completely different from a regular deer.

Before Garrett could answer her question, a sudden 'yelp' came from above. The trio glanced up and saw the source of the yelp: Liza was riding on Seamus' back, holding on for dear life as he descended towards the ground. The green dragon rolled his eyes as he landed softly, lowering his neck so she could climb off. Liza's face lacked any color as she stepped off his neck. Theresa glared at Seamus.

"Seamus, did you go too fast?" she asked.

"Of course not!" Seamus said, quick to defend himself. "I was going at average speed! She's just not use to flying high yet."

"She's as pale as a ghost!" Theresa growled, looking very disappointed.

"I-It's all right, Theresa," Liza said, stopping the argument before it could escalate. "I'm just not...use to being up so high in the sky." The white dragoness didn't back down so easily though.

"Liza, did he tell you to say that?"

"No, it's fine really," Liza said, trying to keep a confident smile. "I'll get over it. I just need a little time."

Theresa glanced over her one last time before turning to Seamus. The two exchanged a wordless stare with one another before the latter turned back into his human form. Sighing in defeat, Theresa held out her hand and said a word in draconic that Aiden couldn't translate.

A small bright light began to take shape over her palm. The light faded slightly, revealing a new weapon: a dagger. The dagger itself was about fourteen inches long and slightly curved. The blade was a shade of forest green that shined brightly in the sunlight. The dagger's guard took form of a dragon's wing, the hilt a dark brown color under it. Its pommel was in the shape of a European dragon, which had a raw emerald in its mouth.

"This is your new weapon, Liza," Theresa said, handing her the dagger. "Its name is Gitanel, the draconic word for earth."

Liza stared in marvel at her new weapon. She observed the beautiful colors that decorated it. Aiden was also surprised by the weapon, admiring its shape.

"It's so light," Liza said in awed. "But it's much larger than any of the daggers I've seen."

"That's because you humans think of small blades that can break easily as the best form for daggers. Daggers aren't meant for light-weight jobs alone. They're also meant for cutting into places a regular blade could not," Seamus explained. "The blade itself might look thin, but don't let appearances fool you. Its metal is as strong as any draconic steel."

Liza smiled as she continued to examine her new weapon. But what caught her attention though was the emerald in the dragon pommel.

"What's this emerald for?" she asked. "Decoration?"

"For a regular human blade? Yes." Theresa said. "But when it comes to dragon blades, gems like an emerald serve as a connection to one of the elements. Fire is red, water is blue, green is earth, yellow is lightning, white is light, and black is darkness."

Liza took a firm grip on the hilt of Gitanel, getting a feel for how she wanted to hold the dagger. She glanced up to Theresa for approval. Theresa smiled and gave a slight nod.

"You just need to begin working on your posture with a weapon, then we'll start your training."

"That shouldn't be too hard." Liza smiled. "Remember, I play sports. Posture is key for them."

"There's a difference between sports and combat," Garrett growled, clearly not amused.

"Leave it be, Garrett," Theresa ordered. "Now, the first order of business is…."

A prickling sensation began running down Aiden's spine once again,. This time, though, he wasn't alone. Theresa, Seamus, and Garret snapped their heads to the right, growling low. Liza stared in confusion at their sudden change.

"What's going on?" she asked.

"Something's coming towards us," Aiden said, doing his best to suppress the prickling on his spine. "Something with extremely strong magic powers."

Liza's face turned gray. The timing could not have been worse. She had barely begun training. Aiden worried for her. He had gotten off lucky when facing enemies, but those didn't have the strength they were sensing now.

The pressure of magic drew closer to the group. As it came closer, Aiden saw that Theresa, Seamus, and Garrett already had their wings open and were armed. Following their example, he quickly brought out Warfang's figurine from his pocket and summoned his own blade. He glanced back to Liza, who looked terrified.

"Whatever happens, stay behind us," he told her. "If anything, we could serve as a distraction in case he tries to attack you."

Liza gave a slight nod as she held Gitanel closely to her. Hopefully there wouldn't be a big conflict; Aiden did not want Liza to be hurt on her first day. If she did, a part of him would forever feel guilty for it.

"Up ahead!" Seamus shouted, spinning his staff around. Theresa slammed the pommels of her two swords together to form Snowfyre. Her eyes glanced back to all of them.

"Stay on your guard," she ordered.

The prickling sensation ran again down Aiden's spine. This time there was no mistaking it; it was the same powerful magic from yesterday. His grip on Warfang's hilt began to feel a little moist as the new being slowly approached them. It must be a mage.

The mage looked to be a middle-aged man, but his choice of wardrobe was not the typical mage wear Aiden often read about. No, instead he wore a pair of black pants, a dark grey t-shirt, and a black leather jacket. His hair, along with his very finely kept goatee, was a darker brown than Aiden's chocolate color.

The mage's most peculiar features, though, were two large scars across his mouth. One cut straight down the center of his lip; the other was a diagonal slash that went from his right cheek to the bottom of his chin. The scars were clear to see, no matter how hard his goatee tried to hide them. He stopped a few yards away from the group. A cold, coy smile grew across his lips.

Deep down, Aiden had a strong gut feeling that this man was responsible for everything that had been happening to him since he had gained Warfang. The orge, the hornets, the goblins, and even Raven. They all mentioned a 'master' of sorts

"So you are the ones my student told me about," he said in a very thick, but clear, Russian accent. "I must admit, I did not believe my student when he told me that the last of your kind was together again. But I am pleasantly surprised."

It felt like forever before any of them spoke. Garrett was the first to break the silence.

"Your…student?"

"I believe that is what I said, no?" The mage crossed his arms over his chest. "Perhaps you might know his name. He is called Raven."

Aiden cursed. Raven! He knew that their first true enemy would somehow appear again one day. But this was not what he expected. Facing off with Raven's master? Now Aiden was really beginning to get nervous.

"We're familiar with the name," Theresa growled. An unchar-acteristic anger flowed through her tone. The mage's cold smile remained.

"Then allow me to introduce myself to you all." He bowed gentlemanly like. "I am Dimitri Cutter, head of the Demonic Magic studies, Master of one hundred demons that answer only to my call. As you probably could tell, I am the one who has been...'testing' you for some time. The orgre that you killed, the hornets, the goblins? All of them were my minions. I truly must thank you for taking care of them by the way. I would have killed them myself with how inept they were."

"Demonic Magic," Garrett snarled. "Your kind of magic is a pure disgrace to the mages of the past."

Dimitri chuckled as he stared back at them. Even though he wasn't showing it, it didn't take a genius to realize how powerful he really was.

"Some might say that," he said, twitching his fingers as he looked at his palm. "But who's to say that the magic I use is the only guilty kind? After all, even the magic used by 'good' mages can be as dangerous."

Dimitri glanced over at Aiden, a cold smile grew across his lips.

"And it seems that his demons left a mark on one of your young wards, dragons."

Aiden's mind relived Zantul's cut. His right arm began to tense, and a familiar feeling ran through it: pain. Aiden dropped to his knees as he grabbed his arm. It was if Zantul's claw were cutting into him once again. He turned back to the powerful mage. There was an unnatural glow around Dimitri's eyes.

Something about Dimitri's stare was causing the pain in Aiden's arm. He felt it would never end. But as his mind nearly went numb from the pain, one part of Theresa's dual ended blade blocked his eyes from the mage's deathly stare.

"Using your magic to cause mental pain on a budding

warrior," she growled, glaring daggers at Dimitri. "Leave him alone, or I'll burn you alive myself."

Dimitri turned his gaze to her now. Aiden watched in silence as Theresa stared right back at him. Whatever he was doing to his arm when he stared at him obviously was not working on her. The mage stroked his goatee slowly.

"You're quick to defend him, Dragoness. That is most peculiar for one of your kind."

"And why is that peculiar to you?" Seamus asked, spinning his staff behind his back, a clear signal that he expected a fight. Dimitri smiled.

"Considering all the evil my kind has done over the years, I figured none of you would be tolerant of humans." His eyes glanced to Garrett. "Well, at least that's true for one of you. Tell me, brown dragon, why do you help train humans when you yourself have great disdain for them?"

Garrett's throat let out a low snarl. He would have jumped at Dimitri and torn him apart, but a glance from Theresa stopped him. The last thing they wanted was a fight with a master mage. Reluctantly Garrett turned back to Dimitri.

"I do not believe in humans, demonic mage," he said in a forced tone. "But the one thing I am is loyal to my leader. And even though I do not approve of this whelp wielding the Great King's blade, I will not question her judgment."

"So you are loyal to your *rexkin's* words?"

"Without a doubt."

Dimitri's lips formed into a smug smile, turning his attention to Liza now. Aiden quickly stood back up, stepping in front of her protectively. It was one thing for Dimitri to use his magic on him, but he would not allow it to happen to someone who just started to learn of the old world and its ways. Dimitri quirked an eyebrow. It looked like he was intrigued by Aiden's action.

"You are standing up to me again just to protect her, are you?" he asked.

"Damn right I am," Aiden answered, pointing the tip of Warfang at him. "I don't care how powerful you are or how many demons you control, you try to use magic on her and I'll kill you!"

Dimitri's eyes narrowed at his threat. Aiden felt both incredibly cool and incredibly stupid. He had just threatened someone who was obviously stronger than he was. He was either going to get really lucky and not be blasted by a spell, or Dimitri would retaliate. He preferred the former.

But as he learned over the last few months, he had no such luck.

Dimitri held his hand towards Aiden. From its palm a black lighting bolt fired straight towards him. Remembering his training, Aiden quickly pulled Liza down with him, with some difficulty, to avoid the spell. The lighting bolt flew over their heads, slamming into the ground behind them. It had just barely missed his hair; any closer and he would have been on fire.

The time for talking was now over. Taking the chance to counter attack Seamus swung his staff. A gust of wind flew towards Dimitri, who put up a blue shimmering bubble shield around himself to avoid being sucked into the gust. Seamus just scoffed as he pointed his staff towards Dimitri. From the tip, several fireballs flew out in full force. Their impact on the shield fared much better than the gust, managing to crack it.

It still wasn't enough to break the shield, however. Garrett growled as he dashed towards Dimitri, his huge axe in hand, and began a ferocious series of attacks. It was hard to see if Dimitri was even straining from Garrett's strength.

Dimitri snapped his fingers casually. The ground began to rumble before splitting open, revealing a large demonic-looking worm. The worm roared as its head and dove towards Garrett.

Without blinking an eye, Garrett held his axe out to the side. When it looked like he was about to be swallowed, the large warrior swung his axe in a slashing arc. The demonic worm gurgled briefly before the lower half of its jaw fell off. Writhing in pain, the large demon fell onto its side, turning into dirt as it died Clearly it was not like Raven's demons that could grow back limbs if they were given a mortal blow.

Dimitri's eyes flashed briefly. An unseen force from behind stirred up the wind. Dimitri pointed at the strongest of the dragons with a confident smile. Suddenly the wind slammed into Garrett. The collision was so strong Garrett had no choice but to slam the hilt of his weapon into the ground. It was just enough to keep him from flying away, but he slowly was pushed away from Dimitri.

Aiden glanced back to Theresa. A small snarl grew on her lips as she spun her Snowfyre. At first he thought she was going to strike out at him in a rage. But he saw that in her eyes, she was waiting. Unlike Seamus and Garrett, she was planning her attack strategy.

"Seamus, Garrett, Aiden," she said, "regroup around me."

Without questioning her, the three of them did as she ordered.

"He's good," Seamus said, glancing back to Dimitri. "Really good. I don't think I've seen a human with that much power since the old days."

"Don't give him credit, Seamus," Garrett growled. "He draws power from forbidden magic."

"Hey, I didn't give him credit! I'm just saying that I haven't seen a human use magic like that in years!"

"Enough, both of you," Theresa said, silencing them instantly. "It's obvious to see that he is far stronger than any foe we've faced since Aiden's training began. We can't let our guards down for a second."

Aiden frowned. He truthfully didn't know how they could possibly beat Dimitri at this point. Theresa and her brothers were incredibly strong warriors, yes, but just how strong was

Dimitri if he could force even Garrett back with just a blast of wind?

"Any ideas then?" he asked. "He's even stronger than Raven, and we barely got out of that fight!"

"Calm down, Aiden," Theresa said, her snarl turning into a regretful smile. "There's no doubt that this Dimitri is skilled, but he hasn't faced a true dragon before."

She turned back to Garrett and Seamus.

"Listen up. The best way to remind him of our position of power is to show him just how strong our kind really is."

Garrett and Seamus nodded in unison as they turned their attention back to Dimitri. Theresa placed a hand on Aiden's shoulder gently.

"I want you and Liza to keep your heads down. Understand?"

Aiden didn't argue as he backed away from the trio. Theresa's eyes narrowed dangerously as she turned to face Dimitri, smoke rising from her nostrils.

"You are strong, dark mage, but you underestimate us."

The three dragons began to grow larger as they entered their transformations. Aiden swallowed a lump in his throat as he watched from the sidelines. During their training sessions, Theresa told him that they only time they assumed their true forms in a fight was when a truly powerful foe came before them.

A blinding flash of light blocked his vision briefly. When it returned, all three of them were now fully transformed. Seeing them like this really put things into perspective for Aiden. They had enough power to destroy an entire city if they wished it, but they never had. The immeasurable amount of control one would require to keep from destroying a city must have been incredibly hard...

Dragons were truly remarkable creatures.

Dimitri on the other hand did not look as impressed as Aiden and Liza. In fact, a cool calculating smile slipped across his face as he stared into the eyes of the great dragons before him.

"I must admit, your power is great - for a race that is practically extinct."

Garrett snarled as he opened his large maw, unleashing a hot torrent of flames towards their new foe. Dimitri held up one hand, using a shield spell to block the flames. While he did, Seamus took the chance to strike back. With a quick spin, the green dragon whacked the demon master away from the group towards a tree.

Dimitri quickly regained his balance, summoning a large, almost obese, demon to soften his impact. The demon's large gut managed to save its master at the right moment. Without even batting an eyelash, Dimitri spoke quickly in a strange language that Aiden could not comprehend.

He would later learn that he spoke a summoning spell in demonic tongue.

Behind Dimitri, three large snake like heads erupted from the obese demon's body. The large creature stood on four legs, easily as tall as the three dragons, had blood red eyes, and frills on the side of their cheeks. Its scales were a mixture of pale yellow and light green color. The dragons seemed to snarl at the beast.

"I take it that all three of you are familiar with the hydra, yes?" He asked. "You should know that cutting its heads off will be useless."

Aiden and Liza watched from the sidelines as the three dragons snarled loudly at the hydra. The hydra in return hissed before spitting what seemed like streams of acid at them. Taking the chance to counter, the trio's mouths seemed to have tiny sparks in their jaws at first, but then unleashed a stream of fire from each dragon towards the streams of acid.

Aiden knew that this was an important battle happening right before them, but he couldn't help but be amazed at the sight. He was actually seeing the three of them breath real fire towards a foe in battle. It wasn't like anything from the stories he read. The fire his mentors breathed wasn't spread out and without a pattern. It was straight forward, like a flamethrower. He also took notice that Theresa's fire was pure white, unlike Seamus and Garrets whose flames were regular reddish orange.

Then his attention turned back to the hydra. The demonic creature was certainly not letting up its stream of acid as it battled his mentors. Aiden began to sweat somewhat. He knew well enough that the way to kill a hydra wasn't to cut off its heads.

"Damn..." He whispered to Liza, "This is not good."

"I...I don't understand. Why can't they cut off the heads?" Liza asked.

Aiden wanted to give her a look for asking a question like that, but he kept the urge back.

"For some reason, when a hydra's head is cut off, two more will grow in its place." He explained, "The only way that I've heard of to kill it is to crush it. But since Theresa and the others are in the middle of keeping its acid at bay, they may not have the chance to kill it properly."

"Then what do we do?!" Liza asked, still clutching Gitanel in her palms. "I meant, what could you do? I just got involved in this whole mess."

Aiden glanced around, looking for a possible opening to get at the hydra itself. As far as he could tell, there was not a way for him a clear shot at the beast. His grip on Warfang began to tremble a bit. Was he even ready for this?

Looking at it logically, it was plain suicide for him to even attack a beast when Theresa told him and Liza to say back. But if the dragons couldn't get an attack at the monster, he was going to have to do it.

"Just think of all the heroes you've read about." Aiden thought to himself. They had faced just as dangerous scenarios just like he was facing. So he had to man up and do something drastic.

Aiden watched the movement of the hydra carefully. He couldn't attack the heads. that would serve no purpose. The tail was out of question unless he wanted to be suffocated by constriction. The sharp claws were posing a serious threat as well, they flashed in the sunlight. Aiden was forced to squint his eyes a bit.

His eyes grew wide with realization. There was a way to defeat the beast without them getting into too much trouble!

"Liza, I got an idea. It's crazy, but it should work!"

"I'm listening." Liza said, eager to hear what he had to say.

"The only way for them to kill this beast is to either burn it, or crush it. But since their flames are too busy keeping its stream of acid back, the burn it option is out of question. Unless..."

He pointed towards the eyes of the hydra, which was too busy to even notice him.

"We blind the beast."

Liza blinked a couple of times in confusion before tilting her head to the side.

"And how do we blind a beast that is just as tall as Theresa, Seamus, and Garrett?"

Aiden smiled proudly as he pointed towards the blade of Warfang. Liza gave him another confused look. With a sigh, Aiden positioned his weapon just right in the sunlight, aiming for the middle head's eyes. This happened to be the head that Theresa's flames were battling.

The sunlight bounced off his sword towards the middle head. The hydra's head squirmed a bit at the sudden light hitting its eyes. Aiden continued to use Warfang to blind the hydra. Finally, his efforts paid off. With an agitated roar the middle head stopped spitting acid.

Just as it did, Theresa's white fire consumed the middle head whole. The white dragoness continued her stream of fire however, not allowing a new head to re-grow where the previous head was.

Aiden glanced back to Liza, who was now standing on her two feet.

"I got it now!" She said, "You take the right head, I'll handle the left!"

Without saying anything else, the two of them aimed the shining metal of their weapons at the remaining hydra heads. Aiming carefully, the two of placed the bright reflections of sunlight from their weapons right at the eyes of the remaining heads. Just as with the first head, the other two roared in agony from being blinded right before Seamus and Garrett's flames consumed them.

The three dragons then aimed their flames right at the body of the hydra. With no heads to fight back against their flames, the body began to burst with flames. Squirming in pain as the legendary dragon fire continued to burn away at its skin. Aiden and Liza watched in both amazement and fear. The flames of the trio were so intense that the only thing that was left of the hydra was its skeleton.

"Well now," A voice came behind him and Liza, "It seems you're not as slow as you appear to be!"

Aiden turned his head quickly to the voice came from. Sitting on top of a large log was Dimitri. Aiden's eyes grew wide in fear. When did he get behind them so quickly? Dimitri stood up.

"Using the sunlight with the metal of your weapon. An unusual way of defeating a hydra, but affective none the less." Dimitri said.

Aiden quickly pointed his weapon at him. Dimitri walked towards him slowly. Liza, clumsily, held her dagger out at him as well. This didn't daunt the demon master though. He just kept walking towards them slowly and menacingly.

A trio of low growls came from behind Aiden and Liza. If he had time to breathe a sigh of relief, Aiden would have gladly done so. Theresa, Seamus, and Garrett's dragon heads hovered above them. All three of them glaring at Dimitri with angry eyes.

"Keep away from them, demon mage." Seamus said.

"If you even think about hurting Aiden, I'll personally make you my lunch..." Theresa said, her voice strangely higher than it was before.

Dimitri stopped walking and glanced up to the dragon trio. With a small sneer he took a step back. Aiden blinked a couple of times. He saw fully well that Dimitri was capable of handling himself. So why didn't he attack them?

"Very well then, dragoness. You win this round." Dimitri said, "This little event has gone on far enough."

With the snap of his fingers, a strange bat like demon flew from above. Bending his knees quickly, Dimitri jumped onto it without any effort. The group watched him carefully as he smiled at them from above.

"I've evaluated what I wanted to know anyway. For now, I'll let you live. But know this. When the time comes, Raven and I will make our move against you all. For now, train your little runts here. For their sake, they better be prepared for the real battle that is coming."

With a quick wave of his hand, Dimitri and his bat flew off into the sky above. Seamus snarled as he opened his wings, prepared to go after him. Theresa however placed a claw on his back. Turning towards her, Seamus tilted his head.

"Let him go, Seamus." She said, "Going after him would be pointless right now."

"But..."

"Not to mention of course, you'll be spotted easily." Theresa pointed towards the sky. "There are not enough clouds for you to use to cover yourself. It's too risky."

Seamus snarled, but eventually pulled his wings back. Theresa turned her head back to Garrett. The large dragon gave a simple nod of his head. Slowly the three of them began to shine with a bright light. Aiden and Liza quickly closed their eyes. As the light dimmed down, they opened them up to reveal Theresa, Seamus, and Garrett in their human forms once again.

"Liza..." Theresa began, frowning a bit, "I'm sorry that you had to see all of that. I understand completely if you don't want to be a part of this anymore."

Liza was strangely quiet. She glanced down at her new dagger for a few moments, then back up at the trio.

"Are you kidding?" She asked, "That was more exciting than any soccer game I've ever been in!"

CHAPTER 20 - THE START OF A SUMMER ADVENTURE

A week had passed since the group crossed paths with Raven's master, Dimitri. Graduation and Aiden's birthday had passed as well. Both of which were left bittersweet since their encounter with the master of demonic magic. The whole thing had upset Aiden. Despite all that he had learned in his training with the dragons, from how to use a sword with Theresa, the magic training with Seamus, and workouts with Garret, he knew now that his power was nothing compared to Dimitri. He hadn't even used any of his true strength in their fight, if he was truly stronger than Raven, Aiden shuddered at the thought of what he could have done.

What caught him off guard the most though was how accepting Liza was after the encounter with Dimitri. Aiden, along with the dragons, expected her to not want to be part of them. She proved them wrong however as she quickly learned how to wield her new dagger in training sessions and even proved to be quite agile. Aiden believed she was so fast because of her experience as a soccer player.

Still, the group as a whole was very troubled by how powerful Dimitri really was, especially Theresa. Even though she didn't show it to the others, Aiden could tell that the battle with him really rattled her. How could he blame her though? He was a master of a magic art she thought was long dead at this point.

As for explaining to his mother and father about some of the scrapes he had gotten during his training, Aiden would often come up with some very strange excuses. At first it was easy for him to say that the scrapes came from exploring the forest and tripping, but then when he got cut he had to be more elaborate. While his mother seemed to fully except these excuses, his father always gave him a knowing look for a bit, then dropped the subject all together.

Still, summer vacation was proving far more fun than he would have ever dreamed it could be. Getting to be with dragons and one of the most popular girls in school, save for Theresa, was a plus. It got him out of the house and away from what his parents would normally want him to do so that was a plus too.

It wasn't exactly perfect though. Garrett made the training sessions more hardcore for him each day. It got so bad that it nearly broke one of his arms from the weight he was expected to carry. When Theresa confronted Garrett about this, the large warrior stated that if he was to truly be a warrior, he would have to adapt.

Easy for him to say. Garrett was a dragon.

As for his relationship with Seamus, the second dragon started to become more or less a big brother to Aiden. Always pulling jokes on him, often giving him some advice on how to control his magic, and teasing him lightly whenever he made a mistake. It was quite different than when the two first met.

Liza, while still new to the group, often found herself talking with Aiden during their breaks. She proved to be a much faster learner than expected, and almost beat him in a sparring match with their weapons once. They keyword being almost.

Eventually, the training sessions during the day were starting to take their toll on him and Liza. The summer sun was getting warmer and warmer, making it harder for them to keep cool. Training sessions would often be cut in half due to the heat and no one wanted to suffer a heat stroke. As expected, Garrett often scoffed at them for needing a break.

The more they trained though, the more eager Aiden became to go beyond just regular training and face actual challenges. Often he would bring it up to Theresa was it was just the two of them walking together, but whenever he asked her she gave the same answer to him.

"Only when you're ready, Aiden." She would say, keeping a sing song like tone whenever she did.

Aiden often would worry that since she and the other dragons had been reunited, their friendship would suffer because of it. However, the wise dragoness took notice of his worry. When the two were alone, she made it clear to him that even though she and her brothers had a strong bond Aiden would be her best friend. That helped ease him.

The biggest turn of events however came during the second week of summer. It all started out like a normal day really. Aiden and Theresa had met up with one another and started off to the regular training spot.

"So, ready for another day?" Aiden asked, keeping Warfang's figurine in his pocket.

"But of course." She said with a smile, "Though I have a special surprise when we get there."

"A surprise?"

"Mmhm. You'll see when we get there." Theresa said with a wink, walking ahead of him.

"H-Hey! Wait a minute, Theresa!" He called out, running after her. "What surprise? Don't keep me in the dark!"

"You'll have to wait."

Aiden groaned in the back of his throat. If it was one thing he hated more than math, it was surprises. And Theresa knew it more than anybody else, save for his parents.

As the two of them continued their regular training spot, Aiden kept wondering what it was that Theresa had planned to reveal. Was it a new technique for him and Liza to learn? Was she going to teach them how to breathe fire? His heart was racing from excitement at what it could possibly be.

The worst part about it though? Theresa knew fully well that Aiden hated surprises. But she kept the same secretive smile she had at the start of the day. She might have been a dragoness, but she was still a girl. And girls always knew how to make boys putty in their hands.

Still he bit his tongue and kept quiet, fighting the constant need to ask what it was. She might have been his best friend, but he didn't want to get eaten or burned by her by accident.

Finally the two of them reached their usual spot. Awaiting the two were Garrett, Seamus, and Liza. The former two were leaning against trees in boredom as Liza was cutting off small pieces of bark from a tree branch.

"Well, look who decided to show up!" Seamus said, "What happened you two? Get lost on your way here?"

"More like having to deal with questions from both of our parents." Aiden grumbled.

"Heh, you mean YOUR parents." Theresa smiled coyly, "My human mother and father know that I don't have to make excuses for any injuries I get during training."

"That's because you're a dragoness!" Aiden said with a slight glare.

"That's true." Theresa giggled, but regained her composure as she turned to the latter three. "All right, everyone gather around. It's time for a meeting."

This caught Garrett and Seamus off guard. Both were expecting her to start the regular training with Aiden and Liza. Aiden himself looked confused but shrugged as he took a seat beside Liza. At least now they were going to hear about whatever surprise Theresa had for them.

The white haired leader sighed as she began pacing back and forth in front of them.

"It's been almost two weeks since our battle with Dimitri." She started off, "Since then I've kept an eye on local news channels and papers whenever I got the chance to. If he and Raven are truly mages, they'll be behind the strangest events in a crime or case that local authorities can't explain."

"Yeah, it doesn't help that Dimitri is a master at the demonic arts either." Seamus said, leaning on his staff slightly. "He could be doing anything and getting away with it."

"Exactly." Theresa frowned, "The two of them can't be taken lightly. So during my time looking at several reports on the internet and local news papers, I found something interesting."

She pulled out from her pocket a clipping from a newspaper article. In it was a picture of a camp site known simply as 'Camp Sky Uprising.' What really caught the group's attention though was the headline above the picture. Printed in big bold words, its message was simple.

Fourth Disappearance of a Hiker puts the Camp on hot ground.

"I've been reading this story for quite some time now," Theresa continued, "For some reason, the camp site has been under fire from the press because four hikers have disappeared and never returned."

"So?" Garrett asked, "Humans get lost all the time. Odds are they got attacked by wildlife or something there."

Theresa's eyes narrowed.

"The thing is though is that there isn't any wildlife that can potentially harm an averaged sized human being. The only predators there are local snakes and some birds of prey, but from what I've read, it couldn't possibly be them."

"What do you mean?" Aiden asked, his curiosity now interested. Theresa turned the article over to her face

"The report here states that the hikers all disappeared from the exact at the exact same location with no reason. There's no trace of a struggle, nor is there any evidence to suggest that they were attacked by a wild creature."

"So you think it has something to do with magic?" Seamus asked.

"Yes. If Dimitri and Raven are behind these disappearances, then they must be using paralyzing magic in order for them to capture prisoners."

"But why though?" Liza asked, "I thought demonic arts didn't involve capturing humans."

"It doesn't." Garrett answered, "But what the humans fail to notice is that these aren't random disappearances."

Aiden blinked a couple of times until realization hit him.

"They're kidnappings..."

"Exactly." Theresa nodded, "But what makes this even more peculiar to the humans, but not to us, is that there is no cry for help from the hiker. They appear one day, then they're gone the next. I have no doubt in my mind that these hikers were taken by our two demonic mages and kept alive for some reason."

"And you believe that we have a chance to stop them and save these hikers." Seamus mused, scratching his chin. "It's plausible to say the least."

"But what can we do?" Liza frowned, "Camp Sky Uprising is a good way from here and even if we flew there together, our parents would start to freak out the moment we're gone for more than just a day."

Theresa smiled. But it wasn't her usual kind sweet or secretive smile. It was the one smile he dreaded. The smile that pretty much stated that she had something in store he would not like.

"I've already thought ahead on that." She said, reaching into her other pocket she pulled out three camp tickets. "A few nights ago, I was talking to my human parents about letting me, Aiden, and Liza go to this camp for awhile. Since they have a summer camp program, we can easily get into it without making them worry."

Aiden nearly froze at those words.

"You can't be serious..." He said.

"I am." Theresa smiled again, "My human father called up your dads last afternoon and talked them into letting you two accompany me to Sky Uprising for a least three weeks. And the best part is? Your dad, Aiden, paid for the tickets. He believed that it would be a perfect learning experience for you."

Aiden's face could have not gotten any paler. He knew absolutely nothing about camping, and dreaded the idea of having to learn during his summer vacation.

"Please tell me you're joking here." He begged.

"Nope. Starting next week, we head off for the camp site." She smiled, "Consider it a belated birthday present from me."

"Uh, Theresa?" Seamus put up a hand, "What about me and Garrett here?"

"Simple. You use your magic to replicate our tickets for the campsite. As long as they look real and can be used to get in, the two of you will have no problem getting into it."

"And what if that fails?" Garrett asked, flatly.

"Well then you fly into the forest, without being detected, and keep an eye out for danger while the three of us engage in the camp activities."

"Oh this should be fun!" Liza said with a smile, turning back to Aiden. "What do you think they'll have? Maybe they'll have sports to play!"

"Ugh, just great..." Aiden groaned, covering his face with his left hand. "You better be right about this, Theresa."

"Heh, look at the bright side Aiden." Theresa smiled again, "You won't have to make excuses to your parents as to why you're scratched up every time you come home."

Aiden grumbled a bit as he took out Warfang's figurine. He couldn't believe what he had just heard. Theresa had planned a summer trip for them that would involve them going into a forest to look for Raven and Dimitri. To make it even more unbearable, he was going to have to participate in camp activities. Groan city.

Still, it couldn't be all that bad. If he could survive training with Garrett, he could survive a camping trip with Theresa and Liza. As he glanced up, he noticed the same kind, warm smile on her face. The one that always assured him everything was going to be okay in the end. Aiden couldn't help but smile back.

She had a way of making his anger leave. Then again, she was also far stronger than he was at this point, so it was best if he didn't argue with her. As the training between them began to resume, one thought was in the back of his mind.

"What will we even see at the campsite anyway? What could have taken those hikers?"

APPENDIX - DRAGONIC LANGUAGE

*E*nglish Dragonic Pronunciation

AFRAID KITHOR (KIT-HOR)
 After Foful (fo-ful)
 Again Bentia (bent-e-a)
 All Span (span)
 Allow Spenzer (spen-zer)
 Although Spafiveenarre (spa-five-en-air)
 Always Spaveteran (spa-ve-ter-an)
 Am Ka (car)
 An Ki (key)
 And Tim (tim)
 Any Kif (keyf)
 Air Floia (flow-e-a)
 Abandon Fiekona (fee-kon-a)
 Are Guo (goo-o)
 As Guto (gu-to)
 Be Lo (lo)

Because Lokhan (lo-kan)
Been Lowen (low-en)
Before Bealom (bear-lom)
Being Lowing (low-ing)
Believe Demanda (de-man-da)
Bird Beasttee (be-st-tee)
Born Feiry (fair-e)
Brother Stragna (stragna)
Bugger Liaron (lair-on)
But Xou (zoo)
By Heel (heal)
Bye Heel (heal)
Can Toa (toe-a)
Calm Queet (queat)
Care Hito (hi-to)
Careful Hitokan (hi-to-kan)
Carry Titoa (ti-toa)
Chosen Denengar (de-nen-gar)
Claim Nevi (ner-vi)
Crap Xot (zot)
Currant Cresion (crez-e-on)
Current Cresion (crez-e-on)
Cyclone Featheroo (fef-e-roo)
Day Veek (v-k)
Dark Rappra (rap-pra)
Decide Hoaliea (hol-e-a)
Dictionary Diarra (die-a-ra)
Discussion Iletian (il-et-ian)
Did Highroal (high-rol)
Die Pearoo (pair-roo)
Differ Haven (hay-ven)
Dispose Depoa (dep-po-a)
Do Jey (j)
Down Tuggr (tug-gr)

Dragon Drakon (Dra-kan)
Earth Gitanel (Gi-ta-nel)
Eight Ipoy (i-poi)
Eighth Ipoyo (i-poi-o)
Eighty Ipoyven (i-poi-ven)
Eleven Difer (dif-er)
Ember Em (m)
Enough Aimabel (aim-a-bell)
Eve Dect (det)
Even Dectven (det-ven)
Female Jilbecken (jil-bec-ken)
Fifth Hityo (hi-ti-o)
Fifty Hityoven (hit-ti-o-ven)
Fire Beut (be-oot)
First Guyger (guy-ger)
Five Hity (hit-ti)
Flow Spatter (spat-ter)
Friend Jid (jid)
Foe Laco (la-co)
For Uranni (you -rain-ne)
Forest Teena (teen-na)
Forth Uranio (you-rain-ne-o)
Forty Uraniven (you-rain-ne-ven)
Four/For Uranni (you -rain-ne)
Fourth Urannio (you-rain-ne-o)
Garden Jeadit (gee-dit)
Get Gag (gag)
Give Kilo (kil-lo)
Glad Sient (si-ent)
Go Sie (sigh)
Good Singl (sing-l)
Guardian Familiu (fam-a-lee-u)
Guess Deed (deed)
Had Tid (tid)

Happen Foulger (foul-ger)
Have Tieg (tieg)
Heal Emalla (e-mal-la)
He Gan (gan)
Hell Hilk (hilk)
Hello Kaby (kar-be)
Help Ihan (ir-harn)
Her Gar (gar)
His Gos (gos)
Him Go (go)
Hold Petir (p-tear)
Hope Jetoo (jet-oo)
Home Dunu (dun-oo)
How Tyan (tie-an)
Huh Rye (rie)
Hundred Weloect (we-lo-et)
I O (o)
Idea Kipit (kip-it)
Idiot Kalen (kal-en)
If Of (of)
In On (on)
Is Os (os)
It Ot (ot)
Just Golt (golt)
Know Xorea (zor-e-ar)
Land Piane (p-ain)
Langue Opilain (of-fil-e-an)
Let Heardl (hear-dl)
Leader Rexkin (rex-kin)
Life Doll (dol)
Lighting Ragnatorm (rag-na-torm)
Like Cuay (q-ray)
Live Dollvie (dol-v)
Lives Dollvies (dol-ves)

Long Whyt (white)
Luck Valo (val-o)
Male Becken (bec-ken)
Mana Kotura (ko-tu-ra)
Many Zane (zain)
Master Kinsaur (kin-saur)
Memory Lockieo (loc-key-o)
Might Tenara (te-na-ra)
My Min (min)
Name Cert (kert)
Never Sandra (san-dra)
Next Gon (gone)
Nice Fasy (fa-c)
Nine Leo (lee-o)
Ninety Leoven (lee-o-ven)
Ninth Leoo (lee-oo)
No Yed (yed)
None Rikie (ric-key)
Not Reo (ree-o)
Now Rew (ru)
Of Ewra (oo-ra)
Off Ewrana (oo-ra-na)
Oh Gad (gad)
Okay Pomain (po-main)
One Zon (zon)
Our Zo (zo)
Or Li (lee)
Other Keddit (ked-dit)
Over Zitter (zit-ter)
Past Beta (bay-ta)
Peace Avena (A-ve-na)
Petition Gemala (ge- ma-la)
Piss Vaoo (var-oo)
Planet Soaku (so-ku)

Poor Fraw (fraw)
Prevent Joarhand (Jo-ar-hand)
Previous Joarietin (jo-ar-e-tin)
Pronounce Joyerition (joy-er-i-tion)
Prop Dryan (dry-an)
Really Funnel (fun-nel)
Release Joinne (join-ne)
Relax Elgane (el-ga-ne)
Remember Canoain (can-o-ain)
Right Ritted (rit-ted)
Rope Ohnalga (oh-nal-ga)
Sake Litin (li-tin)
Sad Ditin (di-tin)
Scary Zanatone (zan-ar-tone)
Second Poite (poi-te)
See Lon (l-on)
Separate Tineat (ti-n-eat)
Serenity Sinotu (sin-o-to)
Serious Silowin (sil-o-win)
Seven Youao (u-a-o)
Seventh Youaoo (u-a-oo)
Seventy Youaoven (u-a-o-ven)
Shelter Wyen (y-en)
Should Shumbel (Shum-bell)
Six Dren (dren)
Sixth Dreno (dren-o)
Sixty Drenven (drenven)
So Ceo (c-o)
Some Merm (merm)
Sorry Forfit (for-fit)
Speech Stutak (stu-tak)
Spirit Shimera (shim-er-ra)
Stand Keya (key-a)
Still Tair (tear)

Stop Nomaran (no-ma-ran)
Sword Ladbe (lad-be)
Take Yakki (yak-ki)
Tantrum Onergall (o-ner-gall)
Tell Kidon (ki-don)
Ten Wari (wa-re)
That Hubo (hub-o)
The Aba (a-ba)
Them Abam (a-bam)
There Abaren (a-ba-ren)
These Abasen (a-ba-sen)
They Abat (a-bat)
Thing Ittye (it-tie)
Third Itin (it-tin)
Thirty Itinven (it-tin-ven)
This Bah (bah)
Though Fiveenarre (five-en-air)
Thousand Veinatim (vein-a-tim)
Three Itoa (it-toe-a
Through Ficenarre (thick-en-air)
To Ter (ter)
Together Tergaggar (ter-gag-gar)
Tomorrow Teragain (ter-a-gen)
Too Ter (ter)
Torture Deertom (deer-tom)
Turn Goar (go-r)
Twelve wave (twa-ve)
Twenty Twaven (twa-ven)
Two Ter (ter)
Under Quake (quake)
Understand Quakekeya (quake-key-a)
Up Vuat (voo-at)
Was Ghan (gr-han)
Water boakuo (bo-koo-o)

Way Vun (voon)
Warrior Eltraga (El-tra-ga)
We Tolua (to-lu-a)
What Bouk (book)
When Bein (bee-in
Where Beian (be-arn)
Why Quic (quick)
Will Dagal (dag-gal)
With Sammoo (sam-moo)
Would Umbel (um-bell)
Wow Fair (fare)
Yeah Sear (see-er)
Year Quiv (quiv)
Yes Seah (see)
You Yokee (yo-key)
Your Yokeer (yo-keer)
(an) Before
(ed) After
(er) After
(ex) Before
(im) Before
(ing) After
(less) After
(ly) After
(r) After
(s) After
(teen) After
(un) Before
(y) After

EXCERPT FROM "THE HARPY'S DEN"

"**Y**ou certain you want to walk out there?" The camp counselor asked.

The man she was talking to scoffed. He was tall, gruff, and grizzled. He looked and acted like he meant business–definitely not the type of person to be messed with. The counselor's question was insulting.

"Of course I am." The man rumbled, with a voice both deep and powerful, "It's just a night stroll, after all. I know the path better than anyone else around."

"Haven't you heard? The last few men who walked out in the middle of the night never returned! All that anyone could find were their jackets or backpacks."

"Ha, must have been wimps then." The mountain of a man mocked, "People who get lost in these woods, don't deserve to be found."

"Hey man, that's really disrespectful to them and their families."

"Please, as if I cared who their families were or what they think."

"Is that so?" The counselor was starting to get a tad annoyed, "What if YOU disappear without a trace?"

"You're making it sound like I don't know what the hell I'm doing," he responded with a laugh, taking out the pistol hidden on his hip, "I always come prepared."

The counselor's eyes grew wide as she reached out and snapped the pistol from his hand. The big man gave her a dark glare, as if she'd struck him. The counselor didn't flinch.

"Are you crazy?!" She hissed, "This isn't just a campsite for adults, it's a summer camp as well! We do not allow weapons here!"

"And that, my sad little friend," The man snatched his gun back from her, "is why those fools disappeared. They didn't have protection."

"Protection from what?! There aren't any major predators out in our forest!"

"Pray tell then, idiot, what's behind those guys vanishing in the middle of the night?"

"How should I know?! We chose this spot because it was isolated from the bears and wolves! The only wildlife we should have are deer, birds, raccoons, and insects!"

"Obviously not if the multiple reports of men not returning are *true*." The man mocked, placing his pistol away. "You might as well face the facts, missy, something's out there, and it's putting a stain on your camp's good name."

The counselor let out an exasperated groan, shaking her head as she turned away from him. It was true that, as of late, her camp was starting to draw a lot of negative attention. Many parents were concerned that their children would end up missing since the reports began. Lately, it had become a surefire topic that turned any meeting into a bitter argument.

She hated to be reminded that her camp's once trusted reputation had fallen under so much suspicion. Worse, still, was the possibility of the camp being shut down due to all the negative press.

"Are you really going to risk your own life just to find what's taking people away?" She asked, "What if you don't come back? We have enough trouble already!"

The man chuckled as he turned towards the forest. "Relax, missy, I'll be fine. I've hunted things that your little camp should be glad aren't local in this area."

And with that, he walked off into the forest. Leaving the counselor by herself. As the image of the man grew smaller in the distance, the counselor shook her head.

"Stupid fool..." Was all she said, returning to her cabin.

Neither one knew it, but this would be the last time they ever saw one another alive. Had he heeded her words, had he turned back, maybe his life could have retained some sense of normalcy. His pride got the better of him, though, as he plunged deeper into the woods. His pride, and something else...curiosity.

To tell the truth, he really was curious to know why several men, and only men, had vanished when taking the trail. The mystery taunted him, demanding an answer.

He wasn't a detective. In all honesty, he didn't like anything to do with the police. They took too long to do a proper investigation and, all too often, they were too late to find any answer at all. He was a free agent who "helped" folks with trouble like this. As such, he took it upon himself to look into any case the police were too incompetent to handle.

The forest around here was as quiet as it always had been. He knew these woods better than most, from growing up in a town not too far from the camp. He'd never heard of anything like this happening before. These woods didn't have any territorial animals that might attack local hunters, or mistake them for prey.

Whatever was disturbing this peaceful forest needed to be

dealt with. And who better than the man who knew these woods better than the back of his own hands?

"All right, let's see if we can find the source of all this trouble." He murmured, quietly reloading his pistol as he trekked deeper into the forest.

The man took no extreme measures as he walked along. No reason to. Even with the lack of incredibly dangerous animals, the forest had its' share of risky moments. Steep holes were commonplace and it was easy enough to get lost if you weren't sure just where you were going. There were also some poisonous plants, like Moonseed and Nightshade, that could kill a grown man who was foolish, or unlucky, enough to digest or come in contact with them.

Maye that was what had happened, made as much sense as anything, the man thought. "Killed by eating plants," the man shook his head, "I wouldn't be surprised if these hikers were some damn city slickers that didn't know anything about forest plants."

Pushing onward into the forest, he kept his pistol ready. The further he advanced, the darker the forest seemed to get. The hooting of owls never ceased, while crickets chirped their songs. The rabbits, despite being silent most of the time, squeaked as the hooting of an owl grew louder. The almost luminescent eyes of the rabbits appeared in a small field nearby.

The man knew what that sound meant. He had seen them hunt rabbits before; he'd grown all too familiar with the fearful bunny cries as the owls swooped down on the unlucky few they managed to catch. The rabbits in the field began to run as fast as they could, while the hooting of the owl grew louder and louder. At first, it sounded like things were normal. Life was just proceeding as it usually did in the woods.

As he turned away, a new sound caught his attention. A shrill, piercing cry came from above. Turning just in time, the man saw a rabbit carried away in what looked like a pair of large talons. At first he thought it was a large owl, but the shrill cry was what really caught his attention.

This was different from any other animal cry he'd ever heard. But, what terrified him most was realizing just what the scream sounded like. It started out like a bird, but as it grew in volume, it became a banshee's cry, the blood curdling scream of a mad woman. Hands shaking, he told himself it had to be his imagination.

Then he heard it again. Another horrific scream as a pair of talons swooped down snatching another rabbit from the field. This time, there was no mistaking it. What first seemed like a bird's cry, rose until it cracked and became a woman's shriek. His eyes grew wide as a third pair of talons swooped down and grabbed another rabbit. This time he saw more than just talons. It was brief, but he saw the body of what looked like a teenage girl in the pale moon light, before its large wings carried it away.

A new feeling rushed down his spine, one he wasn't used to. Fear. Just what had he seen? In all his years, he'd never spied anything so...so impossible! Was it a new species of bird? Some kind of freak of nature? Most importantly, where did they even come from and how had no one realized they were here?

Taking a few deep breaths to steady himself, the man focused. He had to remember the reason he came here in the first place. He was looking for the mystery behind the vanishing hikers. A thought suddenly entered his mind that he didn't want to entertain.

What if these bird-like beings were the reason the hikers had gone missing?

A cold chill rolled down his spine once again. The possibility that they could have been taken by those...things...was quite high. There wasn't, after all, any other large beast of prey in this area capable of taking on a man successfully. And those talons, they were the biggest he'd ever seen.

"Do it for those coming to the camp..." He whispered to

himself, checking his clip to ensure it was full, "Do it to keep anyone else from being taken..."

Gathering his courage once more, he set off across the field. Whatever had grabbed the three rabbits couldn't have gone far. No predator strayed too far away from its food source. Especially anything with the giant talons these new creatures seemed to have.

Silently moving through the forest, he kept his gun raised at all times in case he came across what he was looking for. As he walked, he kept his eyes on the landscape around him and the sky above him. If these birds got the jump on him, he'd never have time to react to an attack from above.

The more he pushed into the forest, the darker and more sinister it became. Each tree seemed to wear a terrible, demented face on their trunk. And the further he went, the more horrible each face looked. His gun hand began to tremble as he did his best to steady his breathing.

He searched for fifteen minutes, finding nothing. Then, suddenly, he heard a loud cracking sound nearby. He jumped, and quickly steadied his hold on his gun. Checking his clip once more, the man turned to his left. It was at this point that he should have listened to his instincts and gone back. But the sight of a campfire glowing nearby overwhelmed that preservation instinct.

Gathering his courage, the man slowly approached the flickering light. Who would start a fire out in the middle of a forest? And worse, away from the camp grounds! The cracking sound he had heard before was getting louder. While that could have meant a lot of things, growing up in Georgia, hunting all his life, he knew just what it was. Someone, or something was cracking bones.

Spotting a particularly large tree, he slipped behind it as quietly as he could. What he saw nearly made his eyes pop out of his skull. There, sitting around the campfire were what looked like three teenage girls! But, he quickly realized something was off about the trio.

In the faint glow of the campfire, he clearly saw what had shocked him before. The three girls had enormous bird-like wings sticking out from their backs and where their hands should have been were large bird like talons. The only thing that looked normal about them were their faces, though even those had a feral, strange look to them.

They looked similar, likely related, but were still distinct from one another. The tallest had pitch black hair, with dangerous red eyes that gleamed in the crackling firelight. Another, smaller than the first, had strange turquoise hair, with a curious set of green eyes. The last, easily the smallest, surely no more than fourteen years old, had sunny blonde hair and kept her pale blue eyes on her meal, only casting glances at the older two.

The man had never before seen anything like this in his entire life. These...girls, if he could call them that, were like something out of a freak show! He was about to ask what the hell they were, but one of them spoke up suddenly.

"This was a good night," the tallest commented with a small nod, "These rabbits are a much better catch than last night's pitiful meal." She cleared her throat and glared at the smallest one, "You should try a little harder next time, dearest sister."

The blonde bowed her head a bit lower and sighed..

"I'm sorry..." she mumbled, with a twinge of a whine in her tone, "I got outnumbered by the wolves." She sniffed and peeked up at her sister, mumbling "Thought there weren't supposed to be any around here..."

"Don't give me that! It doesn't matter if you were outnumbered ten-to-one!" she rose up from her seat, wings flaring up, her eyes narrowed, "You're not some helpless human! You're a harpy, so start acting like one!"

"Oh, give her a break, sister," the girl with the oddly-colored hair giggled, "You were no majestic hunting expert when you were her age, I'm sure," She teased, giggling again when her sister puffed up her cheeks.

The tallest took a warning step towards the middle sister, cheeks still puffed and eyes angrily shimmering in the night.

"Brave words from downy-feathered, soft-taloned fledgling!" she insisted, talons clenched and trembling.

The odd-haired sister shrugged and took a messy bite from her rabbit. She mumbled a low "Mmmm," and cheerfully chewed her food. This only further flustered her oldest sister, causing her wings to flap in agitation.

"Were you listening, little sister? I was talking to you!"

"Yup! I heard you!" she chirped in response, taking another bite. Her mouth still full, she giggled, "I just don't wanna respond when you're being a flutterbrain,"

The oldest sister's eyes widened and she let out a little squawk of disapproval.

"Flutterbrain! You ungrateful, arrogant little-"

"You shouldn't fight..." the small harpy mumbled, taking a small bite of her rabbit. She wilted when the tallest harpy glared at her. Pursing her lips, she mumbled, "Mama doesn't like it when we argue,"

"Ugh! No one asked you! Why don't you worry about catching a bunny of your own, instead of telling me what to do?" the first harpy snapped, crossing her arms across her chest with a huff.

"She's right, you know!" The odd harpy perked up, "If she was here, Mama would have your wings on a wall, Flutterbrain,"

Still puffed up with anger, the tallest harpy snatched another rabbit from the fire. Inspecting it to be sure it had cooked enough, she dug in ravenously, taking her anger out on the poor creature. The smallest harpy peeked up again. After a moment of hesitation, she cleared her throat softly.

"So um...how are things going, you know, overall?" She asked.

"Well, there's enough food for us to last a couple more months," the odd harpy responded, pausing for the two to glance at their oldest sister, who was still fuming into her food. The odd harpy giggled and muttered something under her breath before speaking up, "Some of the game just might not be here anymore, but we stocked up plenty so far!" She assured her.

The tallest harpy swallowed and sighed, finally content, "I'm just shocked that Mama won't let us deal with those trespassers" She commented, glancing down at her food. She shrugged and began to suck on one of the rabbit's bones, "If we really start to run low on food, we could always eat those filthy humans,"

"Sister, you know how Mama feels about humans," the odd harpy pointed out. Clearing her throat, she spoke in a regal tone, "Don't eat the humans!" she giggled at her own impression while her sister scoffed.

The man nearly shouted at the top of his lungs, but he managed to keep quiet. If he gave his position away now, he would surely be dead. Plus, he had to get more information. If these "harpies" were responsible for the disappearance of the hikers, he had to know where they were keeping them.

"Yes, yes, I know, I know," the oldest grumbled in annoyance, sighing and throwing the bone down, "Mama has lectured me more than once about how dangerous humans can get when they set their minds to it," she rested her chin in her claws, "and nothing sets them off more than finding one of their own half-eaten in the forest..."

"I kinda, sorta wish we didn't have to live like this..." the small harpy mumbled, kicking her legs and glancing back and forth between her sisters. He could hear a hopeful tone in her voice, "Why can't we just live with the humans?"

"Are you crazy?" The eldest squawked with a glare, "Humans are trouble! They're all over the place, and they're awful, and they can't even feed themselves sometimes! How are they going to feed us too?"

"Not our problem!" The odd harpy replied in a sing-song tone, "If they want to kill themselves off by using up everything, let them. We're so much smarter and better off than they are. We'll be fine."

"But..."

The odd harpy joined the small harpy, putting her hand on her shoulder. She offered her a soft, sincere smile. The first sincere expression she'd worn so far.

"It's a sweet dream, little sister, but there's no way we can live with the humans, especially now. They're just too ignorant and intolerant. I mean, come on! They still think Bigfoot and Nessie aren't real!"

The small harpy sighed and nodded. With a frown, she peeked up at the oldest sister. At first, she was poking at the rabbits, trying to find something else to eat. She'd frozen now, though, peering off in the distance.

The man froze, his eyes widening in horror. Her gleaming red eyes were locked with his own. Part of him prayed to Lady Luck that she hadn't noticed him. However, as an ember rose up from the campfire between them, her lips pulled back in a snarl and her eyes narrowed dangerously.

"HOW DARE YOU!" the harpy shrieked, her voice echoing through the forest.

Immediately the other two sisters leaped to their feet. The man cursed under his breath as he turned and began running. The cries of the sisters behind him at first were distant, but they gaining on him quickly. He cursed their wings, knowing that they would eventually catch up to him. His only chance was to turn around and fire at them with his pistol.

Realizing he didn't have any other choice, he turned and aimed at the sky above him. Firing about five rounds blindly, he hoped that at least one could hit its mark and take one of the monsters down. The moon's light allowed him to see somewhat, and the silhouettes of the three were just barely visible above him. As he continued to run, he found himself in the same field that the sisters had hunted in before. Without any trees, he could aim properly once again.

Turning around and standing his ground, the man held his gun up and aimed carefully, firing three more rounds into the night air. This time, he had better results: one of his bullets grazed the wing of one of them.

Shrieking in pain, the harpy he shot was the youngest one. Immediately, the older two cried out in anger at their sister's injury, diving toward him in a vengeful rage. The man reached for the next clip of bullets in his jacket, but was stopped by the two sisters as their talons pinned his shoulders into the ground with a force greater than he could have ever imagined. It was all he could do to catch the breath forced from his lungs.

"You dirty-" the eldest harpy had him by the neck, talons digging into his flesh, "rotten, pathetic, stupid, worthless human!" She snarled and tightened her hold, "You think you're going to get away with that?"

"No one hurts our baby sister," the odd harpy hissed. The quirky playfulness from before was gone. Now, her eyes were shining like pools of venom. She motioned toward her talons, flashing in the moonlight, "Especially a filthy coward caught spying on us!"

The man coughed a bit, regaining some of his breath.

"What...did you do...to the hikers?!" He asked, barely able to speak.

"The other trespassers?" The eldest harpy asked. "We took them back to our home, locked them up and threw away the key. Don't worry, you'll be joining them soon,"

The youngest harpy landed in a heap, her wing finally giving out. She moaned softly, sitting up with some effort and trying to get a better look at her injury.

"You aren't gonna kill him, are you?" She pleaded, "Mama will be so mad if you kill him, we're not supposed to kill them!"

"I won't kill him...even though it would be so easy," the eldest harpy assured her. She yanked the man from the ground by his throat, claws digging deeper into his skin, "And I want to. Believe me when I say I want to kill you," she spat, her eyes gleaming red in the dark. Her grip tightened more, her claws piercing his skin. An angry tremor ran through her, and a growl began to work its way into her throat.

The man tried to pry himself from her grip. With what strength he had left, he took a wild swing with the pistol, slamming it against her arm. If she was capable of feeling pain, she didn't show it. The last thing he saw was her eyes gleaming in the moonlight. Then, suddenly his world went dark.

The odd harpy shook her hand, glancing at the unconscious human still hanging in her sisters grip. "His head was harder than I expected..." she mumbled. She cocked her head when her sister threw the human to the ground. The odd harpy gave her sister's arm a warm squeeze. The angry tremorS running through her faded and she relaxed with a sigh. The glow in her eyes faded.

The youngest harpy sighed and stared down at the grass, pursing her lips. She felt terrible, both from the pain of being shot, and from worrying her sisters.

"I'm sorry..." she mumbled. She sniffed, and quickly rubbed her eyes, hoping they wouldn't notice her crying.

The oldest harpy gave the man a swift kick to his side, then quickly walked over to her   fallen sister. The little harpy glanced up, a frown tugging at her lips. Instead of the expected ridicule, the tallest harpy dropped down beside her and threw her arms around her, careful to avoid the wound on her wind.

"No one hurts my sisters," she insisted, kissing her cheek, "You're a weak little fledgling, but you're still mine," she explained, with an awkward, faint blush on her cheeks.

The odd harpy grinned, snatching up the man and fluttering

her wings. She rose up into the air, clearing her throat and calling to the other two.

"Let's go! Mama's going be so, so interested in what we found!" The odd harpy giggled a bit, as the tallest tried her best to lift the small harpy off the ground. By the time she finally managed to heft her into her arms, the odd harpy was struggling to stay in the air, rolling with laughter.

"St-stop laughing!" the oldest shouted.

"I c-can fly…" the youngest mumbled, cheeks flushed bright red. Still, she smiled when her sister insisted on carrying her back. Truth be told, her wing did hurt. And it was a nice change of pace. She'd have to take advantage of her sister's good mood while it lasted.

"Ready to go?" the oldest asked.

The young harpy nodded and with a flutter of their wings, they disappeared into the sky.

ACKNOWLEDGMENTS

This book is dedicated to those who made it possible. To my family, especially my sister, father, and mother, who never gave up on me and pushed me to pursue my dream of being a writer. Mom your belief in me always keeps me going, even when I want to stop!

For my friend Hailey Ivy, the artist who drew the character pictures capturing my vision, I want to thank you for being a great friend. Your artwork of the characters is what really brought this book to completion.

To my editor, Raechelle Wilson, who helped me clean up many things when writing this first book of seven, thank you for teaching me so much with your suggestions and helping me become a better writer as a whole.

Now, on to the next book!

Charlie Rose
   December 2014

ABOUT THE AUTHOR

Living with the stories in his head from the time he could talk, Charlie Rose describes himself as a writer, first, last, and always. In his spare time he can be found on the internet or playing one of his many different gaming systems. He loves animals, Tolkien, and stories - in all their forms. He also loves to hear from his fans. If you want to talk you can reach him by email at chroseiv@hotmail.com.

He looks forward to hearing from you soon!

Books by Charlie Rose

Book 1: Dragonera
Book 2: The Harpy's Den
Book 3: The Mage's Sin
Book 4: The Dangerous Traitor (upcoming)
Book 5: Bane of Dragons (upcoming)
Book 6: The Return of the Dragon King (upcoming)
Book 7: The Final Truth (upcoming)

Made in the USA
Monee, IL
14 March 2020

23150005R00157